ALSO BY ALEXANDRA AMOR

Historical Mysteries

Charlie Horse

(Get your free copy of Charlie Horse at AlexandraAmor.com/Ukee)

Horse With No Name

Juliet Island Romantic Mysteries

Love and Death at the Inn

Children's Animal Adventure Novels

Sugar & Clive and the Circus Bear

Sugar & Clive and the Bank Robbery

Sugar & Clive and the Movie Star

Larry at the Wedding (A Sugar & Clive Novella)

Memoir

Cult, A Love Story

A TOWN CALLED HORSE SHORT MYSTERY COLLECTION

A TOWN CALLED HORSE SHORT MYSTERY COLLECTION

Books 1 - 4

ALEXANDRA AMOR

THE OUTSIDE OF A HORSE

A Town Called Horse Short Mystery

"There is something about the outside of a horse that is good for the inside of a man."
Winston Churchill

CHAPTER ONE

June 1889

The door to Constable Jack Merrick's office was unlocked when Walt arrived on Tuesday morning. This wasn't entirely a surprise; Merrick had sometimes been sleeping in the cell, rather than going home to his empty house.

It was pleasantly warm, even though it was just 8 o'clock in the morning. Walt had finished his morning chores, feeding the animals that were stabled at the livery, cleaning out their stalls, and filling the water troughs. The past winter had been a challenging one. When Walt had first moved to this brand-new town in the new Canadian territory of British Columbia, it had essentially been an outpost, with nothing more to offer than the partly constructed hotel and a general store. The town served the purpose of being a tiny commercial hub for the ranches being claimed in the area. Walt had bought the livery from a man who was "eager to get back to civilization," as he put it. Whereas Walt was eager to be as far from civilization as he could. The town fit that bill superbly.

This June morning was promising to be another absolutely perfect day. He stepped over the threshold into Merrick's office, which was also the telegraph station and the home of the several other jobs that Merrick filled in his capacity as the local law enforcement officer. Right away, Walt could smell the stew that he had dropped off the night before, in an effort to try to get Merrick to eat something. However, as he lifted the lid on the pot that stood exactly where he'd put it on the wood stove the night before, one glance told him that Merrick hadn't touched it. Walt set the lid down and held his hand against the side of the stove, which was stone cold. He glanced into the minute cell at the back of the room and could see that the simple blanket lying on the straw mattress had been used, but right now the cot was unoccupied.

Walt sighed and recognized that he was at a loss as to how to help his friend. Merrick's wife had died four months ago, and Walt was grieving her loss as well. Charlotte had been a charming and beautiful woman, so lovely and polite and refined that Walt had constantly teased her about what she was doing with Merrick.

"Walter," she would say. She always called him Walter. "Merrick is very much like you. Inside that enormous frame and rather thick head beats the heart of a very good man."

Walt would always reply, "We've got you fooled."

Since Charlotte's death Merrick had been inconsolable, and also utterly unwilling to accept any kind of comfort from his neighbors. Merrick might not have been able to see it, but Walt was aware of the 150 or so souls who made up the town all watching Merrick out of the corners of their eyes, making sure he wasn't swallowed whole by his grief. It warmed Walt's cynical Irish heart.

Walt checked the telegraph machine and saw with relief that no messages had come in. Messages meant work for Merrick, and Walt was sure the constable wasn't up to that.

He decided to take the stew back to Caroline Finnegan at her hotel, where it had originated. On second thought, perhaps he'd just take it back to the livery and eat it himself.

When Pastor Thoreson arrived, he found Walt in the jail cell, folding the woolen blanket on the cot.

"I always knew your nefarious character would catch up with

you." Pastor Thoreson grinned at Walt from the open doorway of the office.

"A truly free man can never be contained, Pastor," Walt said.

The pastor, a short, thickening man with black hair and twinkly brown eyes, stepped into the office and glanced around. "The man himself is not about, then, I gather?"

Walt finished folding the blanket and tossed it down onto the cot. He stepped over the iron railing that held the bars at the bottom on the floor, bars that he had forged himself. "He was here last night when I dropped off that stew," he said, pointing to the stove. "Not sure where he's gone to now."

The pastor nodded thoughtfully, an expression of compassion and sorrow on his face. "He's not doing very well, is he?"

Walter Sheehan, livery owner and blacksmith, was usually exceedingly comfortable with himself. Raised on the streets of Dublin, the middle child of twelve siblings, he was self-sufficient to a fault. Put him in any situation—in the wilderness, in a saloon fight, as a stowaway on a freighter crossing the Atlantic—and he would find a way to take care of himself and not only survive but thrive.

However, ask him to talk about his feelings, or his thoughts about someone else's feelings, and the man would freeze up like an Arctic sea in January. He growled some noncommittal guttural noises at Pastor Thoreson, and his eyes darted away as he studiously concerned himself with the wood grain in the floorboards.

He didn't see it, but a smile just barely touched the edges of the pastor's lips, though his eyes were still sad. He shifted the subject to more comfortable ground. "If you have any idea where I might find him, Walter, I'd be obliged. I've got a situation."

Now Walt was able to look up. "What's that?"

"Mrs. Thoreson's sister is in town for a visit and some of her jewelry has gone missing. Apparently, it had monetary, not to mention sentimental, value." The pastor lowered his voice and dipped his head toward Walt. "Mrs. Bell has been married several times, you see, sadly losing all her husbands. But they were all wealthy men and contributed greatly to her catalog of sparkly and shiny things. She is greatly distraught about the loss."

"And you were wanting Merrick to look into it this."

The pastor nodded. "Got any idea when he'll be back?"

Walt glanced at the stew pot on the stove and then over at the cot, thinking. "Pastor, he doesn't spend much time in the office these days. And when he does he's really only here in body, I'm afraid."

Pastor Thoreson glanced at the cot himself, nodding gently. "I wonder if having a puzzle to work on would help him?"

"Perhaps," Walt shrugged.

There was a pause. Pastor Thoreson tapped the hat that he was holding in his left hand against his leg.

"I must be going now, Pastor," Walt said. "I need to get to the forge and get on with my jobs. The stagecoach rigging is about to come apart and they'll be in town later this week to pick up the new one I'm making for them."

Whenever Walt was with the small man he always felt like the six-year-old Catholic boy who had stolen hard candy from this corner store. He always felt as though there was a list of his sins painted down the front of his shirt.

Walt took hold of the office doorknob and with his body language tried to usher the pastor out onto the street.

"If you see the constable, Walter, please tell him I'm looking for him. My wife and her sister are quite distraught."

"I will, Pastor."

Walt pulled the office door closed behind him.

CHAPTER TWO

Nails were the backbone of Walter Sheehan's blacksmith business. The town of Horse was in a state of expansion, which was a boon for everyone, not the least the lumber merchant and Walt, who provided the nails and hinges and door handles for the buildings going up at a rapid clip down the main street. It was boring work hammering out the small iron nails, square in their stem and tapered to a point at the bottom with a flat head at the top. But he was well practiced at it and could produce nearly 150 in an hour. If things got much busier he might have to hire himself an assistant to help out. Doing work like creating a new rigging for the stagecoach was always a welcome break from the bread-and-butter task of making nails. As he had told the pastor, the BX Express stagecoach would be back in town later that day, and it had not been a lie when he'd told the pastor that the rigging had to be ready for them.

As he approached the livery and the blacksmith shop from across the street, he could see the motley crew of three dogs hanging around in front, waiting for him. As he got closer they all stood with wagging tails and wandered over to greet him. He leaned down and gave them all a ruffle on the head and rumbled sweet nothings to them. The dogs did not belong to him, but they were attached to him nonetheless.

With the forge fire started and his tools laid out, Walt began to think about the next steps that he needed to take to create the pieces he needed for the rigging. Part of his mind, however, was still on Merrick. He wasn't the man's babysitter, or his mother, but still Walt didn't like it that he hadn't seen Merrick since the night before. Walt had brought the stew back to the forge with him and put it out of the way on the forge hearth to keep warm. He'd have some of it for his lunch.

Merrick was a strong man, or at least that had been Walt's impression of him in the year or so that they'd known one another. However, Walt had seen more than one strong person undone by grief. His mother was one perfect example.

When Walt's father had died when he was just 12, his mother had retreated into herself and had refused to get on with life. As far as Walt knew she was still that way. His oldest sister, Kathleen, who had been grown and married when their father died, had taken Mrs. Sheehan into her home to live and to heal. That was years ago, and as far as Walt knew his mother was still there, sitting in a chair by the window, wearing her mourning dress, her eyes haunted, looking toward the past, not seeing the present.

As Walt dipped the tongs into the fire with the piece of iron that he was working on and rolled it around, heating it up, he wondered if maybe he should take Merrick hunting sometime soon. Perhaps getting him out in the fresh air and the sunshine, especially now that the weather was good, would clear some of the grief out of his friend's head and heart.

Walt was so deep in thinking about both the past and the present, and the effect that grief has, that he didn't see Mrs. Thoreson until she was standing right in front of him. Head bent, hammer swinging, he was lost in another world and was startled when he suddenly realized that the delicate lady was standing not two feet from his anvil.

"A penny for your thoughts, Walter," she said.

The blacksmith smiled at her and dipped his workpiece into the water bucket beside his anvil. "If you're looking for your husband, Mrs. Thoreson, he just left the constable's office. I thought he was headed in the direction of your home."

If someone had created a pair of fancy china figurines of the kind Walt had only seen once or twice in his lifetime, they would look exactly like Pastor and Mrs. Thoreson. The couple had been married for God only knew how long. Mrs. Thoreson had the same dark hair as her husband, and exactly the same pair of twinkly brown eyes. When they stood together after church on Sundays, they looked more like brother and sister than husband and wife. The same calm, kind expression on their faces. The same expression of delight when meeting a new member of the congregation or saying hello to someone brand-new to town.

Walt had always thought that Mrs. Thoreson was likely quite a stunner in her younger days. Pastor Thoreson, though, wasn't much to look at. He wasn't ugly, just plain. But Mrs. Thoreson was delightful to behold. Petite, with delicate features in a small delicate face. She really did look like a china figurine. And despite her age she didn't seem to be experiencing any of the thickening through the waist that her husband was.

"I'm not looking for Matthew, Walter. I saw him at home. He came back directly after he saw you."

Walt did not consider himself to be an intuitive person at all. However, in this moment he had what he would definitely describe as a premonition: this visit from Mrs. Thoreson was going to turn into a problem for him. He stood silently and waited for her to speak, hoping he was wrong.

Once again, Walt felt like a schoolboy.

Mrs. Thoreson took a little breath. "I understand that Matthew was unable to find Constable Merrick this morning, but that he talked to you about the problem that my sister has encountered."

Walt nodded, and waited some more.

She hesitated and then continued. "We find ourselves in a situation where we need someone to help us. My sister has come up from the coast and we were hoping to have a nice visit. Unfortunately, all this business with stolen jewelry has put a damper on things." She stopped there briefly, hesitating again, and then went on. "I wonder if you might be able to help us, Walter?"

"Me?" Walt frowned, not understanding.

"Yes. You see, my sister is beside herself. I hate to see her this way. What has happened is ruining her time with us. I just thought that maybe, as the constable's friend and confidante, you might be able to lend us a hand."

Walt still didn't quite understand what was happening. "I'm not the law, Mrs. Thoreson. I'm the blacksmith."

"I understand. I really do, Walter. I just thought that, as one of the founding people in our little town, you might wish to right things that have gone wrong."

Walt wasn't sure Mrs. Thoreson's remark about him being a founder was accurate. He felt like someone who had stumbled into a place far enough away from his troubles that he could forget them. That hadn't turned out to be true, but he stayed because he liked the town, most of the people in it, and especially his work, as it mostly involved animals and inanimate objects. He hadn't founded anything as much as he'd just coincidentally been there at the beginning.

"I'm sorry, Mrs. Thoreson. I don't have any authority..."

He was going to continue, but the pastor's wife jumped in. "You don't need any! This is just a mix-up, I'm sure. I'll bet that Victoria has misplaced her jewelry rather than had it stolen."

"Well, then, you can help her with that."

"No, but you see, we can't." Mrs. Thoreson looked pained for the first time since she'd arrived. "Victoria is ..." she was choosing her words carefully now, "...challenging sometimes. She and I have never really been as close as I would have liked. Her third husband died recently and she's feeling abandoned and vulnerable. She would respect the reassurance of someone outside the family in a way she doesn't, exactly, respect Matthew's and my support."

This woman sounds like a real peach, Walt thought. No wonder Mrs. Thoreson wanted help with her.

Walt could tell that if he didn't disabuse Mrs. Thoreson of her ideas right quick, he was going to get sucked into something he had no business being a part of. He was still confused about why she had decided that he, of all people, should help her out with the theft, or the misplacement, or whatever it was, but asking any more questions would be wading deeper into the swamp.

He closed the hatch on the forge fire, set his hammer down on its head on the anvil, wiped his hands on the seat of his trousers, and came around his work area.

"Mrs. Thoreson, it's not that I don't have sympathy for your situation, and I'm very sorry that a damper has been put on your visit with your sister. But you need to understand that I'm not the law in this town. I have no jurisdiction. And I'm..." Walt wanted to say that he was certain that Merrick would be back on his feet in a day or two and would be able to help Mrs. Thoreson. However, he didn't really believe that.

He shook this thought away and, with his hand very lightly on Mrs. Thoreson's left elbow, he escorted her gently out onto the street and walked her a little ways back toward the center of town. Having given his initial explanation, he was quiet now, considering what else there could possibly be for him to say.

Mrs. Thoreson, her innate kindness once again taking over, turned to him just as they walked in front of the open doors of the livery. She looked up at him, a fair distance between their faces. "Walter, you are right. I need to apologize. I've put you in an awkward position, and I realize that now. The jewelry that's gone missing has quite a bit of sentimental value to Victoria and I confess I'm frantic about it. But that's no reason to put you on the spot and ask you to do something that, as you rightly said, is not your job." She looked at him with remorseful eyes. "I hope you can forgive me."

Walt let go of her elbow and smiled at her.

She straightened her shoulders a little bit and give a sharp nod of her chin. "Right then," she said. "God is ever-present in my trouble. I'm sure we will find a way to sort this situation out."

From beside them through the open livery doors Walt could hear the occasional nicker of one of the equine residents of the livery. The three dogs had risen from where they'd been napping in the sun and stood looking at Walt.

Suddenly there was a crash from within the livery building. The dogs' heads all jerked in unison as they looked through the wide doors.

Mrs. Thoreson reached out and patted Walt's forearm. "I'll leave you now, Walter. It sounds like you've got something to deal with."

Walt nodded at her, giving his silent thanks. The crash had come from upstairs where the utilitarian sleeping rooms were for those human guests who didn't want to, or couldn't afford to, stay at Finnegan's hotel. Currently there was no one staying up there, and Walt was slightly alarmed about what could've caused the noise they'd heard. He turned and walked into the shadows of the building.

CHAPTER THREE

Walt grabbed an old shovel from the tack room, and then took the stairs at the back of the livery two at a time. Trouble seemed to follow Walt, wherever he went. It was like it sought him out. He'd gotten used to fending for himself at a very young age. He had been 6 feet tall by the time he was 14 years old, and now he exceeded that by several inches. He'd often wondered if it was his size that drew trouble to him. That certainly did seem to be the case in places like saloons or San Francisco back alleys. And he understood that. Drunk men, men with something to prove, men with chips on their shoulders and men who felt were feeling lousy about themselves and wanted to prove that they were men, would approach Walt and try to incite a fight with him.

When he was still a teenager, he'd unfailingly risen to this bait. Each fight had given him a chance to prove his own masculinity to himself. His brothers had taught him the fundamental basics of fist fighting when they recognized that this was a skill that the boy was going to have to learn.

As Walt got over older, however, and entered into his 20s, he'd finally come to recognize that by fighting those men who were looking to him, he was responding to an obligation to answer questions for them. He had eventually realized that it was not his responsibility to answer those questions. And in any case, nine times out of ten, Walt's aggressor would either walk away with his nose bleeding like a stuck pig, or would hit the ground and stay there while his mates tried to revive him. Walt was big but he was deceptively fast, and this was something that his aggressors underestimated very nearly every time he was approached.

Gradually he had learned that this kind of trouble was a kind he could avoid. He would walk away from these men and refuse to answer their questions for them.

So now, as Walt crept up the stairs of the livery carrying his weapon, he was calm and also resigned. If someone was doing damage to the upstairs rooms, for there was nothing really to steal, Walt would be able to deal with it. At the top of the staircase he turned onto the landing and stood still, waiting, listening. There was silence for a few beats and then he could hear someone muttering under their breath, growling at themselves.

His shoulders relaxed and he loosened his grip on the shovel in his right hand. He walked down the hallway, peeking through the open doors of the rooms. Each one held a very simple single bed on an iron frame that he'd made. Most rooms had a wardrobe standing in one corner and a small dressing table with a wash basin and jug.

The rooms were all empty, so Walt kept on following the muttering sounds that continued. When he came to the last room at the end of the hallway, whose window faced out onto the main street, he found his friend Jack Merrick crouched down in the middle of the floor picking up the pieces of a broken jug and putting them in his right hand.

Walt leaned on the frame of the doorway. "Trying to ruin the place, are you?"

"Just doing you a favor getting rid of this hideous artifact. Did it belong to Noah originally?"

Charlotte, Merrick's late wife, had actually given that jug set to Walt. She had toured the livery one day, seen the rooms upstairs, and recognized that he didn't have enough sets of bowls and jugs for each room. Only a woman would notice something like that, Walt had thought at the time. The next day she had shown up with a wooden apple crate. In it were an old bowl and jug that she and Merrick were no longer using at their house. At first Walt had refused it but Charlotte had insisted. And for the rest of the time he had known her, he would recognize her thoughtfulness as one of the main parts of her character.

Walt was just about to make a stinging retort to Merrick and mention the origin of the jug. But he caught himself just in the nick of time.

"Leave it. I'll go get the broom."

Merrick stood up, a handful of china shards in his right hand.

Even though Walt saw Merrick almost every day, each time he looked at the man's face he was struck anew by the pain etched around Merrick's eyes. It nearly took Walt's breath away. Today was no exception.

But today was unusual in that Merrick made an observation about the outside world. The world outside his own pain. "Was that Mrs. Thoreson I saw you talking to?"

"Were you spying on us?"

"It's easy to track you wherever you are, Sheehan. By the way, I could hear you coming up here, trying to be all sneaky. It was like a herd of elephants was climbing the stairs."

Walt was enormously cheered by this lighthearted teasing from his friend. It had been months since Merrick had said anything of the kind. He grinned and said, "This from the bull in the china shop?"

When the shards of broken porcelain had all been swept up and put in a dustbin downstairs in the tack room, Walt found two bottles of Edgar Finnegan's home-brewed beer that he had stashed away for just such a moment. He held them up to Merrick, who knew instantly what to do. Walt carried the beer bottles, and Merrick grabbed two old wooden chairs from the front of the building and took them outside to where the dogs continued to lie in wait for Walt knew not what.

The two men sat in silence, as only men can, and drank their beer. Walt didn't ask how Merrick was doing. There was no point. His friend was experiencing what would probably be the worst time in his life, if he was lucky. There was no need for the two men to talk about how Merrick felt.

So they sat and watched the world go by. Very occasionally one of their neighbors would ride or walk past and Merrick and Walt would nod hello. Twice the person would meet Walt's eye at the end of the exchange and, with the simple rise of an eyebrow or widening of their eyes, acknowledge that they were surprised and pleased to see Merrick out in the sunshine. It was a sight they had been unfamiliar with these last few months.

"So you're not going to tell me what Mrs. Thoreson wanted." Merrick was leaning back in his chair, his toes pushing the front legs up off the ground. His hands rested in his lap, clasping the bottle of beer.

"It was nothing, really. Her sister has mislaid some jewelry."

Merrick nodded and his eyes wandered away again.

Before Charlotte died, Merrick would've expressed concern about Mrs. Thoreson's predicament, and in a few moments would have thanked Walt for the beer and headed over to the Thoresons' house to see what he could do to help. Not so today. The light that had been there in his eyes for a few moments was gone again. Two steps forward, one step back.

When his beer was finished, Merrick stood and put his chair back inside the livery and left his bottle for Walt to deal with. He nodded his head at his friend and walked down the center aisle of the livery building and out the back door. Walt didn't ask where he was going. These days Merrick just shrugged an answer to those sorts of questions. People had reported to Walt that they'd see Merrick with his big gray gelding, Earl, riding aimlessly through the hills around Horse. Once Merrick was gone, Walt wished he had remembered to offer his friend some of the stew that he brought back from the office. Too late now.

Walt returned his own chair to the spot inside the front door. He took the bottles to the back of the building and set them on a shelf with several others that he would rinse and return to Edgar Finnegan.

He did a quick check of the animals in their stalls. He glanced out the back of the building as well and saw his own horse Nelson, Merrick's horse Earl, and two spare horses owned by the stage-coach company sleeping with sunshine on their backs, each with one back leg pulled up at its hock.

Time to get back to work. Instead of going out the front of the building, he crossed through the paddock at the back of the livery, bent down and climbed through the wooden fence, and then went over to the back door of the blacksmith shop. The familiar smells, the warmth and light in his workshop, provided Walt with the comfort of familiarity. Without having to think about it he walked over to the anvil where he'd left his tools and picked up the project he had been working on where he'd left it.

However, the hammer that he was certain he'd left standing on the anvil was gone. For a moment he looked around at the work area, considering that perhaps he'd done something else with it, even though it was his habit when he was interrupted in the middle of the day to always leave the hammer on the anvil. When he didn't see it anywhere inside his work area, he began looking around the other parts of the shop. He stepped over to the fire and looked all around the hearth. He checked the floor around the cooling bucket of water.

Finally, he spotted the hammer, standing on its head on the much-scarred wooden workbench at the front of the smithy.

Confused, and certain that he hadn't put it in that spot when he'd been escorting Mrs. Thoreson out the door, he took several long strides over and stood beside the workbench. Right away he could see that the hammer had been placed on the table for a specific reason. It was being used as a paperweight to hold down a scrap of paper.

Walt picked up the hammer in his right hand and with his left picked up the note. On it in boxy and untidy printing it said, "You're not the law. Stay out of Mrs. Thoreson's business. Or else."

CHAPTER FOUR

Betty Mitchell opened the door to the general store and leaned the top half of her body out onto the front walkway. "Walter Sheehan are you going to come inside or do you plan to hang about all day?" She smiled at him. "It's easier to do your shopping from inside, you know."

The blacksmith had been pacing up and down in the alley beside the store for some minutes. Betty had watched him through the store's wide front windows, first with amusement, then with some concern.

Everyone in Horse was new to the town. It was a place that was sprinkled with people either looking for new opportunities or running from an old life they were trying to leave behind. Betty had often suspected that Walter Sheehan was one of the latter, though she didn't know him at all well. She did know he was close to the local constable, so whatever his past held, it wasn't enough to make him wary of that relationship. Therefore, she considered him good people.

Betty and her husband, Christopher, had once been close to Merrick and his wife, too. Charlotte had often had the Mitchells over for dinner. Betty had tried to return the favor as often as she could, though she wasn't nearly the cook Charlotte had been. However, it had been months since the last time she'd seen Jack Merrick socially.

And now the local blacksmith was dithering outside her shop, in a most uncharacteristic way.

"Well, are you going to come in or not? I'm letting the flies in holding the door open for you."

Walt had stopped, mid-pace, when she first spoke to him. Now he turned and climbed the step at the end of the wooden sidewalk. He walked toward Betty, eyes fixed on her and his mouth set almost grimly. He came across the threshold while she held open the door.

Betty closed the door behind Walt and went back to her familiar place behind the glass counter. "What can I get you today, Walter?" She was in the middle of folding some linen tablecloths that had just arrived.

"I'm not sure if you've heard, but Mrs. Thoreson has had a spot of trouble over at her house."

Betty glanced up from her folding and then back down. "No, I hadn't heard that. Is everything okay?"

"Not really," Walt said

Betty looked up for a longer moment now, curious. Walt didn't elaborate, and finally she said, "Is there anything else you want to say about that, Walt? You seem tongue-tied this morning." She smiled. "Well, perhaps just a little quieter than usual."

"It's nothing, really." He turned as if to leave. "I'll just... I'll just see what I can do."

"What you can do about what?"

Much to her surprise, a story began to spill out of the large man in front of her involving Pastor Thoreson, his wife Anne, and Anne's sister, a woman named Mrs. Bell.

Betty's hands stilled and she waited until the story seemed to finish and Walt shuddered to a stop. He looked at her when he was finished speaking with something akin to embarrassment in his eyes.

"Why, that's just terrible. How is—" she began, but Walt interrupted her.

"That's not all. I just found this on the table in my shop."

He reached into his pants pocket and brought out a crumpled sheet of paper. He took a step forward from the middle of the store where he'd stood frozen until now and handed Betty the paper across the glass counter.

She smoothed the paper slightly and read the message once, and then again. She looked up at Walt. "That's odd, isn't it? Have you talked to Merrick about this?"

Walt shook his head. Betty thought he wasn't going to say anything more, but then he said quietly, "I'm not sure he's able to help right now."

Betty nodded. "Of course." She looked down at the paper again and then back up at Walt. She realized that he must have been wrestling with whether to tell her what was going on when he was pacing outside. She felt a slow flush of pleasure that he had come to her with this situation. "Are you going to look into this for Merrick?"

"I wasn't going to, but now, with this..." He gestured to the note. "I think someone ought to. Though I don't really want it to get around."

Betty thought some more. "You've been keeping an eye out for him and keeping an eye on his office as well."

"How did you know?"

"It's a small town, Walter." She handed the paper back to him and he folded it twice and put it back in his pocket.

Betty wondered suddenly if he wanted her help. The idea caught hold in her mind like the sudden flare of a match in a dark room. She weighed up Walt's discomfort and his reluctance to come inside and decided she must be right. He must be there to ask her help.

The idea thrilled her. Though she loved her life and the business she ran with her husband, she had never felt exactly challenged by stocking tins of beans and counting apples. It was frightfully tantalizing to think of trying to solve a real-life mystery.

Get a grip on yourself, woman, she thought, squaring her shoulders and trying to tamp down her nerves. *You're leaping to silly conclusions.* She tried to pull her face into a more neutral expression and determined she wouldn't press in where she might not be wanted.

Her hands automatically ran along the edge of the tablecloth she'd been folding, and she adjusted it so the corners lined up. Walt kept glancing at her and then glancing away if she met his eyes. In the silence, she could her Christopher shifting boxes in the storeroom.

Walt made a little motion with his head, deciding something. Betty's heart began to beat a little faster. She could feel the pulse in her throat.

The blacksmith turned and strode across the store floor. "I'd best be going, then." He grabbed the doorknob and pulled the door open. Without looking back, he stepped onto the sidewalk and pulled it shut behind him.

Betty sighed and blew a breath out from between her lips, shocked at how disappointed she was. Maybe Walt hadn't planned to ask for her help at all. Maybe he just wanted someone to know what was going on. Someone who also cared about the town constable, and the pastor and his wife. She chastised herself as she finished folding the tablecloth. "Silly woman."

The bell on the front door jingled once more, and she looked up, hoping she could hide whatever disappointment was on her face from the customer coming in.

It wasn't a customer, however. It was Walter Sheehan again. "I wonder if you'd..."

Betty grinned at him. "I'll get my hat."

CHAPTER FIVE

The Thoresons lived in a two-story whitewashed house on a side street just past the new bank building. As Walt and Betty walked toward that part of town, Walt reflected that he didn't know too much about the Thoresons. He knew they were from the Maritimes and he didn't think they had any children, but he wasn't totally sure about that. Frankly, he had never paid the couple too much attention before today.

Walter Sheehan had been raised Catholic, and had never developed any kind of affection for the church. The nuns in the Catholic school that he went to in Dublin, who had spoken of Jesus' love and compassion, had acted almost entirely without both those two traits. This contradiction had puzzled young Walt, and as he had grown older it had angered him.

Pastor Thoreson was nothing like the nuns or priests from Walt's childhood. He was in fact a Presbyterian minister, a form of spirituality that Walt was entirely unfamiliar with. Walt did know that the man knew how to lay on a good sermon, though. Sometimes on a Sunday morning, if his livery chores were done early, Walt would wander down to the building where services were held and take a seat as far back from the front of the room as he could.

Being in a crowd like that with everyone facing forward listening to the man at the front of the room gave Walt a pleasing reminder of home, even though there was less Latin spoken in Pastor Thoreson's church.

As they walked, Betty asked for more details about the missing jewelry, and Walt filled her in with what he knew. He could tell that she was excited by the prospect of helping him try to figure out what had happened. He imagined this was something outside Betty's normal daily experience, and might look like an adventure to her. As he thought this, Walt realized it was true for him as well. It made a change from hammering steel and stoking a fire.

Mrs. Thoreson answered their knock immediately, almost as though she'd been standing on the other side the front door waiting for them. Her eyes opened wide and she smiled. "Walter. Betty. Do come in." She ushered them into the front hall and closed the door behind them, and then turned and looked at them both for a moment, assessing the situation.

"Are you here to help us?"

Walt nodded and, beside him, Betty murmured assent.

Mrs. Thoreson looked at Walt and he saw relief on her face. In response, he noticed he felt a slight reassurance that perhaps he'd made the right decision.

"I see you recruited some help, Walter," Mrs. Thoreson said, smiling at Betty.

"Yes, ma'am. What I don't know about jewelry could fill a castle moat."

She turned. "Come then," she said. "I'll introduce you both to my sister."

She led them to a parlor immediately to their right. The room was bright, with windows on two sides looking out onto the yard and the garden that were Mrs. Thoreson's pride and joy. There were several pieces of simple but well-made-looking furniture: a small settee, a small feminine armchair upholstered in a flowery fabric, and a larger upholstered chair. This last item was clearly Pastor Thoreson's domain, as there was a low table beside it with an ashtray that held, at Walt's quick glance, at least two pipes. The room smelled very pleasantly of pipe tobacco.

In another armchair set close to one of the windows was a woman Walt assumed was Mrs. Thoreson's sister. She had obviously been crying; her nose and eyes were red and she held a handkerchief in her lap. She was the same tiny size as Mrs. Thoreson, and something about the shape of her nose made it clear that the two women were related. But it was there that the comparison stopped. When she glanced up as Walt and Betty entered the room, there was a severity around her eyes that Walt had never seen on Mrs. Thoreson. The woman was obviously greatly distressed, and, despite his discomfort at being in a fancy parlor with three members of the fairer sex, Walt felt sorry for her.

"Victoria, let me introduce you to two of my neighbors. This is Mrs. Betty Mitchell. she and her husband own the general store here in town. And this," she gestured with her hands to Walt, "is Walter Sheehan, our local blacksmith.. May I present my sister, Mrs. Victoria Bell."

The woman held Betty in her gaze for a heartbeat and then looked at Walt. "My, you're a man and a half, aren't you?"

Walt squirmed internally but bravely held his ground on the woolen area rug.

Without a word, Betty walked across the room and sat in a chair that was close to Mrs. Bell. "I'm so sorry to hear about the incident, Mrs. Bell. Can you tell us what happened? Mr. Sheehan and I would like to see if we can figure out who did this and get your jewelry back."

Mrs. Bell looked at Betty and dabbed at her eyes. Then she glanced away from Betty and back to Walt. "Did Anne say you're the blacksmith? Doesn't this town have a police presence?"

Before Walt could answer, Betty explained. "Our police constable is not available at the moment. Mr. Sheehan and I will do whatever we can to help."

Mrs. Bell didn't look pleased, but whether it was about this or about Betty answering her question, Walt wasn't sure. Her eyes continue to leak tears. She sniffled and wiped at her nose with her handkerchief.

Betty tried again. "Tell us when you first noticed that the jewelry was missing."

"Right away," Mrs. Bell said. "As soon as I arrived in this..." She glanced out the window and made a vague fluttering motion with her hand, and then completed her sentence. "...place." She seemed to want to be derogatory, and Walt assumed she meant the town, not her sister's house.

She continued. "I was unpacking and Anne was helping me," she motioned to her sister, "and when I opened up the satchel where I keep my jewelry, the little carrying case was open, which it shouldn't be, and when I looked inside everything was gone." She began to cry in earnest now, and hiccupped with the effort. Mrs. Thoreson went over and put her arm around her sister's shoulders and murmured calming words.

Betty waited a few moments and then carried on. "And what did you notice was missing?"

Through her tears, Mrs. Bell gave a list. "A pair of diamond earrings that my husband gave me before he died. My first husband, that is. A gold and pearl hair comb. Several necklaces. Two came from Paris." She hiccupped again and swiped at her nose. "My second husband gave me those. Oh, and a little wristwatch."

"And you're sure you had them with you when you left Kelowna?"

Mrs. Bell snapped at Betty. "Of course I'm sure. I take those things with me everywhere. They have tremendous sentimental value. I wouldn't leave home without them."

Betty calmly looked up at Mrs. Thoreson, seemingly oblivious to the tongue-lashing she'd just received. "Did your sister come here straight from the steamship? Did you and Pastor Thoreson pick her up?"

Mrs. Thoreson nodded. "Yes, we were waiting at the dock when the ship arrived."

"Mrs. Bell," Betty turned back to the weepy woman, "when you left Kelowna, did someone take you to the dock?"

"Yes, my dear friend Mr. Simpson picked me up this morning and took me to the dock to meet the ship."

"And when you were on the ship, were you ever separated from your luggage?"

Mrs. Bell sighed deeply and shifted in her chair. She turned so she could take her sister's hand. "Anne, I really need to lie down. Can you show me to my room again?" She looked at Walt again and said, "It's so difficult, all this fuss. I was already exhausted from the journey with that horrid little boat captain. What an ordeal." She lifted her left arm and held it out toward Walt. He automatically took her hand and she rose out of her chair. She continued to clasp his hand in hers, and as she and her sister passed Walt on the way out of the room, Mrs. Bell sighed once more. "I'm so glad you're here to help me. I'm sure you'll find whoever did this in no time."

The two women exited the room and disappeared.

From her chair, Betty looked up at Walt and grinned. "Looks like you've made a new friend." She paused slightly and then continued her teasing. "I'm going to call you Man and a Half from now on."

Walt groaned.

Walt and Betty stepped out of the Thoresons' house after saying goodbye and walked down the short walkway to the street in silence. Walt could almost feel Betty thinking. It was like a heat that emanated off her. She was enjoying herself. Walt wasn't sure if he was enjoying it yet.

Betty interrupted his thoughts. She turned to him as they walked slowly down the street back toward the center of town. "What do you think? I'm guessing we should talk to Sully first." Her eyes were bright, lit up by the thought of working on this puzzle.

Walt looked down at her and nodded.

He could see her thinking again, and then she said, "You don't think Sully could've stolen the jewelry, do you? I know he's a bit of a character. He does come into the store nearly every day, of course, though I don't know him all that well. My sense is that he'd do anything to earn a dollar, but do you really think he would steal from someone on his steamship?"

Walt thought about this for a moment, considering what little he knew about Arthur "Sully" Sullivan. He knew nothing of the man's background, only that he lived alone and ran the only freight and passenger ship that Horse had. Walt had had some interaction with Sully since he'd arrived in Horse, simply because the ship's captain spent most of his spare time drinking at the restaurant in the hotel. The hotel itself was still under construction, but Caroline and Edgar Finnegan had made it their priority to get the restaurant up and running as soon as they'd arrived in town. And they were wise to do so. It was the only place in Horse so far where one could get a decent hot meal. For a bachelor like Walt, this was a godsend. He ate there every day, often twice.

Sully wasn't into eating as much as he was into drinking. Which meant he regularly spent his overnights in Merrick's cell, drying out. The ship's captain always swore that he never drank before a scheduled sailing, and Walt almost believed him.

Betty was still waiting for Walt's answer. He looked down at her and nodded again, and they picked up their pace, heading towards the small one-room cabin where Sully slept when he wasn't a guest at Merrick's barred hotel.

THEY ARRIVED at Sully's cabin about ten minutes later. Walt could feel sweat pooling under his arms and in the small of his back. It was a warm day and Walt was grateful that he had thought to grab his hat on the way out of the livery. He glanced at Betty and saw that her face was slightly red from the exertion of the walk over.

Sully's cabin was slouched on its little patch of land, looking exhausted. The cabin was only three or four years old, but to Walt's eye it obviously hadn't been built all that well. There didn't seem to be a square angle in the place. They could hear the sound of an axe striking wood as they got closer to the cabin.

"He's likely in the back," Walt said.

Without a word Betty altered the trajectory of her march and they curved around the side of the cabin, passing some scragglylooking chickens scratching around in the yard.

Walt's guess had been right, and they found Sully beside a little pile of logs chopping some smaller pieces into kindling.

Sully always reminded Walt vaguely of a rat. He had sharp features on a small face, with deep furrows flowing outward from his eyes and more of them curving around his mouth. He never appeared to be someone who was overly fond of bathing, and today was no exception. He was wearing a much-stained long-sleeved undershirt tucked into some dirty black trousers with a tear in one knee. These were held up by a fraying pair of suspenders. On his feet were ragged boots that looked like they were held together with hope more than stitching. On Sully's head was the incongruous black bowler hat that he always wore. It too was stained and dusty, and Walt reflected that he wasn't sure that he'd ever seen the top of Sully's head. The hat was always present.

The man looked up as his two guests approached. He was mid-swing and his axe landed with a thud, splitting a piece of wood in two. Sully set the axe head down on the ground and leaned the handle on the strange-looking white block that he was using as his chopping block.

"Sheehan," he said. "And Miss Mitchell. This is quite a surprise. What have I done now?"

The question made Walt smile. Sully was indeed usually involved in some sort of trouble around town, whether that was liberating vegetables from people's gardens or riding a horse that wasn't his because, as he put it, "It was just standing there, waiting for me." His transgressions were largely harmless, and Merrick seemed to view him as a nuisance more than an actual danger. He just had his own code of conduct that was slightly outside the boundaries of what your average law-abiding citizen would consider acceptable.

But the captain had a good heart. He showed up every Sunday at the Thoresons' church, no matter how hung over he was, helping put the chairs in place before the service. He always chipped in when a hat was being passed around for someone who had hit a rough patch.

Walt pointed to the strange chopping block. "What is that? Is it a bleached tree trunk?"

The chopping block in question was entirely white, with a round center and three long protrusions sticking out from it at regular intervals. If it had been a clock face, these arms would have been at 12, 4 and 8.

The scrawny captain, who always looked like he could use several decent meals just to get him up to what should be a normal weight for his not generous height, leaned on the handle of his axe. He looked smug as he answered, "That, my friend, is the backbone of a whale."

Walt considered the object, but before he could ask a follow-up question Betty voiced his thought. "Where on earth did you get it?"

"Traded for it." Sully looked proud of himself. "I had an old plow I'd picked up somewhere. This Indian fellow I met wanted it so I got the backbone in exchange. Nifty, isn't it?"

Betty spoke again. "There are no whales in the lake. They're saltwater animals. Where did this fellow get it?"

Sully shrugged, unconcerned with the background details of his acquisition, and changed the subject. "What can I do you folks for?" Walt thought he could detect a slight slurring of Sully's words.

Before Walt could answer, Sully turned and disappeared around behind a little shed where some of his wood was stacked. He reappeared almost instantly with an old wooden milking stool. Graciously he brought it over to where Betty stood and set it down beside her. It wobbled slightly as he did so. "Miss Mitchell, have a seat. You look a little peaked."

"Why, thank you, Sully. That's very kind."

Betty lowered herself down onto the stool, and it wobbled again. Her hands went up in that automatic motion we have when we feel we're falling. Walt tensed, getting ready to grab her if she fell, but she figured out how to position herself on the unbalanced stool and folded her hands in her lap. Walt looked at her and smiled internally. She was listing badly to one side, but was obviously not wanting to offend Sully and kept her seat.

"Sorry I don't have another chair, Sheehan."

"No problem. We won't take up too much of your time. We just want to ask you a couple questions about your trip up from Kelowna yesterday."

Sully appeared to consciously arrange the features on his face. He looked surprised for a moment, but then blinked deliberately. "Fire when ready." He looked over at Betty and winked at her as he said this. Sully, the ladies' man.

"I understand you had several passengers."

"Aye, it was a gorgeous day for a trip. The lake was like glass. Not a breath of air. We made excellent time. The conditions were perfect and the leeward..."

Walt waited patiently while the story about the journey ran its course. He was familiar with Sully's long-winded answers to questions. He had seen Merrick grapple with the man on several occasions. What Walt had noticed was that if Merrick interrupted Sully, the story just continued unabated. Merrick had learned to just sit patiently and wait. Eventually, like a windup toy running down, the story would slowly come to a close.

"... And we saw not three but four sailboats, just settin', waitin' for a breath of air. They're likely still waitin'." Sully guffawed at his own humor. He had been leaning on the axe again while he told the story, and as he laughed his hand slipped off the top. He lurched sideways, but was able to right himself almost immediately.

"Maybe you should have the stool, Sully. Are you okay?" This from Betty.

"Fine. Fine." He waved off Betty's suggestion. "Don't trouble yerself."

Walt waited a beat and then continued. "One of your passengers was a Mrs. Victoria Bell."

Sully thought about this for a second. Walt could see him

picturing the passengers from that journey. "Snooty lady? Bad case of chicken-ass mouth?"

On his right, Walt heard Betty snort, and then she covered her mouth quickly, blushing.

Walt looked back at Sully. "Chicken-ass mouth?"

"Aye, you know..." Sully pursed his lips, puckering them like he just had a sucked on a lemon, "...like that." He continued. "She's a tightarse and it extends all the way up to her mouth."

Though he'd said it indelicately, Sully's description of Mrs. Bell wasn't inaccurate. At the Thoresons' house she had given Walt the impression of someone who, when she wasn't feeling victimized, would want things done her way. He had to stop himself from laughing out loud at Sully's indelicate yet succinct summing-up of the woman. It was incisive and to the point. Very unlike the captain's usual style of communication.

"Unfortunately, some things seem to have gone missing from Mrs. Bell's luggage. "

"Wha'?" Sully stood up straighter and adjusted his hat, though he missed the first time he tried to grab the brim. "The hell you say, sir. Not on my ship."

"That's why we're here. I'm wondering if you saw anybody else near her luggage on the journey?"

The captain furrowed his brow and then shook his head slowly, as though he was thinking, but Walt got the sense he was playing for time. Eventually Sully answered. "I never pay too much atten-tion to the luggage once it's on board, I gotta say, Sheehan. Most people carry their own bags onto the ship, but this Mrs. Bell," Sully shook his head again, chagrined, remembering. "I've never seen anything like it. She stood on the dock with her suitcases beside her, staring up at me across the gangplank. For the longest time I couldn't figure out what she wanted. I had a little trouble with the steam engine going down, so I was messing about with that. When we were just about to get underway she started shouting at me from the dock." He shook his head again and let out a snort of his own. "It turned out she wanted me to go down and carry her luggage up onto the ship. I'm the captain, for Christ's sake, not the porter. She had a snooty-ass man standing with her. I don't know what his trouble was, but he couldn't be arsed to carry her luggage up onto the ship either."

Though Walt was amused at Sully's description of Mrs. Bell and her companion, he also felt slightly uneasy with the story. He had no doubt that Mrs. Bell would behave in such a way. It aligned with the character he'd met just a few minutes ago. But something about Sully's delivery was bothering Walt. Sully was reminding him of a poor actor in an amateur production. Complicating this was Walt's strong suspicion that Sully had been into the grog already this morning. His odd reactions to Walt's questions might simply be an effect of inebriation. Walt decided to set this to one side for now and asked, "What about the other passengers on the ship? Who else came up with you on that trip?"

"It were a small crowd, which was too bad for such a beautiful day. Let's see. There was a young fellow coming to work at Finnegan's. I think he said he was Caroline's nephew or somethin'. And then there was a couple, a young man and woman, who were traveling up to claim their land.

"And that was it? Just the four passengers?"

Sully nodded. Deep in his chest, Walt felt a stirring of pleasure. He realized he was looking forward to talking to the other passengers and getting to the bottom of things. Thinking he had enough information to go on, he was about to say goodbye when Betty spoke up from her wobbly seat. "Sully, I've never been on your ship. Can you tell me where you store the luggage when you're underway?"

There was a pause while Sully thought about this. And then he said, "I can do you one better, Miss Mitchell. I can show you."

LAKE OKANAGAN IS a deep lake and not very wide. It runs north and south for roughly 135 miles between Penticton and Horse and then beyond. Traveling by steamship in this part of the world was infinitely easier than traveling by road. It was quicker and much easier on the body than jouncing around in a stagecoach for days on end.

Before he had acquired the steam engine that now powered the SS *Mary Elizabeth*, named after the captain's mother, Sully had rowed people up and down the lake when they wanted to get from one place to another. In those days, he could only take one passenger at a time, and it took up to five days to get to Kelowna. He and his guest would stop each night as darkness fell and spend the night on the shore, and pick up the journey again the next day. More than once Sully had been known to get into his cups on the overnight portions of the journey, leaving his passenger to do the rowing the next morning.

But late last year through means Walt was sure were slightly suspect, Sully had managed to acquire the tiny little steam engine the now powered his slightly larger boat. He could take up to five passengers, and this had greatly improved his financial position, although Walt saw no evidence of that in the outward appearance of Sully's life. The man still dressed in the same old ratty clothes and wore the same tatty bowler hat. Walt suspected that all Sully's profits ended up in Finnegan's till.

When Walt, Betty and Sully reached the dock, Sully proudly, although a little unsteadily, ushered them down to where his ship was moored. Walt had never taken the journey with Sully, and had never seen him in his element like this. The man positively glowed. He walked Betty from stern to bow, explaining all the features of what was really quite a rudimentary ship. It was like a bathtub with a steam engine set not quite at its center. The little engine was about three feet tall and had a diameter of about a foot and a half. Walt was amazed that it could make the journey all the way down the lake and back.

Sully climbed on board and pointed out to Betty and Walt the bench seats in the stern, where the passengers sat.

Betty picked up her line of questioning again. "Where would the luggage go?"

She had followed Sully onto the dock, while Walt stayed on the shore. In answer to the question, Sully moved forward and showed Betty a spot just ahead of the steam engine.

"You want the weight up front like that," he explained. "Most passengers don't have very much with them. It's rare that I get a someone like Mrs. Thoreson's sister, who had two suitcases plus a trunk."

"And the passengers mostly stay seated throughout the journey?" Walt raised his voice so it would reach them, trying to imagine the relative positions of everyone in the ship during the long journey.

"Aye, they do mostly. Unless we've got someone with a delicate stomach." Sully grinned at Betty, and jerked his thumb toward Walt. "If that happens they sometimes move about, trying to ease their troubles. And if that doesn't don't work they tend to be leaning over the side, if you get my meaning."

Walt understood. The one and only time he'd been on a ship, traveling from Ireland to San Francisco, he had lost two stone, unable to keep food down. He had been green around the gills for the entire journey. He had sworn he would never go out onto a body of water and a boat again.

"So for this particular journey the four passengers that you had, including Mrs. Bell, just stayed where they were in those seats?" Walt pointed to the bench seats.

"That's right. The lake was so smooth and calm, we made excellent time. Everyone just sat quiet-like and minded their own business, it seemed to me." Sully burped as he finished speaking, and then winked at Betty once more. "Excuse me, Miss. My lunch must not be sittin' right."

Your liquid lunch, you mean, Walt thought.

CHAPTER SEVEN

When Walt arrived at Finnegan's restaurant, the lunch crowd was in place. Entering the restaurant, he could smell Caroline Finnegan's beefs stew, and he also thought he caught a whiff of fresh-made bread. He realized he hadn't eaten since his small bowl of oatmeal that morning, and determined that lunch was in order.

The restaurant was at present the nicest establishment in the town. Caroline and Edgar Finnegan had invested deeply when they had designed and built it. The floors were dark-stained wide wood planks. The bar at the far side of the room gleamed with layers of varnish that Finnegan himself had applied day after day and honed to a glasslike finish. The tables around the room were furnished with leather-backed chairs. This was no backwoods saloon where ladies of ill repute would ply their wares. Caroline Finnegan insisted that everyone minded their manners when they were in her establishment. Including her husband, who knew better than to swear when his wife was around.

Walt recognized several drovers from the outlying ranches. They must be on a day off to come all the way into town for lunch, he figured. Mayor Billy Jones and his wife Millie were seated at a table for two in the window; if you couldn't find Billy in his office, you could be sure you'd find him here, smoking a cigar and pretending to listen to his wife.

Edgar was behind the bar pouring coffee as Walt approached. The proprietor nodded at Walt, and when he finished pouring he pushed the coffee cup into Walt's hands. "Afternoon, Sheehan. What can I get you?"

"I'll take whatever you're serving for lunch."

Finnegan nodded. "And what about a spot of whiskey? I've got some lovely new stuff in."

"No thanks, Edgar. Just the stew for now. And then I'd also like to talk to your wife's nephew."

Finnegan had started to move away and now he turned and raised his eyebrows at Walt. "Bertram? What do you want to talk to him for?"

"I want to ask him about his journey up from Kelowna yesterday on Sully's ship."

Finnegan frowned slightly but nodded and disappeared through the swinging doors that led from behind the bar into the kitchen.

Walt turned and leaned his elbows on the bar and sipped his mug of coffee, which was hot enough to scald his tongue and so strong you could likely stand a spoon up in it. Just the way he liked it. He thought about this business of investigating a crime, reflecting that it was possible he was actually enjoying himself, despite his initial reluctance to get involved.

He thought about Sully and the man's propensity to stray across the line into illegal territory. He wondered if that could include stealing a passenger's jewelry. Sully had certainly had opportunity. Walt reflected that the passengers sat a fair distance from where he operated the steam engine. The business part of the ship was where Sully would be positioned, and passengers would likely not think anything of it if he was messing about near their luggage, which was positioned just ahead of the engine.

Walt wondered though what Sully's motive could be. He was undoubtedly more financially sound than he been for quite some time. Then again, one never knew what kind of debts another person owed in their life. Finances were never something that Walt spent all that much time thinking about. He had food and shelter and a business that he enjoyed running. He never lacked for customers at either the livery or the blacksmith shop. Being the only game in town certainly helped, and that was also Sully's position. Unless a traveler wanted to spend days on end having their spine jolted in a stagecoach or a wagon, getting up and down the lake on Sully's boat was by far the best option available. It was quicker, easier and more enjoyable than any other mode of transportation.

Behind him Walt heard Finnegan set down a plate on the bar and he turned to tuck into his lunch.

"Bertram will be out in just a few minutes."

Walt picked up his fork and started to eat.

CAROLINE FINNEGAN'S nephew emerged through the swinging kitchen door while Walt was still working on his stew.

"Sheehan, this is Caroline's sister's boy, Bertram. Son, this is Walter Sheehan, local blacksmith and depraved character." Finnegan winked at Walt. "Pay him mind and answer his questions."

"Yes, sir." The boy, for he couldn't have been older than 16, was in a body that very nearly reached 6 feet tall, though it was stick thin. He had light brown wavy hair that Walt's mother would've said was desperately in need of a haircut. His forehead and cheeks were spotted with the red pips of adolescent acne. He was an attractive boy, but obviously shy, and had trouble meeting Walt's eyes. He stood on the business side of the bar and held a dishtowel tightly in his hands, as though he was trying to prevent it from escaping.

"Your uncle tells me that you came up to Horse yesterday on Arthur Sullivan's steamship."

The boy nodded.

"I want to ask you a few questions about that journey. Is that okay?"

The boy nodded again. Walt wondered if he had a tongue.

"Tell me about the start of the journey. What happened when you arrived at the dock in Kelowna?"

Bertram looked at him with questions in his eyes and then shrugged slightly. "What do you want to know?"

"For example, there was a woman traveling alone. A Mrs. Bell. I don't know if you remember her." The boy nodded, so Walt continued. "Was she on the ship when you boarded?"

"No."

Walt wondered how to get more than a one-word answer out of this young man. He realized he needed to ask open-ended questions. "Tell me about what happened when you arrived. Start when you got to the dock."

The boy had been glancing down at the counter, using his dishcloth to wipe at an invisible spot on the gleaming hardwood. He shrugged again and Walt had to resist an urge to rip the dishcloth out of his hands and swat him with it. But finally the boy spoke. "Mother took me to the dock. We arrived early, and Captain Sullivan wasn't there yet. Mother's always early for everything. The captain arrived about ten minutes later, maybe fifteen. He invited us on board as soon as he had tied the ship up. Mother said goodbye and then she left. That was it." Bertram quickly glanced up at Walt and then glanced away again, perhaps checking if that was the sort of information what was looking for.

"So no one else was on board when you got on board."

The boy nodded. "That's right."

"And you say you remember Mrs. Bell. What happened when she arrived?"

Bertram thought about this for a moment. "She arrived in a closed carriage with a man dressed like a banker. The carriage driver lifted her luggage down off the rack and set it there beside her on the dock."

Walt encouraged the boy. "Go on. You're doing fine."

"She and the man in the fancy suit stood there waiting."

"Waiting for what?"

"For the ship to arrive."

Walt nodded. "What happened when Sully docked?"

"She stood waiting while he got tied up, and then after a little while she called up to Mr. Sullivan. She wanted him to come down and get her luggage."

"And did he?"

The boy shook his head. "No. They argued back and forth, and then Captain Sullivan said that that wasn't part of the service that he offered and that the lady should get her own suitcases onto the boat soon because we were leaving right quick." Walt could only imagine how much that had impressed Mrs. Bell.

"But her luggage did eventually get onto the ship," Walt said. "What happened?" He wanted to hear the boy tell his version of the story.

Another shrug. "I went and got it."

Walt waited for more information to be forthcoming, but there was none. "How many pieces of luggage did she have?"

"She had two suitcases. Heavy ones." Walt was thrilled with this bit of exposition. "And she had a trunk. I took the two suitcases up to the ship no problem. But then the trunk was going to be too big for me to carry by myself. I was debating about what to do when a man offered to help me."

This was new information to Walt. "What man?"

"The man who also came on board. I think his name is Smith. He and his wife sailed with us."

This must be the couple that Betty had gone to speak to. Interesting that Sully hadn't mentioned any of this to Walt and Betty. Walt took a second to wonder what that meant, but then turned his attention back to Bertram. "So you and Mr. Smith carried the trunk together up onto the ship." The boy nodded, confirming. "And where did you put it?" Even though he knew the answer to this question, Walt wanted the young man to confirm what Sully had told them.

"Captain Sullivan instructed us to put everything up front, ahead of the engine. There were some crates that we had to shift around, but we got it stored."

"You just set the trunk down and then what?"

Bertram looked at Walt with questions in his eyes. "Then nothing," the young man finally said. "We set sail about five minutes later and that was it. I didn't speak to Mrs. Bell again. She certainly didn't thank me or Mr. Smith for our effort. I got the impression in fact that she was unhappy with the lack of amenities on the vessel."

"What you mean?"

"Well, at one point she was asking what there was to eat. Captain Sullivan told her she could eat whatever she wanted as long as she had brought it with her. That didn't seem to please her. And then a little later in the journey, I heard her say something to Mrs. Smith under her breath about noticing that there weren't any washing-up facilities available on board."

This made the corners of Walt's mouth turn upward. Sully's ship was as basic as they came. It had a gunwale and sides and the few seats that he'd seen for passengers. But that was about it. No cabin. No roof cover. He could only imagine how hot it would get sailing on it in August.

"Was there anything unusual that you noticed about the journey, or anything that happened between the other guests that made you curious or caught your attention?"

At last the boy's interest seemed to have been piqued. He stopped rubbing at the countertop and looked up and met Walt's eyes for perhaps only the second or third time. Walt almost held his breath, waiting to hear what the boy might have to say. There was a long pause and Walt remained absolutely still, not wanting to spook him.

But he was disappointed. Bertram eventually shook his head

and said, "Can I go now? Auntie has lots of washing up for me to do."

He was not wrong. At that very moment, Caroline Finnegan burst through the swinging doors carrying a small wicker basket and came along the length of the bar to stand beside Bertram. She glared at Walt. "Are you done interrogating the boy, Walter? I'm not paying him two bits a week to stand here and jabber."

Walt looked at the boy and nodded his head. Bertram disappeared like a rabbit down a hole.

"Sorry for the trouble, Caroline," Walt said.

"Finish your stew," his hostess said gruffly. But she pulled a roll out of her basket and put it on his plate.

When Betty Mitchell was nine years old, she had run away from home. The reason escaped her now, as she walked down Cedar Street. But she did remember the feeling of freedom that came with her temporary leave of absence from her family home. By the time it had started getting dark, she was cold and hungry, but still had too much pride to go home and apologize to her parents. So she had shown up at the home of her best friend, a girl who was also called Betty. And though the day's adventure had ended unceremoniously, with her father coming to get her and her mother sending her to her room without supper, she still remembered the feeling of being on her own, out in the world, and the thrilling terror that had sent through her.

She and her husband had come to Horse with the intention of setting up the general store that they now owned and lived above. The town itself was an unknown entity. Who knew if it would catch on and grow, or wither away like the towns of the gold rush farther north in British Columbia. They were taking a chance, and it was not easy. They lived week to week, just barely making ends meet, and sometimes not even doing that. But for Betty the worry of getting by was balanced by a thrilling feeling similar to the one she had had on that September day as a nine-year-old. The outcome was unknown. She was free and living outside the boundaries of normalcy that had defined her life up until then.

And now, she felt this way about helping Walt figure out who had taken Mrs. Bell's jewelry. She smiled as she walked, wondering if she could officially be described as a thrill-seeker.

Betty's mother, who wrote to her without fail twice a week, never neglected to mention any bad news that she'd heard about other failed businesses on the frontier. Betty's mother and father lived a very comfortable life in Ottawa. They had both been born in that city, and not only had they never left it, they had never traveled more than 50 miles away from it. It was incomprehensible to them both why their daughter would want to live on the far side of the country, about as far away as you could get from Ottawa without falling into the Pacific Ocean. For Betty, though, that was exactly why she lived here with her husband. It fed her soul in a way that nothing else did, and she loved rising to the challenges that came up for her and Christopher nearly every week.

These thoughts followed her up the walkway to the Smiths' place. She went up the steps and across the porch without hesitation and used the brass door knocker shaped like a fox's head to rap three times on the front door.

The door was answered in a few moments by Mrs. Smith, a woman Betty knew only from the grocery store.

At church on Sunday mornings, Betty could count the number of female heads inside the building almost on one hand. Six months earlier she had barely been able to do that. Any time a new couple arrived in town and the female half of the equation added to the number of women in the town, Betty rejoiced. She was starved for female company, and the addition of Mrs. Thoreson, and the even the odious Mrs. Jones, had made her life that much sweeter.

Adele Smith, however, was another story. This was a woman who only ventured out of her house to come to Betty's general store. For weeks Betty had invited her to the various feminine gatherings around town—the sewing circle, the afternoon teas, the canning gatherings in the fall—but Adele Smith had declined to come to a single one. Eventually Betty had given up asking her, though it went against her nature to do so. Her middle name should have been Inclusion.

"Mrs. Mitchell. How may I help you?" Adele looked surprised and also a little wary.

"Good morning, Adele. I understand that your husband's younger brother and his new bride are staying here with you."

Mrs. Smith hadn't invited Betty across the threshold, but she nodded, agreeing.

"I wonder if I might speak to them?"

"About what?"

Mr. Smith, who Betty thought was named Thomas, appeared behind his wife. "Who is it, Adele? Oh hello, Mrs. Mitchell. How are you this afternoon?"

"Very well, thank you. I was just asking if I could speak to your brother and his wife."

Mr. Smith was much more accommodating than his wife. "Of course. Come on in."

Though her husband had made the invitation for Betty to enter the home, Betty noticed the lady of the house hesitating before opening the door fully to allow Betty to step inside. And with the door closed behind her, it was Mr. Smith, not his wife, who ushered Betty into the little sitting room that was directly beside the front door. He got her settled and was just about to speak when his wife asked her question again "What is this about, Mrs. Mitchell?"

The Smiths' personalities were so much at odds that Betty was unsure how to proceed. They didn't provide a united front, which meant that she wasn't sure whom to address first, or which of them would ultimately decide whether or not to grant her request.

In the meantime, while she figured this out, she addressed Mrs. Smith again. "I understand that Thomas's brother and his wife came up from Kelowna on Arthur Sullivan's steamship yesterday.

And also on that journey was Pastor Thoreson's wife's sister, a woman named Mrs. Bell." She let this information settle in with the couple and then carried on. The next part of her question was delicate, and she didn't want to appear as though she was accusing the younger Smiths of anything. "There's been some question about some property of Mrs. Bell's that has gone missing."

Right away Betty could see that she was wading into dangerous waters. Mrs. Smith stood a little taller, and clenched her hands a bit more tightly in front of her.

Betty bravely continued. "Pastor and Mrs. Thoreson have asked Walter Sheehan to speak to the other guests from the steamship and find out if they know anything about what might've happened to Mrs. Bell's luggage."

Mrs. Smith blinked. "So why are you here?"

"I'm helping Walt with his enquiries."

"Enquiries? What on earth? Are you coming into this home accusing our family of stealing something?"

"Now Adele," her husband said soothingly. "I don't think that's what Mrs. Mitchell is saying."

"I think that's exactly what she's saying. I have no idea who this Mrs. Bell is, or what has gone missing, but I know for certain that James and Eunice had absolutely nothing to do with it. I don't appreciate you coming in here and casting aspersions."

Betty could feel her own back being put up, so she took a deep breath and prepared to defend herself. Before she could, Mrs. Smith leapt in again.

"And by the way, why are you here talking to us? If anything really has gone missing, shouldn't this be police business? Where's Constable Merrick?"

"Well, as you may know, Constable Merrick is struggling somewhat these days with the loss of his wife. He's taking some time—"

Mrs. Smith interrupted her. "Shouldn't somebody official be doing his job for him? Who are you to be asking these questions? Stomping around the community, accusing people of stealing, without any authority."

Betty felt she was losing ground rapidly. She had a sensation like she was sliding on an ice pond, unable to point herself in the direction she needed to go. Adele Smith was absolutely determined to be offended.

"Mrs. Smith, I don't mean to—"

But Betty couldn't get a word in. Adele Smith launched into a tirade the likes of which Betty hasn't seen before.

"Wait until I tell Millie Jones about this. She will be *apoplectic*. Here you are, dragging our good name though the mud…"

Betty tried again to break in. "Not at all, Mrs. Sm—"

"…and spreading who knows what kinds of lies and gossip around town. I've never been so shocked in my whole life."

During the barrage from his wife, Mr. Smith stood silently, looking down at his feet. Any civility that he had brought to the meeting was now gone.

Mrs. Smith took a breath and then lowered the boom. "Please leave, Mrs. Mitchell."

Betty tried negotiating. "I'm so sorry to have upset you. If I could just have two minutes with—"

"Good day, Mrs. Mitchell."

The room was heavy with silence. Betty glanced at Mr. Smith, but he was determined not to meet her eyes.

Mrs. Smith stepped out of the parlor and opened the front door. Betty exited the house with as much dignity as she could muster.

"We'll just see if I've got any of that Keen's mustard you like so much next time you're in my store," Betty muttered to herself as she headed toward the street.

CHAPTER NINE

Betty found Walt at the livery, and unusual for him, he wasn't working. On the infrequent occasions when their paths had crossed before this, he had always been either mucking out a stall or working at the forge in the blacksmith shop. Today he sat entirely still on a wooden chair in front of the livery.

It was mid-afternoon, and the sun was losing some of its power. Betty was feeling sweaty, dusty, and disgruntled, though also, she realized, bizarrely fulfilled. She was enjoying helping Walt try to solve this puzzle, although she didn't have any good news for him.

The tall Irishman had his elbows resting on his knees and seemed to be staring down at the dirt between his feet. He must have heard Betty's boots on the dirt, for as she approached he looked up. He immediately stood and disappeared into the livery, reappearing again instantly with a second wooden chair, this one with two of its back rungs missing. He set this down and gestured for her to have a seat.

"I gather you haven't solved our mystery," she said to him.

He shook his head. "And you?"

Betty shook her head as well. "What do we do now?"

"Damned if I know. This is Merrick's area of expertise, not

mine." Walt thought for a moment, and then turned his head toward Betty. "What did the Smiths have to say?"

Betty answered his question with one of her own. "Have you ever encountered Mrs. Smith the elder?"

Walt shook his head.

"She comes into the store a few times a week to get her groceries, of course. I always thought she was somewhat brusque during those interactions. But today took things to a whole new level."

Walt raised his eyebrows at Betty. She assumed that was the only encouragement she was going to get. He was not a verbose man.

Betty shared the story of her experience with Mrs. Smith, concluding with her expulsion from their house.

Walt grunted and gave her a wry smile. "Did you even get to talk to the younger Smiths?" he asked.

She shook her head.

The blacksmith thought about this for a moment. "Do you think she was covering something up with all that blustering?"

Betty had been considering just this on her way from the Smith house. "I'm not entirely sure. My sense is that that's just her personality. Her husband didn't react to her outburst at all, except to put his head down and endure it. He didn't do anything to stop her, which makes me think that he's used to her behaving that way. I think if her behavior had been unusual he might have tried to reason with her." Betty looked over at Walt, who was watching her closely. "Does that make any sense?"

Walt nodded. "Yep."

"But on the other hand, she did press me about what authority I had and asked about Merrick. It reminded me of the mention of 'the law' in the note you found."

Walt nodded, thinking.

"What about your conversation with Edgar's nephew?" Betty asked.

He made a small gesture with his hands, rolling his palms up into the air and then clasping them again. "Nothing really of interest there. The boy is extremely shy and uncertain of himself. He wouldn't say boo to a goose, as the saying goes. I just can't see him having the nerves of steel that it would take to steal something out of Mrs. Bell's luggage with such a strong chance of being caught there on the boat. He said that he didn't notice the other passengers doing anything suspicious."

The two new friends sat quietly, contemplating their fruitless afternoon. Betty was starting to feel the pressure of needing to get back to the store. Christopher would be wondering where on earth she was. But she stayed for a few more moments, relishing how different this day had been from how her days normally unfolded. She thought about the people involved in this little mystery. She pictured each of them—Mrs. Bell, Sully, the different passengers on the ship. Eventually she turned to Walt again. "So we've got exactly nowhere."

"Yep," Walt said again.

"You're not Constable Merrick."

Walt froze with the door to Merrick's office halfway open. The mayor was standing over the constable's telegraph desk, looking at the tape. He had turned to greet Walt when he'd heard the door open.

The mayor always reminded Walt of a snowman with tree trunks for legs—his very round torso with its round head stacked on top. All he was missing was a carrot nose. Today the mayor was wearing his usual dark suit and dark waistcoat with a white shirt and dark tie. However, in concession to the summer weather, he had on a fawn-colored hat with a wide brim and an accompanying wide sweat stain around the band.

"What gave me away?" Walt tried to affect a genial mood, but he was concerned to find the mayor in Merrick's office.

Until yesterday, Walt had believed that no one had noticed he was trying to cover Merrick's absence. However, Betty had obviously seen what he was doing. And her comment about how small Horse was had rattled Walt. He had hoped that Merrick would pull himself together before now. Walt had been surreptitiously covering for his friend for a little over two months. Finding the mayor checking the telegraph paper sent a chill up Walt's spine. How much longer before Merrick's superiors in Victoria caught wind of what was going on?

"I understand there was a spot of bother over at the Thoresons' yesterday." The mayor took a puff on his cigar.

"Was there?" Walt hoped his expression was innocent.

"Something about missing luggage. Or money. Was it money?" The mayor looked up to the ceiling, trying to remember. "Honestly, Sheehan, I wasn't really listening when Millie was telling me at breakfast."

Walt nodded, feigning sympathy for the married man's plight. Inside his guts were roiling; he hoped the mayor would leave immediately, if not sooner. Walt always suspected he was a terrible liar, and if the mayor asked more questions about Mrs. Bell he was afraid he would reveal what he and Betty were doing. And subsequently get Merrick fired. No doubt word was getting around the town anyway, especially considering how Mrs. Smith had reacted to Betty the day before. But though the mayor was friendly he wasn't the sharpest pencil in the box. Walt had counted on Billy's naturally oblivious state to do most of the heavy lifting in his cover-up.

Just for something to say, and to distract the mayor, Walt asked, "Where is your wife this morning, Mayor?"

"She's getting together with that Mrs. Bell who arrived in town the other day."

Walt's guts churned some more. "Do they know each other?" he asked cautiously.

He had woken this morning with an unfamiliar sense of dread. He was navigating a situation he'd never encountered before, and didn't have the first clue about what to do next. Betty had tried to be helpful yesterday, though her session with the Smiths seemed to have stirred up a hornet's nest more than anything else. And his own conversation with Bertram hadn't been any more helpful. He was at a loss about how to proceed now. Their inquiries seemed to have reached a dead end. And now here he was, caught red-handed, as it were, arriving in an office where he didn't belong.

The mayor was glancing around that very office, and Walt was hoping to keep him distracted, to prevent him from noticing that Merrick wasn't actually there.

Billy answered Walt's question about Mrs. Bell and his wife's relationship. "No, not that I'm aware of." The mayor seemed to finish his inspection and pulled up one of the guest chairs in front of Merrick's desk to sit down. He eased into position, squeezing his ample buttocks between the arms of the chair, letting out a small sigh. "But Mrs. Bell is a big part of the temperance league in Vancouver, and I think Millie wanted to press her for information about how they're organizing things."

It was an open secret that Mayor Billy liked to participate in nearly every illegal or frowned-upon activity available to a grown man. He loved to play cards and was a regular attendee at Edgar Finnegan's weekly poker game. He'd lay a bet on just about anything—when the stagecoach would arrive, how many piglets a sow would deliver, when the first snow would fall. Most of all, the mayor loved his cigars and whiskey. He, and many others in town, referred to Finnegan's restaurant as the mayor's office.

It was also a well-known fact that the mayor's wife spent most of her waking hours trying to stamp out these same activities. How she had never figured out that her husband was one of the people she was working against defied explanation. The only answer Walt had, when he gave it any thought, was that Millie Jones was so wrapped up in herself and the dramas that played out inside her own head, that she didn't notice what her husband was up to. Walt wondered if Billy had worked out some kind of a system or strategy for distracting his wife so that he could get away from her at the times when he wanted to gamble and drink the bootleg whiskey that Edgar Finnegan always seem to have flowing from behind the bar at his restaurant.

The mayor was continuing to talk about his wife's desire to start up a branch of the temperance league in Horse. Walt listened, but with only half an ear. He was trying to figure out how to get the mayor out of the office, knowing that if Billy was planning to wait for Merrick he could likely wait several days and never see the constable. While the mayor sat and babbled on about Millie's connections in Vancouver and her trips up and down the lake to meet with the temperance ladies in Kelowna and Penticton, Walt remained frozen in the center of the room, his hands jammed in his pants pockets, wondering how to get the mayor out of the office.

While Billy's voice droned on, like the rushing of a stream over rocks, in another part of Walt's brain there was something troubling him. Something that the mayor had said had triggered a thought, but it had whipped by so quickly that Walt hadn't caught it. He let go of his focus on the mayor entirely, though he continued to look at the man, and let his mind drift away, hoping that the thought he had missed would come back to him.

"Wouldn't you say so, Sheehan?" The mayor was looking at Walt, waiting for an answer to goodness only knows what question.

Luckily, Walt's friends and neighbors were used to his reticence to speak. He made a slightly noncommittal gesture with his head, a cross between a nod and a shake.

"I completely agree with you," the mayor said. He gave a wheezy laugh and took another puff of his cigar. "Well," he said, struggling to his feet. "It looks like Merrick must be out fighting the good fight somewhere. I'll have to catch up with him later."

Walt breathed a small sigh of relief and followed the mayor over to the doorway.

"If you see the constable, don't send him to the house..." the mayor began.

Walt grinned and the two men spoke together. "Send him to Finnegan's."

As the mayor walked away, the thought that Walt had been chasing landed with a thud.

CHAPTER ELEVEN

Walt couldn't swim, and water in any volume larger than a bathtub always made him nervous. He usually made a point of staying away from the dock where Sully moored his steamship, but today he had no choice. He had gone to the captain's house only to find it empty, and the yard empty as well, except for the chickens. As it was still relatively early in the day his chances of finding Sully at the dock were higher than they'd be once the clock struck 12.

Once more, the lake was like a sheet of glass, but this made Walt no more comfortable. Reluctantly he stepped up onto the wooden planks that formed the dock. He was hyper-conscious of the small waves, more like large ripples, that lapped at the sandy shoreline.

There were times when Walt had been traveling on the freighter that brought him from Ireland to North America when his seasickness had got so bad that he had actually considered throwing himself overboard as a form of relief. He knew that he'd have been dead within minutes, weighted down by his boots, clothes, and coat. It was only the companionship of another young man that had kept him alive during some of the most wretched days of his life.

Now, walking along the dock, he was grateful that it only went out into the water about twenty feet. He tried to focus his eyes straight ahead, closing off his peripheral vision so that he couldn't see the clear blue depths on either side of him. He could see Sully in his ship pottering about and whistling. Sully was a great whistler, and any time he wasn't talking he seemed to have his lips pursed, breathing a tuneless melody. The captain looked up as Walt got close.

"Mr. Sheehan, once again I have the pleasure of a visit from you." Sully's tone was jaunty; however, Walt could see flickers of worry and concern in the man's face.

Walt walked to the edge of the dock and didn't so much lean on one of the tall pilings there, which came up to about his waist, as cling to it.

"Why didn't you tell me about the whiskey, Sully?"

Sully worked hard at looking innocent. He formed a "Who me?" expression on his face, with a dash of shock thrown in for good measure..

"Don't waste my time, Sullivan," Walt said. "I'm about to throw up just standing on the dock. Come onto dry land and tell me the story."

"Finnegan likes dealing with me because he knows the goods will always arrive in one piece. When they get shipped up via the stagecoach, he loses nearly half the inventory but he has to pay the distributor for the full amount."

They had walked off the dock and down onto the beach and were now sitting on a log that had washed ashore. Walt had his legs stretched out in front of him and his ankles crossed. Sully was sitting hunched over himself, with his hands squeezed between his knees, looking about as wretched as Walt had felt when he was on the dock.

It had been Billy's mention of the temperance movement that had started Walt's mind working. Then the mayor's parting shot about being found at Finnegan's had tied everything together.

"But you don't have a license to distribute the liquor."

Sully shook his head. "Too much paperwork. I get it from a bloke in Kelowna, who gets it from one of his mates on the coast. We just work out the arrangements between ourselves."

"Does Merrick know about this?"

Sully shook his head. "Finnegan and I have had this arrangement since before Merrick arrived in town. The previous constable used to take a kickback to look the other way, but Finnegan assessed pretty early on that Merrick was not the type of fellow who would go along with that kind of arrangement."

Walt nodded his head, agreeing.

Sully continued. "So we just try to keep it real quiet-like. I never deliver the boxes of liquor during the day. And we never talk business in the restaurant. Finnegan also keeps it quiet from Caroline, although I think she knows but just turns a blind eye. She's a shrewd businesswoman, that one. Anything that helps their bottom line is okay with her, as long as it's not completely illegal."

"This *is* illegal, though."

Sully made a waggling motion with his head and sat up a little straighter. "Sort of. Finnegan does have a license to sell it. It's my distribution license that's not in place. Plus, it's a—whaddaya call it? A victimless crime."

"I guess that depends. You'd have to have a debate with one of the temperance ladies about that."

"Exactly my point. That Mrs. Bell looks like she'd eat me up and spit me out without batting an eyelash if she found out what I was doing."

"So that's why you didn't offer to help her with her bags and her trunk."

Sully nodded. "Mrs. Thoreson had told me before I left to go down to Kelowna that her sister was in the temperance league. It's just my luck that that happened to be the exact same trip that I was picking up a new load of spirits. I was in a small panic all the way down, but luckily I said a prayer to St. Christopher and it worked out that the driver was at the dock waiting for me when I arrived."

Walt thought about this for a moment. The timing didn't add up. "Mrs. Bell told us she was waiting on the dock when you arrived. Come to think of it, Bertram said the same thing."

"I changed docks. The place where I pick up the ... shipment is separate from where I get the passengers."

Walt had no idea if this was true, and of course there were not many ways to check. He decided to assume Sully was telling the truth this time. "When I asked you yesterday about your observations on the trip back up here, and you acted all shifty-like, that was just because of the whiskey on board?"

"Yeah. I guess that was it. It showed, did it?"

Walt nodded, feeling dejected. He realized that now that he'd tied up this loose end with Sully, he was back at square one.

The two men were quiet for a moment. A seagull walked along the sand, eyeing them for food but trying to look aloof at the same time.

Sully broke the silence. "St. Christopher was really with me that day. When we arrived back here those two biddies from the local temperance league were at the dock waiting for us. I nearly swallowed my tongue when I saw them standing here. I thought they'd got wind of my shipment." Sully took a deep breath, remembering his fright. "But it turned out they were just here to meet Mrs. Bell."

This was new information to Walt. "What two biddies, er, ladies? I thought Pastor and Mrs. Thoreson met Mrs. Bell?"

"They did. That is, they were there too. But there were these two other women as well."

"Do you know who they were?"

Sully shook his head. "I don't know their names. But I know

they belong to the temperance league. I've seen them quarreling with Finnegan over at the hotel."

Walt was cheered somewhat. This gave him a new lead to follow. But there was one other thing that was bothering him. He decided there was no time better than the present to address it. He glanced at Sully and then glanced away, looking straight out onto the silent lake and tempering his tone as much as possible so that what he was about to say didn't sound like an accusation. "What did you really make of that note that I showed you yesterday?"

"The note?" Sully began digging a little hole in the sand with the heel of one of his boots. "I don't know. Why do you ask?"

"You can't read, can you, Sully?" Walt turned his head back towards the captain. Sully looked up at him and their eyes met.

"Boy oh boy," Sully said. "You're sure giving Merrick a run for his money in the detective department."

CHAPTER TWELVE

When the first few buildings in Horse were being erected, it was one of the town's priorities to put up a building that would could be used by the whole community. Pastor Thoreson and Mayor Billy had organized the building of a structure that now served several purposes. It was the church the pastor used on Sundays. It was the town hall whenever there were meetings or elections held. It was the dance hall and the place where community festivals were held, like the harvest festival in the fall. And Walt had also heard rumors that it would soon be a schoolhouse as well, now that several families with children had moved into the area.

With a little bit of trepidation, Walt headed up the staircase to this building that was normally referred to as "the hall." Before he had even got to the third step, he could hear the chattering of the women inside the building. His foot hesitated momentarily, and he wondered if he might put this interview off for another day. But then he had a sharp conversation with himself, accused himself of being chicken, and kept on climbing.

The front doors were wide open, letting the fresh June air in. Today's event was a sewing circle, organized by the mayor's wife,

Millie Jones. Scattered around the room were several clusters of women, seated in chairs, with one form of needlework or another in their laps. There was one tiny circle of about five women who were all working on the same quilt; they each had a different portion of it in their lap and were seated so that their knees were very nearly touching each other. In another group Walt could see Mrs. Thoreson furiously knitting, her needles whirling in the air. The ladies were concentrating on their work and it took several moments for them to notice that he was standing in the doorway.

This was a moment he appreciated. He was able to look over the crowd, spotting faces that were familiar to him, like Mrs. Thoreson and also Mrs. Bell; but there were some faces that were unfamiliar to him as well. Based on the horses and rigs that were outside the building tied to the hitching rails, Walt assumed that some of the ladies were likely from the ranches that surrounded Horse. Perhaps this was their one day to come into town to socialize and to buy any groceries or supplies that they needed.

There was nothing like a room full of women. It created a sound unique unto itself, and Walt remembered it from his childhood when he and his brothers would be sent outside to play while his mother, older sisters, and aunts would all gather to cook or to sew together. It brought back memories for him, and for a brief instant he could even smell the scent of his mother's clothes and skin, as if she was standing there right beside him.

Walt was just about to address himself to the room when Millie Jones leapt out of her seat and came rushing toward him.

"Walter Sheehan, as I live and breathe. I can't believe it. Have you come to do some needlework with us?"

Walt smiled. He hadn't experienced Millie before as a person with a sense of humor, but perhaps he had underestimated her.

"Good morning, Mrs. Jones." They began to exchange a few pleasantries. Walt asked after the mayor, even though he had just seen the man, and he could see Millie struggling because Walt didn't have any family for her to ask after. She asked about his work, and then stumbled to a halt. For perhaps the first time Walter had ever witnessed it, Millie Jones was at a loss for words.

"I wonder if you could help me out, Mrs. Jones." Walt was conscious that the room had grown silent, a completely different atmosphere now from the one he'd entered. All eyes were pointed toward him and Millie. "I wonder if I might speak to Mrs. Pine and Mrs. Sharp. I understand that they're friends of Mrs. Bell's."

Walt had stopped into Betty's store on his way over and got the names of the temperance ladies from her.

Millie, who was shaped almost identically to her husband, that is, about as round as she was tall, perpetually kept her hands clasped across her ample stomach. She turned her head and glanced around the room, apparently finding the faces that she was looking for. "Give me one moment, Walter."

Walt took a step backward, hoping to melt into the shadows cast by the vestibule at the front of the building that he had just come through. However, his intention to somehow become invisible, all six feet three of him, was rendered impossible. He heard the scrape of a wooden chair on the floor and looked up to see Mrs. Bell approaching him, weaving in and around the chairs scattered about the room, her gaze unwaveringly set on Walt's.

"Mr. Sheehan. What a pleasure. I'm so pleased you've came in to talk to me." She seemed to have recovered fully from the day before.

"I'm here to talk to Mrs. Pine and Mrs. Sharp. I understand from Captain Sullivan that these two ladies came to meet you at the dock when the ship came in. You didn't mention that when Mrs. Mitchell and I spoke to you yesterday." He let the statement hang there, curious to see how much she would share.

For an instant there was a wary flash in Mrs. Bell's eyes. Walt was watching her closely, and even so it was gone so quickly he wondered if he'd imagined it. She dipped her head down slightly and then looked up at him again through her eyelashes. The self-pitying woman he'd met the other day at the Thoresons' was gone. She stepped half a step closer and put her left hand on his forearm.

"My, my, you're all business, aren't you, Mr. Sheehan? I'm so pleased that you're looking into this little spot of bother for me. It makes me feel so safe."

Her flirtatious behavior had Walt a little tongue-tied. He wasn't used to women treating him this way. He wasn't very often in the company of women, so they rarely got the opportunity. And if they did, he usually just ended up escaping through a back door. Walt opened his mouth to say something but nothing came out.

Millie Jones rescued him. She arrived back at his side with two women somewhere in age between Mrs. Bell and Millie Jones, likely their late forties. Millie introduced Mrs. Pine and Mrs. Sharp, although she didn't specify who was who, and Walt asked if he could speak to them about having met Mrs. Bell at the ship. The women looked at one another and had a short conversation with just their eyes, and then they turned back to Walt, nodding their heads in unison.

The other women in the group had started to chat again, and the noise level in the room was rising once more. "I wonder if we might step outside?"

The women nodded again. Walt motioned with his hands and ushered them through the vestibule and out onto the landing of the staircase up to the hall. His intention had not been to have Mrs. Bell join them, but she did. For half a second Walt debated about asking her to leave them alone; however, he calculated that this might cause more trouble than it would save. He didn't imagine that Mrs. Bell was someone who would take being dismissed very well.

"Thank you for helping me out, ladies. I'm sure you're as anxious as I am to solve this puzzle of where your friend's jewelry has gone."

The woman who Walt thought was Mrs. Pine spoke up first. She glanced at her friend Mrs. Bell and then back at Walt. "We'll do anything we can do to help, Officer."

Walt was about to correct the woman about his role, but Mrs. Bell leaped in before he could open his mouth. "Oh, Sylvia darling, this man isn't a member of law enforcement. He's just a kind citizen assisting a helpless woman in need." As she finished the sentence Mrs. Bell looked at Walt once more and gave him a coquettish smile.

Walt cleared his throat and carried on. "Did you ladies know each other prior to Mrs. Bell's arrival in Horse?" It seemed as good a place to start as any.

Mrs. Pine spoke up again. "No, not at all. But we belong to the same temperance league. One of my friends down on the coast who belongs to the chapter that Mrs. Bell belongs to wrote me and told me that she was coming out to visit her sister. So Gladys and I went along to welcome her to town and to let her know that there were women of like mind here in this little backwater place."

Walt assumed that Gladys was Mrs. Sharp, the other lady who had so far said nothing. "As you know, what we're trying to do is figure out what happened to Mrs. Bell's missing jewelry. When you got to the dock, what was happening? Were the all the passengers still on board?"

The two middle-aged temperance ladies looked at one another and then Mrs. Pine spoke again. "They were, yes. The gangplank hadn't been lowered yet. And there was a fellow helping the captain tie up the ship on the dock. We waved at the woman we assumed was Mrs. Bell and then just waited until the gangplank was lowered."

"And then you went up the gangplank and onto the ship to meet her?"

"We did."

"Why not wait on the dock for her to come down?"

This seemed to stump Mrs. Pine for a moment, so Mrs. Sharp stepped in. "It seemed the friendly thing to do."

Walt nodded, trying to keep them comfortable and keep them talking. "And when you got on board, was there anything unusual that you noticed? Anything at all that struck you as odd or out of place?"

Both women seemed to think about this for a moment.

Mrs. Bell leaned over and touched Walt's forearm once again. "This is just *so* lovely that you're working so hard to help me out, Mr. Sheehan. I do *so* appreciate it." Walt was conscious of the light pressure of her hand on his arm, and also of a slightly sweet smell that emanated from her. For a man who was used to being surrounded by the smell of horses, manure, and men who hadn't washed in weeks, Mrs. Bell was something of a shock to his old olfactory senses.

Mrs. Sharp spoke up again. "I can't think of anything that we saw that was unusual. We were focused on welcoming Mrs. Bell. There was some shuffling around while Captain Sullivan moved everyone's luggage closer to the gangplank. And it was crowded. It's not a big boat and there were already four passengers plus the captain, and then when we arrived there were six. We endeavored to get out of the way as soon as we'd welcomed Mrs. Bell."

"We exited the ship almost immediately," Mrs. Pine added in. "A young gentleman who seemed to be traveling on his own kindly carried one of Mrs. Bell's pieces of luggage down with him onto shore."

This was an important part of Walt's line of questioning. He wanted to know what had happened to the luggage at this moment of disembarking. "What happened to the other two pieces? There was a trunk and another suitcase." He looked at Mrs. Bell first, and then at the other two ladies.

The three women looked at one another and thought back to the events of the day. "I think Captain Sullivan and one of the other passengers carried the trunk down the gangplank and up the dock to Pastor Thoreson's cart." This from Mrs. Sharp. Walt was somewhat pleased that this detail matched what Sully had said. It removed one question from his mind, although it raised another.

"Pastor Thoreson was there as well?" Walt knew the answer but he wanted to hear the ladies' explanation. "I thought you ladies were picking Mrs. Bell up."

"No, we were just there as the welcoming committee, as it

were. Pastor and Mrs. Thoreson were there to take Mrs. Bell back to their house, of course."

Walt nodded, not really understanding why one woman needed so many people to greet her. He focused on the logistics. "What happened to the other suitcase?"

"I'm not sure," Mrs. Bell said, frowning slightly. "Gladys, do you remember?"

The other two women shook their head, but Walt could also see them thinking.

"Did Captain Sullivan go back and get that one and bring it down as well?" Mrs. Bell asked.

"I think perhaps Matthew maybe went up the gangplank and got it. Do you remember that, Sylvia?"

"I think that's right." Mrs. Bell looked up at Walt once more, and, much to his relief, she spoke to him more directly this time, and with less flirtation. "I think that's right, Mr. Sheehan. You'll have to double-check with Matthew, but I'm pretty sure when Captain Sullivan was returning to the ship Matthew went with him and got the last suitcase and brought it back to the cart."

Walt nodded, thinking. This conversation had only deepened his frustration. The suitcases and trunk had never been left unattended. If they had gone straight from the ship to Pastor Thoreson's cart and then, undoubtedly, straight from the cart into the spare bedroom at the Thoreson home, how could anything have gone missing?

CHAPTER THIRTEEN

"Walter. I didn't expect to see you this evening." Betty Mitchell stood in the back doorway to the general store.

Walt glanced at the carrot in her right hand. "I'm interrupting your supper preparation. I'll come back."

"Don't be silly. What is it?"

He took a step back from the doorway toward the two shallow steps leading up to the covered porch that came off the back of the store. "I'll talk to you tomorrow."

He turned to leave but her hand latched onto his forearm with a surprisingly strong grip.

"Walter Sheehan. Don't be silly," Betty said. He thought she sounded like one of the schoolteacher nuns from his childhood. "Come in and have supper with us and tell us what's been going on with your investigation. You can't leave me hanging like that."

She turned and led him into the store's back room and then up the stairs to her and Christopher's apartment.

"That's some grip you've got there." Walt could still feel the pressure on his arms.

"It's what I get from moving stock around all day." Betty bent her arms at the elbow and raised her clenched fists above her head. "Strong like man," she said, laughing.

~

WALT HAD NEVER BEEN up to the apartment above the store, though he had wondered how it was laid out. As they emerged at the top of the stairs they were in a long hallway that ran left and right in front of them. It smelled wonderful up here. Walt had been right: he had caught Betty in the middle of her dinner preparations.

She talked over her shoulder as she walked away to her left, motioning Walt to follow. "Christopher has just gone to deliver some pears to the hotel. They were late arriving. Come and talk to me in the kitchen until he gets back and then we'll have supper."

She turned right and went through a doorway. Walt followed and found himself in a large, warm kitchen that was filled with light. At one end of the room was a window that, from where he stood, Walt could tell looked out over the main street. That meant that it was facing west and was catching the late afternoon sun.

Betty had a stack of vegetables on a table. He could hear the wood crackling in the cooking stove and there was a large pot gently bubbling on one of the front burners. Betty pulled out a wooden kitchen chair, similar to the old broken-down ones at the livery, except this one was painted white to match the table and looked nearly brand-new. She motioned for Walt to have a seat.

Around the walls of the kitchen were shelves that housed delicate china cups and plates. Along the wall where the stove stood was a shelf with several sizes of metal tins, a teapot, and, at the far end near the window, a collection of candlesticks. It reminded Walt of his mother's kitchen at home. The smells and the sound of Betty chopping made him feel more homesick than he had in years.

"Tell me about your day," Betty said. "What more have you discovered about our little mystery of the missing jewelry?"

Walt thought for a moment. "First of all," he said, "did you know Sully can't read?"

Betty stopped chopping, her knife hovering above the carrot. Then she bent to her work again. "That does make sense."

"How?"

She kept chopping but explained. "When he comes into the store he never has a list with him like some people do. Although you never do, either; nor do many of the men who come to the store. So that has never raised too many questions for me. But the other thing is that he never asks for anything by brand name. For example, if he asks for washing soap and I ask him which brand he wants, he never has a choice and he always just tells me to choose. Which doesn't sound so odd on its own. But there had just been a little tickling wonder in the back my mind." She looked up at Walt. "Why do you ask now? How did that come up today?"

"It was eating at me that when we spoke to him yesterday he got fidgety and was acting strange when I handed him the note I'd found in my shop. I was down at the docks talking to him about something else, and it occurred to me to wonder if he'd been able to read what the note said. He couldn't."

Betty paused for a moment. "So I suppose that eliminates him as a suspect, doesn't it? If he can't read the note he couldn't have written it."

"Exactly."

She seemed to hear the disappointment in Walt's voice. "Were you thinking that it was him who had stolen the jewelry?"

At this moment they heard the screen door in the store below fall shut and steps in the stairwell. Christopher's voice came to them. "Betty? Are you up here?"

"In the kitchen."

Her husband's boots thumped up the staircase and then he bounded into the kitchen. He wrapped his arms around Betty's waist and planted a big kiss on her neck. Giggling, she gently pushed him away. "Sweetheart, Walt Sheehan is here. He'll be joining us for supper."

"Walt!" Christopher exclaimed, seeming to notice the blacksmith for the first time. "What a thrill. You have to try this new beer I've got."

Christopher Mitchell always reminded Walt of a puppy dog. He was perpetually cheerful, friendly, and optimistic. He had the perfect temperament for someone who worked with members of the public all day every day. Where Betty was friendly and smart and helpful, Christopher was all these things plus he had an innate enthusiasm that made being around him almost inebriating. He bubbled like champagne. Walt had often wondered if the man ever had a bad mood or a sad day. His enthusiasm for everything was almost relentless.

Before Walt could say anything, Christopher disappeared out of the room and clattered down, and then back up, the staircase. He reappeared momentarily with two dark brown bottles of beer in his hand. He handed one bottle to Walt and they raised them toward each other.

"Sláinte," Walt said.

"Cheers," Christopher said.

Betty continued with her meal preparations and Christopher chatted to Walt about the price of oats and the possibility of a new spur rail line that was rumored. Walt listened but had trouble concentrating. His mind was still chewing on the problem of Mrs. Bell's missing jewelry.

Finally, Betty said, "Go sit down, you two. Let's eat."

Once they were seated and the men both had full plates in front of them, Betty enquired after Merrick.

Walt swallowed. "I haven't seen him since yesterday morning."

Betty sat in her chair and picked up her fork, though she didn't begin to eat. "How do you think he's doing?"

"He's not eating." Walt looked at the full plate in front of him. "And every time he disappears like this I wonder if he'll be back." As he spoke, Walt felt a tightening at the back of his eyes. Until he'd said these things he hadn't fully realized how worried he actually was.

"We'll keep our eye out for him, won't we, Christopher?" Betty looked at her husband and he nodded, chewing thoughtfully.

"Let us know if there's anything you think we can do for him," Christopher said.

The group ate in silence for a few minutes, and then Betty asked Walt to continue telling her what he'd found out that day. Walt glanced at her husband, wondering how much he could say. Betty interpreted his look. "He knows everything, Walt. Say whatever you need to say."

Between mouthfuls, Walt told them about the rest of his visit with Sully, including the not-quite-legal whiskey he had had on board.

Christopher interrupted Walt's tale. "It's great whiskey, by the way. Have you had any?"

Walt shook his head and then continued. "When I was talking to him at the dock this afternoon, Sully happened to mention the 'temperance ladies,' as he calls them. He mentioned that they'd gone to meet Mrs. Bell as well when she arrived." Walt looked at Betty. "Do you remember him telling us that in his yard yesterday?"

Betty shook her head. "No, I'm sure he didn't say anything about that. Who met her? Mrs. Sharp and Mrs. Pine?"

Walt's eyes grew a little wider. "Yes. How did you know?"

"They're the most active of the temperance league. Irritating old birds but mostly harmless."

The trio continued eating and when the men had cleaned their plates, Betty asked if they wanted more. Walt was too shy to say yes, so Betty filled his plate again anyway. He didn't object.

"So I'm completely stumped," Walt said as he buttered the slice of bread Betty had given him. "If the suitcases were never out of anyone's sight, and it appears as though no one on the ship interfered with them, when did the jewelry go missing?"

The dining room was quiet. Then Betty asked, "Was Mrs. Bell at the hall today?"

"She was, and quite content, it seemed. Much happier than she was when we saw her yesterday."

"Did she flirt with you?" This from Christopher at the end of the table.

Betty seemed embarrassed. "Darling, don't say that."

But Walt was intrigued. "Why do you ask?"

"She came into the store today with Pastor Thoreson." Christopher looked at his wife. "You must have been making lunch up here. They were wanting to buy a new wristwatch for Mrs. Bell to replace her missing one, but we didn't have anything suitable for her. We don't really carry things like that. She'd need a jeweler in a larger center than this. Although maybe it's—"

Betty interrupted her husband. "Christopher, I don't think Walt wants to hear about our stock problems. Why did you ask if Mrs. Bell had flirted with him?"

"Oh, right. Well, it's just that she's possibly the most flirtatious woman I've ever met. She was glommed onto the pastor the whole time they were in the store, and yet somehow she managed to flirt with me as well. Made me decidedly uncomfortable, I must say."

A tiny light was flickering in the dark recesses of Walt's brain. Christopher kept talking but Walt tuned him out, trying to catch hold of what was bothering him. He was broken out of his trance when a voice called from downstairs. "Hello?"

Christopher stood up and went to attend to the visitor. Walt could feel Betty watching him, but she was quiet, letting him think. Her husband returned, his eyes alarmed.

"Who was it?" Betty asked.

"Jane, the girl who cooks for the Thoresons sometimes. There's a problem at the house and Mrs. Thoreson sent her to find Walt."

CHAPTER FOURTEEN

When Walt and Betty arrived at the Thoresons' house, Walt took the stairs to the front door two at a time and banged on the door. No one answered but they could hear shouting inside. He looked over his shoulder at Betty, wondering if he should enter the house. He had one hand on the front doorknob. Without him saying a word, Betty nodded, understanding and granting her approval. Walt turned the knob and they stepped inside.

The shouting was coming from the same parlor where Walt and Betty had been a day earlier. He closed the front door behind them, and he could tell that it was Mrs. Bell who was doing all the shouting. The two amateur detectives stepped into the parlor and right away Mrs. Bell came almost running across the area carpet toward them. "Oh Mr. Sheehan, you've come to save me. Please help me convince my brother-in-law about what's really happened."

The Thoresons were standing side-by-side over close to the wood stove on the longest wall of the room. At a quick glance Walt could see that Mrs. Thoreson wore an expression of anger, shock, and disappointment. Mr. Thoreson, on the other hand, just looked poleaxed. Walt had never seen the minister look so stunned.

"Tell them!" Mrs. Bell shook her finger at her sister and

brother-in-law while she shrieked at Walt. "Tell them the truth. I've been trying to tell them and they won't listen."

"What truth is that, Mrs. Bell?" Walt deliberately tried to keep his tone calm. It was something he'd seen Merrick do in situations fraught with emotion.

"Tell him it was her. Tell Matthew that it was his beloved wife who stole my jewelry."

Walt heard a quiet gasp behind him from Betty.

"Victoria, you're being irrational," Mrs. Thoreson said. "Why don't we all calm down and try to work this out."

He looked around the room at the three faces in this drama and knew that what he was about to say would change this family group forever. He felt guilty about that, even though he wasn't the one who had set this chain of events in motion.

Walt looked at the woman who stood in front of him, shaking, with tears rolling down her face. "Why don't you tell them the truth, Mrs. Bell? Why don't you tell them it was you who stole your own jewelry."

IT WAS like Walt had set a bomb off in the room. Mrs. Bell started shrieking anew, louder and more shrilly than before, raising the level of her dramatics, it seemed, in order to direct attention away from what Walt had said. He made an enormous effort to tune her out and turned his gaze to the couple on the other side of the room to gauge their reactions. He saw Pastor Thoreson take half a step sideways until his left shoulder and hip were touching those of his wife. He reached around behind her, squeezed her left shoulder, and pulled her into him. This kind of demonstrable affection was unusual, especially among members of the clergy. But it seemed entirely appropriate to Walt, and he knew in that moment that Victoria Bell had failed in her aim.

That aim, it seemed, had been to divide the Thoresons and capture Mr. Thoreson for herself.

The shrieking continued, and it was getting on Walt's nerves so badly that he had to make a concerted effort to stop himself from slapping the woman. Betty took charge of the situation then, and, ignoring Mrs. Bell entirely, took Walt by the elbow and pulled him away so that the two of them could sit on a little loveseat. The other couple followed suit and sat together on a matching loveseat opposite Walt and Betty's. Walt noted that they sat very close together, and that Mr. Thoreson still had his arm draped around his wife's shoulders. Mrs. Thoreson's expression had changed from one of shock and anger to a look of deep sadness.

Mrs. Bell began to storm out of the room. She was flailing her arms and yelling about injustice and the absence of qualified law enforcement officers and hick towns.

"Sit. Down." Walt's normally deep baritone had deepened even further and now sounded almost like a growl.

Mrs. Bell stopped mid-sentence, and Walt thought that maybe he had brought her to her senses. But to no avail.

"This is utterly ridiculous! I can't believe I'm having to put up with this. When is the next ship back to Kelowna? I'm never returning, I can tell you that much. What a mess!"

Walt stood and took one step over to where Mrs. Bell was putting on her performance. He towered above her and positioned his body so that he was standing in her personal space. She took half a step back and he leaned in further. "Sit. Down."

This time she did as he requested.

Walt returned to the sofa where he'd been sitting with Betty and leaned his elbows on his knees. He looked over at the Thoresons. "I'll begin at the beginning," he said, feeling slightly ridiculous, but also pleased with himself and Betty. Pleased that they'd figured out what was going on. "I always felt there had to be a motive for your sister coming to visit you, Mrs. Thoreson. It's a long way to come from the coast, and an uncomfortable journey, especially for someone as used to comfort as your sister. You said yourself that you two have never been very close. So I wondered why all of a sudden Mrs. Bell would show up in, as she puts it, this hick town."

Mrs. Thoreson nodded, encouraging Walt to go on.

The next part embarrassed him, but he pressed forward. "I had noticed that Mrs. Bell was a bit, er, flirtatious with me." Walt could feel his face heating up. "And then something Christopher Mitchell said this evening confirmed that this was a pattern with her. It's not every woman who can meet and marry three husbands in one lifetime."

There was another small nod from Mrs. Thoreson, and a huffy noise from her sister.

"And then earlier today when I was at the hall talking to Mrs. Pine and Mrs. Sharp, you," he looked at Mrs. Bell, "made a point of mentioning to those two ladies that I was not the law here in Horse. That was bothering me and I couldn't figure out why, but then I realized it reminded me of the phrasing on the note that was left in my shop.

"As well, the more that Betty and I looked into the question of when Mrs. Bell's jewelry could've gone missing, the more I was convinced that there just wasn't an opportunity during the journey or even shortly thereafter for anyone to have access to her luggage. So that left me with the conclusion that the theft had to have happened once the luggage arrived in the house."

Mrs. Bell leapt out of her chair and waved her arms at Walt. "That's what I've been saying all along! I was just trying to convince Matthew of that very thing when you walked in! Why won't anyone listen to me?"

Everyone in the room, by some sort of silent agreement, stared at Mrs. Bell and said nothing. The accused and accusing woman waited momentarily, and then, perhaps realizing that no one was going to respond to her theatrics, plopped down again in her chair, defeated.

Walt turned to the Thoresons again. "It seems that the missing jewelry issue was created by Mrs. Bell herself in order to cast aspersions on you, her sister, and drive a wedge between you, which might enable Mrs. Bell to then step in and offer some comfort to you, Pastor Thoreson."

Pastor Thoreson gave a quick glance over at his sister-in-law and then brought his eyes back to Walt and Betty. "I can see that now. I wouldn't have believed it an hour ago."

CHAPTER FIFTEEN

Walt was back to working on nails. In a way it was relaxing. More so, certainly, than trying to catch a thief. He could put his body on automatic pilot and let his mind wander away, thinking about other things. He dipped what was probably close to his seventy-fifth nail of the hour into the bucket of water that was always down beside the anvil and was used for cooling the hot objects that he was creating. The iron made its pleasing sizzle as it is he dipped it into the bucket, and the little cloud of steam rose up magically.

His shoulders and back were starting to get sore from being in the same position for so long. He decided it was time for a break. Walt set down his tools and closed the bellows on the fire, leaving just a small gap for air to continue to circulate, and left the shop.

The walk to the constable's office was quick, and Walt was thinking of other things as he strode along the dirt street. Mrs. Bell had left town in disgrace the day before, still protesting that she had been wrongly accused. The missing jewelry had not reappeared despite her sister and brother-in-law questioning her. Walt assumed it was secreted away and would materialize again only once Mrs. Bell was back home.

Mrs. Bell's protestations had been loud and long, but Walt was sure he was right, and the Thoresons agreed with him. Mrs. Thoreson had brought him a freshly baked pie that morning. She had apologized for dragging him into what had turned out to be a family drama.

"No apology necessary," he had said.

There were dark circles around her eyes and she looked sad. "My parents always spoiled Victoria," Mrs. Thoreson said by way of apology and explanation. "They let her get away with almost everything. She was sickly as a child and I don't think they ever got over that. It eroded her character. They didn't do her any favors."

"If it's any consolation, I think your sister is the type of person who bounces back."

"Oh, I know that, Walter. She won't be single very long at all. It will only be a few weeks before I receive a wedding announcement." She sighed. "Unfortunately, our relationship won't recover as quickly."

Mrs. Thoreson had gone on and explained more about her history with her sister. Walt's discomfort had made him want to stop her but she seemed to need to explain. "Victoria and I grew up with Matthew. Did you know that?"

Walt shook his head.

"My husband's family lived just a few blocks away from us when we were growing up and the three of us played together as children. As we grew into teenagers, I started understanding that what I felt for Matthew was more than friendship, but I had assumed that my feelings were mine alone." She glanced out the door of the livery, remembering. "But when he returned from seminary college and before he headed out to his first posting, we grew even closer."

"And that's when you decided to marry."

She nodded and stayed quiet.

Walt had filled in the blank for her. "But your sister never got over the fact that Matthew chose you over her."

"That's right." Mrs. Thoreson had wiped a tear from her eye and then looked up at Walt once more, her gaze strong, though still sad. "Enjoy the pie, Walter. And come for supper one of these days."

~

WALT NODDED to the driver of a team of horses pulling a wagon full of lumber. Another house being built, he assumed. He stepped up onto the sidewalk in front of the building that held the constabulary office and was so lost in his thoughts about family and Mrs. Bell's betrayal that he didn't notice the office door was open until he was almost on top of it.

He hesitated in mid-stride. It was likely Mayor Billy in there again, and Walt was running out of ways to distract the man about Merrick's absence. He thought about turning and walking away, but then heard a familiar voice call from inside. "Sheehan? Once again, you're like a herd of elephants. I can hear you coming from a mile away."

Walt smiled to himself and stepped into the open doorway. He leaned forward and looked inside the office. Merrick was seated behind his desk, opening an envelope with the blade of his pocketknife. Walt's relief at seeing his friend doing his job for the first time in weeks was tempered slightly when he noticed Merrick's cheekbones were even more pronounced than they'd been when Walt had last seen him three days ago.

Those three days had been the longest that Walt had gone without seeing the constable. He had been worried. He had tried not to let it affect him, and had not mentioned it to anyone else, not even Betty. His relief now made his throat close.

But the blacksmith showed none of this as he sat down in the chair opposite Merrick. He tried to think of something jaunty to say, to break the tension in his own body, but he came up empty. So he simply sat and was quiet.

Merrick was the first to speak. "I hear you solved the spot of bother over at the Thoreson place."

Walt nodded.

"What happened?"

"What do you know?"

"I just saw Caroline Finnegan and she said that it turned out it was this Mrs. Bell who stole her own jewelry. Is that right?"

So Walt filled Merrick in. He hoped he didn't sound too pleased with himself for having solved the puzzle. As he spoke, he realized that he had enjoyed the whole experience much more than he thought he had at the time. It was interesting trying to work out people's motivations. And in a way, it was pleasing that the puzzle had been almost impossible to solve, with the suitcases never being out of Mrs. Bell's sight.

"Betty Mitchell was a huge help," Walt said.

"Aye, she's a sharp cookie, that one."

Walt nodded. "She's wasted as a grocer's wife."

"Oh, I think Christopher is actually a grocer's husband. She's the brains behind that business."

Walt smiled. Merrick was no doubt right.

The two men lapsed into silence. Outside a wagon rattled past, its metallic and wooden noises reminding Walt that he needed to finish the rig that he'd promised the stagecoach outfit.

"You've been covering for me." Merrick was looking at the paper in his hand while he addressed Walt.

"Not really. It was a small business with the Thoresons."

"I don't mean that. I mean not letting anyone know I haven't exactly been on the job lately."

Walt leaned back in his chair so that he could gaze out the open door. "I knew you'd be back when you could be."

Merrick pulled a few of the papers on his desk into a pile. "I thank you anyway, Sheehan. You're a good friend."

Walt was quiet, watching a chickadee hop around on the hitching rail outside the office. "I'd be much obliged if you'd not disappear again without letting me know where you're going." His voice was calm and steady, and his tone was without blame or shame.

Merrick was quiet for quite a few moments. Walt heard a tearing sound as he opened another envelope with his knife. From the corner of his eye, Walt saw Merrick nod his agreement. Then he said, "You got any of that stew from the other day?"

the end

WATER HORSE

A Town Called Horse Short Mystery

CHAPTER ONE

July 1889

Merrick was dreaming about Charlotte, his wife. He dreamed about her often these days. She was calm and loving, the way she had been in life. But in the dreams she always had a smile on her lips, a smile that made him think she had a secret that she was keeping from him. Nothing too terribly awful – perhaps a surprise for him that she didn't want to reveal quite yet.

On this night, he dreamed that they met in a railway car, which was bizarre because he had never traveled on the railway with Charlotte. When they had come to Horse two years earlier, they had come up from the coast on a stagecoach.

The train car was rudimentary, with wooden seats and metal luggage racks. In the dream he was sitting on one of the seats, rocking slightly with the motion of the train. She had magically stepped into his view; one minute he was alone in the car and the next there she was.

His body flooded with relief.

There she was. Not gone, but here. She walked over to him silently. He stood and she put her arms around his neck. He hugged her to him and held on to her so tight. He could feel their chests pressed together and feel her breathing. They stood there like that while the train clickety-clacked around them. He and Charlotte were completely silent; no crying, no talking. He just held on to her and breathed.

Then a voice came into the dream. Someone calling his name. At first, he thought it was Charlotte speaking to him. The voice caused him to pull out of the hug he was in with her. When he did so, she disappeared.

He heard his name once more and in the dream searched the train car for her, glancing around wildly, even up to the ceiling.

"Merrick. Wake up."

He cracked his eyes open and then slammed them shut again against the glare of a lantern, just a few feet away.

"Get that thing away from my face, for Christ's sake," he said, deeply disappointed. He could still feel Charlotte there with him. He could smell the scent of soap in her hair. And yet here he was, awake, and without her.

Whoever held the lantern backed up a few steps, boots scratching on the wooden floor. Merrick resigned himself to his reality and opened his eyes halfway. It was Robert Parker, the local doctor, holding the lamp.

Based on the blackness that surrounded the doctor outside the halo of his lantern, Merrick assessed that it was still in the deepest hours of the night.

"What's going on?"

"There's a fire down at the docks."

"In one of the buildings?"

"No. It's one of the boats down there."

Merrick raised his torso up off the bed. He was fully clothed, including his suit jacket, which was now disastrously wrinkled. He reached for his boots and began pulling them onto his feet. "Do you know what ship it is?"

"We think it's the *Mary Elizabeth*."

Merrick, fully awake now, grunted and looked up at the doctor. "Really?"

Dr. Parker nodded.

"Shit."

Boots on, Merrick stood, tugging at his waistcoat and jacket to bring them into something resembling alignment. He picked his hat up off the floor and put it on his head. He walked over to the opposite side of the jail cell and nudged the iron leg of the bed frame that was there, opposite to the one where he had been sleeping. "Sully. Come on. Wake up."

The steamship captain was lying on his back with one arm thrown over his eyes. Merrick could smell the alcohol vapors from his breath as he snored. Merrick kicked the bed frame more assertively this time. Sully snorted and his head jerked up off the pillow.

"Whozat? What's happening?"

"Come on, Sully. We gotta go. Your ship is on fire."

CHAPTER TWO

Someone had brought Sully a wooden chair to sit on and planted it on the beach close to the dock where the *Mary Elizabeth* was normally moored. Sully was sitting with his head in his hands, moaning. Merrick assumed it was partly with grief over the loss of his ship and partly from his hangover.

The day was hot already, and it wasn't yet nine AM. This would be Merrick's second summer in the North Okanagan, and he still wasn't used to the hot, dry weather. He was from the Ottawa Valley, where the summers were humid, such that you'd soak through your clothes ten minutes after putting them on. This heat was different. In a way he found it more manageable, but the previous summer he had also felt like he was living in an oven for much of the time.

Once they were able to get Sully up on his feet and out of the cell in Merrick's office, Dr. Parker had led the way. At first they were guided by the light of the doctor's lantern, but very soon the light being thrown from the lake was what showed them the way. They could see the burning boat from several blocks away. Sully gasped and started to run, though he stopped after a few very short shuffling steps. Merrick imagined that the pain in his drunken head would only tolerate so much jostling.

When they arrived at the dock, the men who were there, including Mayor Billy Jones and Walter Sheehan, the town blacksmith and Merrick's closest friend, had wisely pushed the boat out away from the dock and were standing, watching it burn, as though it were a bonfire at a New Year's Eve celebration.

It was beautiful in a way. The bright orange and red flames lit up the night, and their reflection danced on the black surface of the night water.

Walt nodded at Merrick as the three men arrived on the dock.

"How did it start?" Merrick asked the group in general.

It was Mayor Billy who answered. "No idea, son. It was me that saw it first. I couldn't sleep. Too damn hot. So I was out for a walk. The funny thing is I heard it before I saw it. I heard the crackling when I was a couple blocks over. I couldn't figure out what it was for the life of me for quite a while. But then I followed my ears down here and eventually could see the glow and smell the smoke." The mayor looked over at Captain Arthur 'Sully' Sullivan. "Very sorry about this, Sully."

Clearly Sully was in shock. He hadn't said a word and just stood with his hands hanging loosely at his sides, looking out at the ship that was not only his pride and joy, but his livelihood as well.

Captain Sullivan was an enterprising man. Merrick hadn't known him for very long, but he had heard stories told of all the various enterprises that Sully had started or become entangled with. These included, but were not limited to, gold panning, cattle ranching, cattle transportation, and shoe sales. His latest venture had been captaining the *Mary Elizabeth* up and down Lake Okanagan, transporting freight and people. He had started a few years earlier with a rowboat, and would literally row the goods and passengers down the lake to Penticton or Kelowna. It took five days and at the time Sully had had the shoulders and arm muscles of a circus strongman. But then, by means that no one was entirely clear about, he had somehow acquired a small steam engine. The engine was about three feet high and about a foot and half in diameter and he had had it installed on a slightly larger boat that he'd built. He had christened her the *Mary Elizabeth* after his mother, and this was the vessel that was aflame in front of them on the lake.

The small knot of men stood silently listening to the crackle of the wooden ship as it slowly dissolved into smoke and soot in front of their eyes.

"Did you see anyone else around here, Mayor?"

Mayor Billy shook his head. "Not a soul."

When Sully started to quietly cry, Merrick sent Dr. Parker to find a chair and they pulled Sully off the dock and onto the beach.

~

MERRICK WASN'T MUCH of a swimmer himself, but he was willing to lend a hand.

Once the sun had started to rise, and the fire had extinguished itself in the waters of the lake, it was Walt who said, "There's no reason we can't retrieve the engine."

Merrick had wanted to dismiss the idea. He was still annoyed that his dream had been interrupted. But he realized Walt was right. The boat had burned just a few feet away from the top end of the dock; the lake was probably only ten or twelve feet deep at that point.

The men from the town had consulted one another and determined that it would be possible to retrieve the engine and probably fix it up and get it in running order again. Mayor Billy had clapped Sully on the back and assured him that all would be well very soon. Sully's head was still in his hands. This news didn't revive him.

There's nothing like having a new and interesting problem to solve that will get men excitedly working to find the solution. Word had spread around town at lightning speed, like it always did. The crowd at the beach had grown and included virtually everyone who lived in Horse. Mrs. Thoreson, the pastor's wife, ever thoughtful and sublimely organized, had brought two picnic baskets filled with bread and cheese and preserves. The townsfolk busied themselves setting up tables and chairs and picnic blankets on the beach. This was the most exciting thing that had happened in months. Two or three children, daughters and sons of new residents, ran up and down the beach, shrieking with delight, thrilled to have a day off from the normal routine of chores and schoolwork.

Walt and Dr. Parker had gone to the nearby boathouse to retrieve a small rowboat. The idea that the men had come up with was to row out to where the boat had burned and have someone dive down to the floor of the lake, secure a rope around the engine, and pull it to the surface.

Merrick wasn't entirely convinced this plan would work, but he was fully supportive of the effort to try it out. Sully's transportation service on the *Mary Elizabeth* was absolutely essential for the commerce of the town. In the fair weather, when the lake wasn't frozen, the passenger service helped people get quickly back and forth from this remote place. They could travel up the lake in a few days, rather than two weeks or more of jolting, profoundly uncomfortable travel in a stagecoach or wagon, which was required if you came over land.

And Merrick felt for Sully as well. Since he had acquired the steam engine he had prospered. The one thing he had noticed was that Sully spent fewer nights in Merrick's jail cell, drying out. Although last night was an exception.

Sully had just come off several back-to-back trips up and down the lake, and had been looking forward to several days off. He'd kicked off this break with a long evening spent at the Finnegans' hotel bar. Merrick had been sitting in his office, dreading the idea of going home to his empty house, when Edgar Finnegan had delivered Sully just after midnight, dropping the captain onto a jail cell cot with a well-practiced heave. Having Sully there was the perfect excuse for Merrick; he would keep an eye on him and sleep on the other cot in the cell, thus avoiding the unwelcome task of going home altogether.

Now Walt, his blacksmith arms pulling the oars effortlessly, propelled the small boat smoothly toward the dock where Christopher Mitchell was waiting. Christopher and Walt held the boat steady, Christopher from the dock and Walt from the boat itself, while Edgar Finnegan climbed on board. Dr. Parker said he was a strong swimmer and the other men took him at his word. He had stripped down to his underwear, and his bleached white torso looked incongruous among the clothed men who surrounded him. Merrick handed the men two lengths of rope, coiled up like snakes.

When everyone was settled, the men pushed off. Walt steered them out along the glassy surface of the lake until they were roughly over the position where the *Mary Elizabeth* had burned. Pieces of blackened wood floated silently on the small ripples created by Walt's oars.

Awkwardly, Dr. Parker climbed over the side of the rowboat, tipping it precariously. The other men held on until he let go and dropped into the water. He took a moment to get his bearings and then reached an arm out. Edgar Finnegan handed him one of the pieces of coiled rope. The doctor had to hand it back to Finnegan.

"Hang on to one end, Finnegan. And then hand me the rest."

Finnegan did as he was told, and when the doctor had the rope secured over one shoulder he took a deep breath and disappeared under the surface of the water.

Merrick could hear chattering and conversation behind him on the shoreline. Betty Mitchell was standing beside Sully's chair, keeping everyone company and eating an apple. She smiled at Merrick and gave him a little wave. He waved back and then turned to watch the water once more.

He could still feel the fabric of Charlotte's clothes against his hands and the pressure of her chest on his. The feeling of the dream was so real and palpable it made him ache from head to foot. He had been having a dream similar to this one at least once a week since Charlotte had died. It never failed to be a bittersweet occurrence. While the dream was happening he was the happiest man in the world, a man relieved of the burden of grief and soul-crushing loss. Then when he awoke, he had to come to grips with that loss all over again. Confusingly, this was tempered by the lingering memory of holding Charlotte close to him, and he would often spend the rest of the day wrestling with the double-edged sword that the dream presented.

Dr. Parker's head burst through the surface of the lake and Merrick heard him take a deep breath as he rose.

"I found it," he said, pushing water out of his eyes. "It's going to take me a few more tries to get the rope around the engine." He was holding on to the edge of the rowboat, explaining this to the men inside, but Merrick heard and he assumed everyone on the beach heard as well. Dr. Parker glanced over to where Merrick was standing at the end of the dock and gave him a thumbs-up. Merrick nodded to the doctor, who then took another deep breath and disappeared once more.

It took close to an hour and many dives from Dr. Parker to get the rope into position. And then when that was done, it took several more tries from the men in the boat to pull the engine up. Ultimately, they had to tie a second rope around the engine so that it was balanced horizontally while they hauled it up to the surface. Otherwise it just slipped out of the knot that the doctor had tied to it.

Pulling the engine out of the water and up into the rowboat had provided yet another challenge, but they did it. Dr. Parker wouldn't fit in the rowboat once the engine was on board, so he swam to shore, flopping onto the sand to be ministered to by the town's female population, something Merrick was certain he enjoyed very much. He deserved the attention. What he had done was remarkable.

Sully had remained immobile throughout this whole exercise, leaning into his hands and only once walking over to the lake's edge to splash water on his face.

The rowboat pulled up alongside the dock. The men on board tied it up and then pulled the gleaming engine up onto the dock itself, its brass casing shiny with lake water. Then Sully came down the dock, walking slowly at first and then breaking into a trot. He threw his arms around Edgar Finnegan, who was closest to him.

"I can't believe you did it."

"Thank the doc, Sully. It was his idea."

Sully glanced down the beach to where Dr. Parker was seated with a towel over his shoulders and a piece of cake in one hand and a mug of tea in the other. Sully yelled his thanks and the doctor raised his mug, toasting the captain.

Several other townspeople surrounded the engine on the dock now and began speculating about how to get it back up and running. Sully was clearly relieved, and Merrick was happy for him. What had started out as a very dark day now had some hope.

Merrick stood to one side on the dock, listening. What he knew about steam engines could fit inside a thimble. Instead, his mind was focused on wondering how the whole event had happened in the first place. Had it been an accident? How does a ship spontaneously burst into flames? He glanced out to the lake's surface, where the little collection of burnt sticks and boards bobbed, slowly spreading outward. Whatever had happened, there was no evidence for it now. The entire vessel had been burned to a crisp.

Sully must have followed Merrick's gaze. "You're going to find out who did this, right, Merrick?"

Merrick glanced down at the man standing beside him. Sully was bareheaded for perhaps the first time in Merrick's memory. Normally the captain wore a dusty, dirty bowler hat perched at a jaunty angle on his head. He must've left it in the cell in the rush to get down to the waterfront.

Before Merrick could answer, Sully's attention was suddenly pulled away. He looked to his left, down the length of the dock, and Merrick watched his expression turn from one of curiosity to one of fury. Sully spun on his heels and began running back up the dock.

He reached the end of the dock, leapt onto the beach and raced not to his left or right along the shoreline, but straight ahead, up toward the street that paralleled the lakefront. There Merrick could see a couple, a man and a woman, walking toward the waterfront. He couldn't hear any words that were spoken, but the man opened his arms in a welcoming gesture, as though he wanted to give Sully a hug.

But as Sully approached him, Merrick noticed with alarm that he was hardly slowing down. Instead, Sully continued running full tilt and as soon as he got within an arm's length of the couple, he pulled back his right hand and punched the man square in the nose.

CHAPTER THREE

Dr. Parker wasn't pleased at being pulled away from the ministrations of Mrs. Thoreson, Betty Mitchell, and the other women. He shrugged into his coat jacket, pulled his trousers over his wet underwear, shoved his feet into his boots, and stumped over to the little street brawl.

The woman who was with the man with the now bloody nose had slapped Sully as soon as her companion had hit the ground, rocked back by Sully's punch. She had slapped him once and then again and then, after a short pause, had begun battering him about the head and chest with open palms. Walt and Merrick had to pull her away from Sully, while she shrieked and let loose a few very unladylike words.

Merrick's first instruction was to get the doctor's attention onto the man. Next, he waved Betty Mitchell over and asked if she would escort the woman to the doctor's office.

Dr. Parker and Walt helped the man to his feet and prepared to escort him down the street and along the several blocks to his office. The doctor instructed him to keep his head tilted back, and each one held an elbow so that the man could walk without seeing where he was going. Blood continued to pour from his nose as they walked. His shirt front and jacket were liberally splattered.

Merrick himself held onto Sully's elbow and marched him behind the two ladies. The three separate groups were like a little parade walking the side streets.

Merrick shook Sully's elbow as they walked. "What was that about?"

Sully's face was red and furrowed with anger and indignation. "He did it. He burned the *Mary Elizabeth*."

Merrick glanced at Sully with raised eyebrows. "He did? How do you know?"

"I'm sure of it. That good-for-nothing, treacherous bastard. He's always into some scheme and I'm sure he's behind this."

Merrick was still confused. "How do you know that? Who is he?"

"He's my half-brother, the shitheel."

MERRICK LED SULLY straight into the doctor's office but sat him on an upholstered chair in the living room, which did double duty as his waiting room. Walt was standing in the doorway to the doctor's examining room.

"Keep an eye on him, will you?" Merrick said, indicating Sully.

Walt nodded and went and sat on a chair close to the captain, who was massaging the knuckles of his right hand.

Betty and the woman, who Merrick assumed was Sully's brother's wife, were standing to one side in the examining room while Dr. Parker packed the man's injured nose with cotton and instructed him to keep his head tilted back and press on the bridge. The man was sitting on Dr. Parker's examining table now, but when he had been walking Merrick had noticed that he was slightly shorter than average height. He had a large protruding belly that reminded Merrick of a drawing of St. Nicholas he'd seen once. With his head tilted back and his face covered in blood, it was hard for Merrick to see if there was any resemblance to Sully. At any rate, this man was much more amply filled out. Sully always looked as though he had missed his last six or seven meals.

The woman, who was still holding onto Betty's elbow, was extraordinarily pretty. She had hair that was so blonde it fairly glowed. It was gathered loosely at the back of her neck and then hung down her back halfway to her waist, tied in a loose braid. She had porcelain skin and bright blue eyes, and wore a dress that was a shade of blue that brought out the color of her eyes spectacularly. On her head she had a straw hat with flowers placed around the headband, and she was carrying a small fringed purse with a chain handle.

Betty Mitchell, who was in her own right a pretty woman, looked as plain as a doorknob standing beside this specimen of feminine beauty. Betty was wearing her black grocer's dress with its white apron. Her light brown hair was swept into a bun at the back of her neck, and her face was flushed, probably from exposure to the sun that morning, but also from the exertion of walking up from the lake. She looked at Merrick now with questions in her eyes, and he wanted to say to her, "I have all the same ones."

He looked at Parker. "Is it okay if I ask the patient a couple of questions, Doc?"

The doctor nodded, and continued wiping blood off his patient's face with a damp cloth. Parker looked completely ridiculous with his jacket on and no shirt underneath. His wet hair was askew, as were his whiskers, which also contained a few crumbs from the cake he'd been enjoying.

Merrick addressed the man sitting on his examining table. "I understand you're Captain Sullivan's brother."

From the living room Sully shouted, "Half-brother!"

The man spoke up. "Arthur's right. We're half-brothers. Same father, different mothers." The man tilted his head slightly so that he could look at Merrick and held out the hand that wasn't pinching the bridge of his nose. "Clarence Horan," he said. "Plead to meed you." His diction was affected by the cotton in his nose

The hand that was offered was his left so Merrick did an awkward grasp-and-shake with his right hand. "What brings you to Horse, Mr. Horan?"

The woman standing with Betty spoke up before Horan could. "He came to see his brother, didn't he? Quite a fine how-do-you-do." For such a delicate creature, the woman had a surprisingly deep and husky voice, which, to Merrick, only made her more attractive.

"I gather there's some sort of bad blood between you and your brother, Mr. Horan," Merrick said, looking back at the man on the table.

Once again, from the living room, Sully shouted, "Half-brother. And you're goddamned right there's bad blood. Ask him about my gold pocket watch."

Merrick took two steps over to the doorway of the examining room. "Walt, could you take him outside, please?"

Walt nodded and stood up. He glanced down at the captain. Sully stood without comment, though he glared furiously at Merrick while he did so, and the two men exited the house.

Merrick stepped back over to the examining table. "Now, Mr. Horan, why don't you tell me what you're doing here in Horse and what might've provoked your brother – sorry, half-brother – to punch you on the nose."

"Well, Constable, if you know my brother at all you know that he can be a little fractious." Horan was able to tip his head forward now and had to both speak and breathe through his mouth. The tufts of white cotton billowing out of both nostrils seemed to be doing their job. The bleeding had stopped. The skin around Horan's eyes was already starting to turn dark blue.

Horan had curly brown hair with a deeply receding hairline that formed two valleys of bare scalp reaching back from his forehead. His face was puffy, and this seemed to be its natural shape, not the result of his altercation with Sully. His nose was wide with a bulbous end – a good target, Merrick thought ruefully. And his puffy cheeks made the man's eyes appear small and sunken slightly into his head.

Now that he had a better look at Horan's face, Merrick remarked to himself once again that he didn't see much resemblance between this man and Captain Sullivan. However, Merrick did recognize the same mischievous glint in Mr. Horan's eye that he saw so often in Sully's.

"Am I all done here, Doc?"

Dr. Parker nodded. "Come back tomorrow and I'll unpack that nose and we'll see where we're at."

Horan nodded and hopped down off the examining table. He pulled his jacket and his waistcoat straight and stood up tall. He flashed a wide, shit-eating grin at Merrick. "That's a fine welcoming committee you've got here, Constable."

MERRICK LED the way and the four trooped outside, blinking as they adjusted to the bright sunlight.

"I don't think you need me anymore, do you, Merrick?" Betty Mitchell asked.

Merrick shook his head at her, his thoughts on Sully, the burned boat, and now this half-brother complication. Betty nodded and walked away, back toward the lakeshore.

Sully and Walt were standing beyond the little picket fence that surrounded Dr. Parker's front yard. When Sully saw the group emerge from the house, he came running through the gate, brushing past Betty, and launched himself once more at Clarence Horan. Walt came running after him and grabbed him just as Merrick was stepping in to put his body between Sully and Horan.

Merrick never seen Sully so worked up. The captain, when he was sober, had a lot of energy and was never still for very long. Merrick suspected this was another reason for the absence of an ounce of extra flesh on Sully's bones. And when he was drunk he was as mellow as mellow could be, and usually ended up falling asleep face first on Edgar Finnegan's bar. He never picked fights or was an angry drunk, so this side of him bent on attacking his brother was a total surprise to Merrick.

Walt stood with one beefy forearm pressed against Sully's chest so that Merrick could interview the two men. "Sully, you're going to have to calm down."

"You tell him to calm down," Sully said, which didn't make any sense. He continued, "Arrest him. Arrest him right now. He's the one who burned the *Mary Elizabeth*."

Horan looked from Walt to Merrick. "Who is *Mary Elizabeth*?"

"My ship, you asshole. You know perfectly well that's who she was. You set fire to her, burned her right down to ashes. Admit it."

"Now, Sully," Merrick said calmly, trying to defuse the situation. He began to speak again but Sully interrupted him, shouting.

"Is it a coincidence that this turd shows up on the exact same day that the *Mary Elizabeth* goes up in flames? I think not. Case closed, Merrick. Here's your culprit right here. Arrest him, I said."

Almost without effort, Walt's arm was doing a good job of keeping Sully from lunging forward again. Sully was like a bird flapping against the bars of a cage.

Horan straightened his suit jacket once again and flicked something off his lapel, an incongruous gesture considering his jacket was covered in blood and would likely have to be thrown away. He looked at Merrick. "I assure you, Constable, I have no idea what my lunatic of a half-brother is talking about. Mrs. Horan and I have been touring the province and we heard that Sully lived here, so we thought we would come by for a visit."

"When did you arrive?" Merrick asked.

"Yesterday."

"Aha!" Sully shouted. "See?" His eyes were wide and frantic, looking back and forth from Merrick to Horan. "I told you. I told you it was him. You arrived yesterday, you say? Just enough time to figure out which boat was mine and set her on fire this morning."

Merrick made a calming gesture with one hand toward Sully.

"I'll ask the questions," he said. "Where are you staying, Mr. Horan?"

"The finest establishment in town seems to be the Stratford Hotel, so we have a room there."

Mrs. Horan had been completely silent throughout this whole encounter. Merrick glanced at her and noticed that she appeared to be slightly bored.

"And you arrived yesterday? Did you come over land?"

"Yes. We caught the stagecoach coming over from Lumby. We were very fortunate they added another trip; otherwise, we would've had to wait several days. And I was anxious to see my baby brother." With this comment Horan gave Sully a smile, though it was without warmth.

"Arthur's mother said that he was living here. She mentioned that he had a successful shipping operation, but I didn't believe her. Arthur has never been a success in anything before." He looked away from Merrick and gave Sully the cold smile once again. "I guess that truism still holds, now that your so-called ship has been burned to a crisp."

At this, Sully burst past the containment of Walt's arm and threw himself once more at his brother. He jumped on top of Horan, latched himself around his neck, and tried to pull him to the ground.

It took Walt and Merrick several moments to pull the two men apart. Merrick was surprised at Sully's strength, given the man's tiny frame. He was reminded of the legend of Sully's days rowing up and down the lake.

"Alright, Sully that's enough. Back to the clink for you." Merrick held Sully's arms behind him and turned him so they could walk away.

"See you later, little brother," Horan called after them.

"Half-brother!" Sully shouted over his shoulder.

CHAPTER FOUR

Sully was fuming. He paced, shouting at Merrick through the bars of the cell.

It was rare that Merrick ever had to close the door to the cell and use the lock. When he and Walt had escorted Sully in there he had asked Walt to hold the door closed while he searched for the key for several minutes. He found it buried under some paperwork in a drawer of his desk.

Merrick inserted the skeleton key and turned it, the tumblers clicking into place. "Sully, you're going to have to calm down while we get to the bottom of this. You shouting and attacking people isn't going to help us figure out who burned the *Mary Elizabeth*."

"That goddamned asshole did. You saw the look in his eye. You can tell, right?" Sully came over to the bars of the cell and pushed his face through one of the gaps. "You're a good judge of character, Merrick. You can see that he's a thieving, conniving, lying bastard, can't you? It's written all over his face."

"Sully, I prefer not to judge people based on appearances. If you want to calm down and speak rationally I'll be willing to listen to what you have to say."

Sully made an exasperated noise and pushed away from the

bars of the cell, and began pacing in a circle around the enclosed space, muttering to himself and flailing his hands about. Merrick decided that, like a wound-up toy, the best possible thing he could do was to let Sully unwind. Then, when he was calmer, they could have a conversation.

Walt took a seat in one of the chairs opposite Merrick's big oak desk that was the centerpiece of the constable's office. Merrick turned and looked at him and saw the amused glint in his eye; it was often there, but was cranked up a little today. "You're enjoying this, aren't you?"

"It sure beats shoveling horse shit, I'll say that."

Merrick turned toward his desk and took a deep breath. He wanted to spend some time organizing his thoughts. The *Mary Elizabeth* was important to the commerce in Horse and he meant to find out what had happened, even if it was an accident. Before he could sit down, the door to the office swung open and there stood Edgar Finnegan. He stepped inside and glanced over, noticing Sully still circling in his cell like a mad tiger.

"Emergency town council meeting, Merrick. The mayor wants you there."

"When? Now?"

Finnegan nodded. "Yep," he said. "The mayor and the other counselors, including myself, want to figure out right away what to do about replacing the *Mary Elizabeth*. It's important we get things rolling as soon as we can."

Merrick nodded.

"All right." He thought for a moment. "Walt, can you possibly stay here and keep an eye on Sully for a couple of hours? I don't want to leave him alone given the state that he's in."

Walt nodded. "No problem."

W alt hadn't had breakfast. He had been roused by someone banging on the front doors of the livery that morning long before dawn. He had grabbed his clothes off the floor, dressed quickly, and run down to the waterfront, the same as virtually everyone else in town.

He thought that Merrick kept a canister of oatmeal here in the office for days when he wasn't able to eat before he left home. Although, Walt reflected as he searched the small cabinet in one corner of the room, these days he expected that Merrick was having his breakfast here at the office more often than not. From what Walt had observed, the constable was spending most nights on one of the jail cell cots.

Walt had never been married, so he had no frame of reference for what his friend was going through since Charlotte had died. He imagined that sleeping, wherever he could find rest, was the best part of Merrick's day.

He found the tall tin canister of oats and a little cast iron pot. It didn't look especially clean, but then Walt wasn't especially fussy.

Despite this reflection about Merrick's grief this morning,

Walt was actually cheered. He had been observing all morning that Merrick had been completely engaged both at the waterfront and then at Dr. Parker's office. This was the first time that Walt had observed this since Charlotte had passed away five months earlier.

In fact, Walt had spent much of his time during that five months covering for Merrick. It was just what you did for a friend in need. Walt didn't expect or need any acknowledgment of that, but he was heartened to see that perhaps he could back off the things that he had been doing for Merrick – surreptitiously delivering the mail, retrieving the telegraph messages that came through, and distributing those as though he was Merrick's messenger and not his stand-in.

He poured water from the kettle into the pot and then began fiddling around inside the wood stove preparing a fire. The kindling caught and began to crackle, and he pushed the stove door nearly closed, leaving it open several inches to allow air flow. He remained crouched down in front of the stove, watching the flames lick up the kindling and grow. Gradually he added a couple of larger pieces of wood from the basket beside the stove. Once the fire was going, he closed the door almost entirely and found the lid for the pot. He stood over it, waiting for the water to boil.

Out of habit, while he waited, he glanced around the office. He walked over to the telegraph table and noted that there were no new messages. He saw that Merrick had sorted the mail that had come in the day before into several piles. Knowing Merrick, these would be organized according to the sections of the town.

Walt heard the water in the pot began to bubble and he turned to go back to the stove, preparing to scoop a measure of oats into the pot. Just as he turned, his eye was caught by something. He hesitated and looked down at the telegraph desk again. What had caught his eye was a piece of mail was addressed to Jack Merrick, Town of Horse, British Columbia.

Feeling slightly guilty, Walt looked at the return address, a town he'd never heard of in Ontario. The name above the town was Mrs.

C. Merrick. Walt thought for a second and then realized this was probably Merrick's mother.

He could hear the water continuing to boil but took another moment to lift up the letter and look at the one below it. The next letter down in the stack had the same return address. Walt's fingers lifted that envelope as well and found a third. And then a fourth. And a fifth.

He fingered through the entire stack and realized they were all addressed to Merrick from someone who was likely his mother. They must be letters going back several months. Unopened. Unread.

CHAPTER SIX

"Merrick. Thanks for coming in, son."

Mayor Billy was seated on one of the chairs that had been set up in a small circle in the hall building. The front and back doors of the building had been left open, allowing small breaths of air to circulate, although it was still very warm inside.

As befitting a small town, the council was small as well. Present were the mayor and the town's four counselors: Edgar Finnegan, who had walked over with Merrick; Christopher Mitchell; Clement Small, the tailor; and Tommy Blair, the shoemaker.

There was a sixth chair occupied by a man that Merrick didn't recognize. He was slender with light brown hair and eyes that reminded Merrick of an eagle's. The man was dressed in a suit like the rest of the men present, but Merrick could tell at one glance that this was no ordinary suit. Merrick estimated that whatever the man had paid for the suit would probably cover Mayor Billy's wages at the bank for three or four months.

The mayor had his usual cigar clasped between the thumb and forefinger of his left hand. The cigar was extinguished for now, but that never seemed to bother the mayor; he'd likely carry it around for the entire day, lighting it only occasionally. It was like a child's security blanket.

"Come and have a seat, Constable," Mayor Billy said, his round face creased with lines of worry Merrick didn't normally notice.

Merrick sat in one of the unoccupied chairs.

The mayor gestured to the man that Merrick didn't know. "Mr. Moore is here from the Canadian Railroad Company. He was just telling us that CRC is considering plans to start up a larger steamship on Lake Okanagan that could carry a couple hundred passengers as opposed to Sully's five."

Merrick nodded his head in greeting to the nattily dressed Mr. Moore.

Moore cleared his throat. "I was just saying to the mayor and the other counselors that CRC is definitely interested in creating a more sustainable and efficient way to get passengers and freight up and down the lake."

Merrick wondered if any of the other counselors thought the timing of Mr. Moore's appearance merited interest. "How long have you been in Horse, Mr. Moore?"

"Just arrived two days ago," the man said. "Lovely little place. Your dock is inadequate for our needs, of course, but that's no problem at all. We would be willing to invest in building a larger one that would be capable of dealing with the large steamships that we're considering adding to our transportation offerings."

Moore's way of speaking made Merrick feel he was being lectured. The railway man's tone was slightly condescending, as though he was doing the town a favor by being there.

Without prompting, Moore continued. "It's a darn shame about Mr. Sullivan's ship. I just heard about it now from Mr. Finnegan. Will Mr. Sullivan be moving on to find greener pastures?"

Merrick thought this a slightly presumptuous question. He suddenly felt defensive of Sully, the man he'd just arrested, but tried to keep his expression neutral.

Mayor Billy jumped in before Merrick could speak. "That's

what we're here to discuss, Mr. Moore. Arthur Sullivan has provided a valuable service to Horse for several years now. We couldn't have started building the town without him. The counselors and I want to talk about the future direction that we might be able to take with Mr. Sullivan."

"I understand." Mr. Moore nodded, with an expression of civility and wisdom on his face that Merrick didn't entirely trust. Merrick got the feeling it was an expression he was used to practicing. "I just wanted to drop in and let you fellows know that CRC is most definitely interested in partnering with Horse to create greater opportunities for commerce and expansion. We are certain that this new territory is the future. And we'd love to be a participant in that growth with you fellows."

Mr. Moore stood up and put his hat on. "Thank you for so much for letting me speak to you gentlemen. I appreciate it. You know where to find me when you're ready to have a longer dialogue about the opportunities available to you."

He nodded to each of them and left the building.

"Now, Merrick," the mayor said, rolling his cigar between his fingers. "Any early thoughts or observations about the tragic loss of the *Mary Elizabeth*?"

Merrick shook his head. "Sully's brother is in town. I'm not sure if any of you knew that."

Beside him, Edgar Finnegan nodded. "He and his wife are staying at our hotel."

"Well . . ." Merrick was about to push the chair that he was sitting in up on its back legs, the way that he did with almost any wooden chair he sat in. He restrained himself at the last moment and settled his boot heels back down onto the floor. "Sully is convinced that it was Clarence, his brother, who burned his ship. It seems there isn't a lot of fond feeling between them."

"What do you think?" Mayor Billy asked.

"It's too early to tell. I talked to the man and his wife very briefly at Dr. Parker's office but I need to speak to them again. I'm not sure what his motive would be, other than the apparent tension between the siblings. That doesn't seem like enough reason to ruin someone's livelihood."

The counselors were quiet, giving Merrick a moment to think. Now that he had met Frank Moore from the CRC he was wondering if his suspect list had just been expanded. He wasn't yet ready to voice that concern, but to his surprise Christopher Mitchell did it for him.

"What about CRC? Suddenly they seem to have a vested interest in eliminating the competition on the lake." Christopher looked around at the other men, his bright blue eyes concerned.

"Well, now, Mitchell," the mayor frowned, "let's not be rash. It's one thing to look for new business opportunities and another thing entirely to illegally eliminate the competition. I can't imagine a large and fruitful company like CRC would get up to such shenanigans."

"Maybe that's how they became large and fruitful," Christopher retorted.

"I think it's a valid question," Clement Small put in, defending Christopher. "When did Mr. Moore say he arrived in town? Two days ago? So he was here last night when the boat was set on fire."

Edgar Finnegan spoke again. "He went out for a walk after supper yesterday. I didn't see him return."

The room was quiet, though Merrick could almost hear the thoughts crystalizing in the counselors' minds. Soon they'd have their pitchforks out.

"Removing Sully from the equation would certainly make us more keen to cut a deal with CRC, wouldn't it?" Clement Small looked around at each man in the circle. "We're between a rock and a hard place now. No way to ship goods up and down the lake. How are you going to stay open, Mitchell, without any food on the shelves of your store?"

"Moving goods overland certainly complicates things," Christopher conceded.

The mayor was looking more pained every moment. "Come, come, now, gentlemen. I think we need to leave these questions to our constable." He gave Merrick an almost pleading look. The mayor was a peacekeeper and was always deeply uncomfortable at any sign of conflict or ruffled feathers. This was not a great personality characteristic in a politician, but it served Billy well in his home life. "You'll keep us apprised of whatever you find out, won't you, Constable?"

"Of course."

"Thank you." Billy looked away from Merrick and back to his counselors. "Let's deal with this issue of the ranchers moving cattle through town."

Merrick understood that the requirement for his presence at the meeting was now finished. He stood and put his hat on and nodded at each of the men. As he was just about to step through the open front door, out into the bright sunlight, Mayor Billy's voice came to him. "Try to keep Sullivan from assaulting anyone else, will you?"

CHAPTER SEVEN

Merrick returned to his office and relieved Walt.

Sully had calmed down somewhat in the hour that Merrick had been gone. Merrick carried one of the wooden chairs over to the cell and sat down to talk to the *Mary Elizabeth's* captain, looking at him through the iron bars.

"Is there anyone other than your brother – sorry, half-brother – who might have wanted to get rid of your ship?" Merrick kept his thoughts about the CRC man to himself.

Sully was sitting on the same cot where he'd slept the night before. He had his elbows on his knees and his head hanging down, looking pitiful now that his anger had subsided. He shook his head.

"No vengeful debtors you might owe money to? No jilted lovers? No angry husbands?" Merrick offered the last suggestion as a bit of levity, but Sully didn't take the bait.

From between his shoulders, Sully asked, "Could it have been an accident?"

"I don't see how, really." Merrick rubbed his chin. "I'll go down to the lake later this afternoon and have a look for ...well ...clues, I suppose. It seems unlikely to me that the ship would just catch fire on its own. I'm fairly certain it must have been deliberately set."

Sully looked up for the first time since Merrick had sat down. "Are you going to arrest Clarence?"

"No, Sully, I'm not. I'm going to talk to him. But I can't arrest the man simply because you two don't get along."

Sully sighed and hung his head again.

Merrick continued. "What can you tell me about that? Why were you so angry? He doesn't seem nearly as worked up about you."

The captain made a quiet rueful noise but didn't answer.

Merrick tried again. "You said something about a gold watch earlier. What was that about?"

Sully mumbled something, but with his head bent down Merrick didn't hear him.

"Say again?"

"I said he stole it, like he did almost everything valuable of mine. We were kids. The watch was the one thing I had of my father's." Sully gave another little sigh. "*Our* father's."

Merrick was about to ask more questions when Sully continued. "Our father was a cad." He looked up at Merrick and the constable nodded, encouraging him. "He married women and then left them. It was like an obsession with him. Clarence and I have other half-brothers and sisters all over the place. Probably some we don't even know about. Anyway, one day when I was about fourteen Bruce – that's his name –came to visit. He was looking for a place to stay and thought my mother would take him in. He was probably on the run from the law or from people he no doubt owed money to. Mother threw him out as soon as she realized what he wanted." Sully smiled for the first time in hours. "Before he left he gave me a small pocket watch and asked me to take care of it for him."

The office was quiet. Outside, Merrick could hear a wagon rolling down the street, the driver calling to someone. He waited but Sully didn't continue. "And Clarence stole this watch from you?"

Sully made a snorting sound. "Of course it was fake."

"The watch?"

"Yep." Sully looked up at Merrick and then sat up straight on the cot. He was quiet for a few moments and then continued. "Bruce said it was gold but I knew it was fake as soon as I saw it. Brass maybe. I knew it." He shook his head, the memories of a fatherless fourteen-year-old boy clouding his eyes. "But it was the one thing he'd ever given me. The one thing. He left, you see, before I was even three. I have almost no memories of him a'tall, except these visits he'd sometimes give us. Years in between them. Years." Sully shook his head. "And always asking for something. Ma used to call him The Fox, because he was like a fox in the henhouse, she'd say. Always looking to take something. Never up to any good."

Sully stood now and jammed his hands in the front pockets of his trousers, his shoulders slumped, his eyes downcast. Merrick waited, quietly. "Anyway, about six months after that visit, Clarence and his mother showed up, looking for Bruce. Ma couldn't help them. She had no idea where he'd gone or where he was. Clarence always bullied me anytime I saw him, but I didn't mind that so much. It's what big brothers do. After he and his mother left I had a funny feeling in my gut. For days, I couldn't figure out what it was. And then, about three days after they'd come and gone I suddenly had the idea to check on the watch. I kept in an old tea tin, wrapped up in a handkerchief." Sully looked up at Merrick. "It was gone. The tin was there but the watch had gone."

"Did you see Clarence after that? Ask him about it?"

"Oh, sure. We'd see them every few years. A few of Bruce's wives and kids even spent one Christmas together. I asked him but Clarence always denied knowing anything about the watch." Sully took two paces and leaned one shoulder against the bars of the cell. "He has that smile, though. Did you see it? It's the devil's smile. That's what I used to call it. He looks so pleased with himself and so..." Sully searched for a word, "...I dunno. Dangerous or something. He'd just smile that smile at me and claim he didn't know nothin' about that watch."

"It must have been quite a shock when you saw him at the lake today."

"You're telling me!" Sully's eyes opened wide and he pulled away from the bars, his voice animated for the first time in many minutes. "I knew as soon as I saw him he must be the cause of all this trouble. It's no coincidence he's here, Merrick, I'm telling you. Where Clarence Horan goes, trouble follows."

Merrick stood and returned the chair he'd been sitting in to its usual spot in front of his desk. "Leave that to me, will you, Sully? I'll get to the bottom of this, but only if you stay out of it and don't muddy the waters, attacking people."

He found the key and unlocked the cell, pulling the door open. Sully walked across the office and took his tattered bowler hat from the top of the coat rack. He placed it on his head at the slightly jaunty angle it always occupied. Merrick assumed there was a circular groove in Sully's head that the hat band had created.

Sully reached out to shake Merrick's hand. "I'll stay out of your way until this business is sorted out."

Merrick thought the odds were about fifty-fifty Sully would do as he promised.

Merrick found Sully's brother Clarence Horan and his wife Louise having a late lunch in the restaurant at the Stratford Hotel.

The restaurant was busy, busier than Merrick seen it before. He didn't see the mayor and Mrs. Jones, so he assumed the council meeting was continuing. The Joneses were a fixture at Finnegan's restaurant. Mrs. Jones was reputed to be the worst cook west of the Rocky Mountains. Merrick had been invited to the Joneses' once for supper when he had first arrived in town as the new constable. He could attest to the fact.

The Horans were sitting at a round table for eight right in the center of the room. Merrick thought it an odd choice for a couple to sit at such a large table, but it enabled him to join them. It became obvious fairly soon why the couple had chosen that table. They definitely needed to be the center of attention.

Merrick was struck once more by Mrs. Horan's beauty. He was a man who had thought that his wife was the most beautiful woman in the world, and he still believed that. But he confessed to himself that Mrs. Horan would have given Charlotte a run for her money.

Louise Horan was glamorous in a way that Charlotte had not been. Charlotte's beauty had come as much from within her as without. Whereas Louise Horan, at first glance anyway, had tremendous beauty on the outside. Merrick wondered what her insides were like. He intended to find out, and asked the same question to himself about her husband.

He did think it odd that the couple had shown up at exactly the same moment that the *Mary Elizabeth* had been burned. For now, Clarence Horan was at the very top of Merrick's suspect list.

Unfortunately, he'd taken an instant dislike to Clarence Horan, which was affecting his objectivity. Sully's assessment of the man's devil-like smile was totally accurate. Horan had been smarmy and condescending with Sully, which, despite the family connection and obvious history, seemed beyond the habit that brothers often had of giving each other a hard time. Merrick had two brothers himself and knew intimately how hard he and his siblings could be on one another. But, in his experience, this teasing had always had an undercurrent of affection. It had never felt malicious in the way Horan's interaction with Sully had felt.

Clarence hadn't expressed any sorrow or regret on Sully's behalf, and Merrick found this lack of compassion annoying. He wanted Clarence to be the culprit, but he knew he had to keep those feelings tightly sequestered and away from his professional objectivity.

"Join us for lunch, won't you, Constable?" Clarence Horan dabbed his the side of his mouth with his napkin and swiped it along the underside of his mustache. His bruised eyes and swollen nose looked incongruous paired with his quality suit and what looked like a fairly expensive gold watch chain. Not to mention the two tufts of cotton sticking out of his nose. Horan was maintaining a dignified air, but it was comical looking at him.

Merrick's stomach rumbled, so he thanked Horan, realizing he could kill two birds with one stone: eat lunch and interview his prime suspect at the same time. He sat and placed his hat, crown down, on the chair beside him. The smells of cooking wafted out from the kitchen, reminding Merrick that he hadn't eaten yet that day, other than a scone that Betty had thoughtfully given him at the lakefront. He could smell meat cooking, and also undertones of a fresh pie that must be baking. As he sat he caught a whiff of candle wax and smoke, though the lamp at the table was unlit. He felt slightly ridiculous sitting with just two other people at such a large table.

Caroline Finnegan was at his elbow almost immediately with a bowl of venison stew and a basket with two freshly baked buns. She placed these in front of Merrick and walked away without a word.

Before Merrick could begin speaking, Clarence took the reins of the conversation. "We enjoyed a walk through your charming town just before lunch, didn't we, Louise? I must say, this is one of the loneliest places I've ever had the good fortune to visit." When Horan said *good fortune* his tone was one of irony.

For an instant, Merrick felt a twinge of irritation. He wanted to be in charge. But then his better angels whispered in his ear, telling him that letting Horan take the ball and run with it might reveal more about his character than anything that Merrick could extract from him. So Merrick ate and let Horan tell several stories about the various places he'd lived and worked. If all the stories were true, Horan rivaled Magellan for all the parts of the world he'd seen.

Meanwhile, Louise Horan remained quiet. She finished her meal and Caroline came and removed their dishes. Merrick glanced at her occasionally and each time he did she was watching her husband, but if Merrick had guessed he would have said that her thoughts were far away.

"Rub my shoulders, would you, honey?" Horan said to her at one point.

Louise stood up, putting her napkin on the table, and went around behind her husband's chair. This seemed to be a well-practiced routine. She helped Horan remove his jacket and she folded it neatly and placed it over the back of her own chair. And then she proceeded to rub his shoulders while he continued to regale Merrick with his experiences in the Far East. Every once in a while the man would wince and suck in his breath and say, "Oh, yes. Right there, sweetheart."

Though the routine seemed practiced for the Horans, it embarrassed Merrick. He kept his eyes on his stew as much as possible.

Horan drew a breath at one point, pausing in his narrative about the price of silk. Merrick used the opportunity, now that his lunch was finished, to leap in and start asking some questions.

"What brings you to Horse?"

Technically, Merrick had interrupted Horan, and the man made a point of showing Merrick that he had noticed. He paused with his mouth partly open and raised one eyebrow at the constable. But he acquiesced and answered the question.

"As I mentioned, we were touring the province, ostensibly looking for a parcel of land to claim. Weren't we, Louise?" He didn't wait for an answer from his wife. "But what we discovered – yes, right there, sweetheart, that's the spot – is that neither my lovely wife nor I are suited for working on the land, shall we say."

He chuckled, amused with himself, and then continued. "We looked around at several ranches and at several parcels of land between here and Enderby. But the thought of my beautiful Louise living in a shack while we built the proper house... I just couldn't bear it." Horan glanced up at his wife, who, once again, appeared to be miles away. When her husband's eyes met hers she came back to reality and smiled at him. As soon as his head was turned back toward Merrick, though, her expression dissolved once more into one of absence rather than presence.

"I gather that you and your brother haven't been close for quite some time."

"That's very true, Constable. You're clearly a very observant man." Merrick knew when he was having his ass kissed and he never liked it. "There are ten years between Arthur and me, and as we mentioned we had different mothers, so very different upbringings. Arthur lived mostly with his mother, whereas I spent most of my growing up with my own mother and her second husband. We would see each other occasionally, but as we got older those occasions were fewer and farther between. And then when Sully moved up here we lost touch entirely. It was only when Louise and I ran into Sully's mother a couple of months ago in Vancouver that she mentioned that this was where her son had landed." Horan looked up at the ceiling and gave a small moan of pleasure as his wife leaned into the top of his left shoulder with one of her thumbs. "There are times I wish Mrs. Sullivan had been my mother as well. Lovely woman..."

Before Horan could descend into a long story about Sully's mother, Merrick interrupted again. "Did you know that Sully was running the steamship? That that was his business here in town?"

"I did, yes. His mother mentioned it, and when I told the barkeep in Lumby that we were headed over this way to see my brother I used Arthur's name. That fellow let us know as well that Arthur was the steamship captain."

"And when you arrived at the lakefront this morning, was that the first time you had seen Sully on this trip?"

"It was. We just arrived yesterday, as I mentioned earlier, and were quite exhausted from the journey. We spent the evening here in the hotel, relaxing. I knew that we would be able to find Arthur eventually and I wanted Louise to have a quiet evening. It's been quite taxing, hasn't it, darling, traveling around in these backwoods?"

Merrick glanced up at Louise, but she didn't look like she was planning to answer her husband's rhetorical question. "And you stayed in all evening?"

Horan nodded. "Yes."

Merrick looked up Louise again. "What about you, Mrs. Horan? Were you in all evening as well?"

She nodded and smiled. "Yes, of course. Where else would I be?"

"What did you do in the evening?"

Louise Horan continued to press her thumbs into her husband's shoulders. "We read. Clarence fell asleep in his chair, as he usually does." This was said with a gentle tease.

Horan's eyes were closed while he enjoyed his massage. "It had been a very long day of travel, you understand, Constable."

"Oh, pooh, Clarence." For a moment, Louise Horan's face became animated. "That's no excuse. You always fall asleep in front of a warm fire. You barely read one page before your head dropped."

Horan's eyes opened now and he looked at Merrick. "My wife is right, Constable. I cannot tell a lie. I suffer from the futile complaints of a satisfied man. I am well fed, well kept," he reached up and patted one of Louise's hands, "and have few worries in life, financial or otherwise. I am guilty of being so content that the influence of a warm fire and a good glass of port put me right to sleep."

Merrick forced a smile in response to Horan's self-congratulation.

There was nothing else he could think of to ask the Horans. They were each other's alibi, which was inconvenient.

Caroline arrived at Merrick's shoulder and took his stew plate away. She replaced it with a dessert plate holding a large piece of apple pie, still steaming from the oven.

"Caroline, you are my one and only, you know that, right?" Merrick grinned at her.

She snorted softly and turned and walked away. "If I don't feed you, who will?"

Fair point, Merrick thought. Charlotte hadn't been the best cook in the world, but she had been enthusiastic about keeping him well fed. Another thing he missed. Add it to the list.

He glanced up at the Horans and wondered about asking a few follow-up questions. But his warm pie beckoned. Further questions could wait.

CHAPTER NINE

A breeze had picked up, in contrast to the absolute stillness that had been present when the *Mary Elizabeth* had been found burning earlier that day. Was it only that morning that Dr. Parker had roused Merrick and Sully out of the jail cell?

Merrick walked thoughtfully down Pine Street, which led to the waterfront. He wanted to have another look at the scene of the crime, so to speak.

As he walked, he realized with a startle that it had been a couple of hours since he had last thought of Charlotte. This thought made him pause mid-stride. He felt a strange mix of relief paired with renewed grief at thinking of her again, and also guilt that she was fading from his life.

When Charlotte first died, he had been unable to process the information for at least a week. He was actually unsure now how long this period of what he would describe as insanity had gone on. He had few memories of the time, and only vaguely recalled that Walt had checked on him every day and escorted him to the hall for Charlotte's service. He thought back to that time now and seemed to remember that for several days, maybe more, the house that he had shared with Charlotte was always full of people. Betty Mitchell had seemed to be in attendance much of the time. And he vaguely recalled several other people whispering and moving about his kitchen. They had tried to keep him fed but he had been incapable of eating.

Two days after the service, Merrick had begun a daily practice of taking his big gray horse, Earl, out for a long ride. Over the next several months, he and Earl had watched the spring arrive in the North Okanagan landscape. The snow had gradually melted until it was just patches on the ground here and there, under the trees. Crocuses and other spring flowers had bravely raised their heads above the ground, despite the still near-freezing temperatures. They had had another couple of snowfalls in April but these didn't last. Soon the deciduous trees had begun to show their bright green new growth.

Prior to Charlotte's death, Merrick had never understood the expression 'mad with grief,' but he did now. There were many days when he had contemplated setting Earl loose and simply lying down on a hillside somewhere and letting the elements and perhaps the bears coming out of hibernation take care of removing him from this earthly plane. He had also contemplated several times walking into the lake, his pockets full of rocks.

But he hadn't done any of these things. It was his job that had prevented him. That and Charlotte's voice in his head. She had told him throughout this time, in loud and assertive ways, her voice as clear as a bell, that he was better than that, that he could carry on. He hadn't believed her then, and he still wasn't sure he believed her now, five months later. But because he loved and respected his wife, he was willing to give her the benefit of the doubt. He didn't find it surprising at all that in this, the worst time of his life, her voice was proving to be the steady presence that was helping him to pull himself back together. The memory of her steadfastness and the understanding that the strength of her character was what was pulling him through were at times sometimes more painful than the grief he felt at her loss. The world should have taken him instead. She was definitely the better person and would have done the world much more good if she had been here instead of him. It was a difficult thing to grapple with the lack of control over that circumstance. He hadn't been able to save her, and now she had tasked him with saving himself.

And so he noticed with surprise on this sunny July morning that there was a glimmer of hope inside him for the first time in many months. He wasn't just going through the motions of being alive. Here he had a possible mystery in front of him, and he was actually enjoying trying to solve it. He felt guilty about this, but then he heard Charlotte's clear voice say, "Don't be ridiculous, Jack. You were born to do this work."

The wind that had kicked up was creating tiny whitecaps on the lake, and as Merrick arrived at the dock he saw that the detritus from the remains of the *Mary Elizabeth* had spread outward and was disappearing. Nature was taking care of cleaning up the mess that had been left behind by the fire, as nature usually does. He could still see the occasional piece of blackened wood being tossed around on the small waves. But the tight circle of debris that had been there earlier was now almost entirely gone.

He had his head down and was examining closely the wooden planks of the dock, looking for any clue or any remnant of something that had been left behind by any possible perpetrator. He was concentrating so hard that he didn't hear Frank Moore approach him.

"Looking for clues, are you, Constable?"

Merrick looked up, pleased to see Mr. Moore, whom he wanted to speak to, but also curious about why the man would classify the event as a crime.

He asked the question.

"Well, it seems to me that most vessels don't spontaneously combust, wouldn't you say?" Moore looked at him with curiosity and Merrick thought he could detect a glint of anger in the man's eyes.

"I'm hoping it was an accident," Merrick said. "I'd hate to

think that someone would do this deliberately. Perhaps it was an errant cigar butt. Or perhaps even a rogue lightning strike." Merrick knew both these options were highly unlikely, and that he was grasping at straws.

Moore was making him anxious, which bothered him. The man had a strange effect on him. He felt unsettled and, looking back, he realized he'd felt the same thing when they'd been at the town hall. As near as Merrick could put a finger on it, he felt that Moore was playacting and that he was supposed to step into place and perform his role as well. But Merrick didn't know what play they were in, and he preferred to stay in his own reality. It was disorienting, and he wondered if Moore had this effect on everyone or just on him. Was the railway man always like this or was it just now? And if it was just now, then why?

Merrick rose to his full height from his crouching position. "How long have you been in town, Mr. Moore?"

"I think I mentioned that at the hall, Constable." Moore stared at Merrick, refusing to answer the question. Merrick waited, giving the man an opportunity to be less creepy, but he refused it.

"Could you remind me, sir?"

More smiled, a big wide conciliatory smile, one that said 'I win that round.' "I arrived two days ago, via the very steamship that we do not see before us." He gestured toward the empty spot at the end of the dock. "It was a beautiful day and a gorgeous trip and I was grateful for every moment on the water. I'm a sailor myself, but I must say that traveling by steamship is certainly faster and a much more efficient mode of transportation."

"You're a sailor, are you?"

"Indeed. I grew up in Victoria, there on Vancouver Island. And my father was a sailor himself. He had me out in little dinghies almost as soon as I could walk. I imagine that, during my childhood, I spent more hours on the water than on land." Moore looked very pleased with himself about this accomplishment.

"And when did you get into the railway business?"

"Yes, my other passion for trains. I would've rather got a job as a ship's captain. But my mother wouldn't hear of it. She said she didn't want her son traipsing around the world, never to be heard from again. So I took the second best option that was available to me and began working for CRC about ten years ago. It is exceptional employment, I have to confess. And I think my mother was right to steer me in this direction, although I'm not sure I would ever tell her that." He winked at Merrick, implying the shared experience of overbearing mothers.

"When did CRC become interested in expanding its business into steamships on Lake Okanagan?"

"The idea came up about a year ago, and we've been investigating it ever since. The question, of course, with a large corporation like CRC, is could such a business be profitable. I don't think the accountants have the powers-that-be entirely convinced yet, but I am. Especially now that I've seen this part of the lake. Clearly, with the ranches and farms springing up everywhere and the seemingly endless opportunities for growth in this area, I think the company would be foolish not to expand in this direction."

Merrick nodded, thinking. "And what about the smaller companies, like Arthur Sullivan's, those people who will not be able to compete with CRC?"

"Well," Moore opened his palms to the sky in a gesture of futility, "at some point we all have to make way for progress, don't we? Things are changing at a rapid pace and, frankly, I can't wait to see what the future holds."

Merrick noticed that Moore hadn't exactly answered his question about Sully's business. He changed tack abruptly, hoping to unsettle the man. "Where were you last night at around two AM?"

If the question had the effect of unsettling Moore, he didn't show it. "Why, asleep in my bed, of course. Like pretty much everyone else in town." Moore smiled at Merrick. Checkmate.

Merrick couldn't think of any other questions he wanted to ask the man, but he did want to get onto the shoreline and examine it for any signs of foul play. "Will you continue to be here in town for a day or two, Mr. Moore?"

"I hope so," the man said jovially. "Being here is almost as good as being on vacation."

CHAPTER TEN

The town council had determined that the priority for the community was to get Sully's transportation business back up and running as soon as possible. CRC might indeed be looking at adding a steamship service to the lake, but Horse's needs were more immediate than that.

The morning was bright and sunny again, with a few very wispy clouds on the horizon. Merrick arrived at the dock at first light to find that many of the town's men were there already, preparing to refit an old ship that had been abandoned. Merrick smiled to himself as he saw the convivial atmosphere: men joking around with one another, teasing one another, excited to work today on something meaningful and collaborative.

Life on the frontier was not easy. It was a challenge mentally, physically, and emotionally. This was a new land to the European settlers, and it was being forged out of nothing. Everything was a challenge. The people who were operating the brand-new ranches that surrounded Horse found that ranching was much more diffi-cult than they had imagined it would be. The winters were long, cold, and dangerous. The country was filled with predatory animals; there was a black bear lately that had been wandering through town on a regular basis, looking for scraps of food. Getting to and from any other place was difficult and also sometimes dangerous. It was a modern age and tremendous change was happening everywhere, making life easier; however, here in the middle of nowhere, staying alive was still often a day-to-day struggle.

The town of Horse had arisen as a commercial hub for the ranches that were being claimed in the surrounding area. The population continued to grow every month, and Merrick was pleased to be involved with such a vibrant, growing community. He only wished that he had Charlotte to share it all with. She had been the one to encourage him to take the job in Horse. Her family had been dead set against her even marrying Merrick, but she had always had her own mind and got her way in the end. Merrick had known at the time that he was not really good enough for her. She was refined and well educated. He was the son of a farmer who had made his way west on a lark and had landed the job as a police constable almost by accident. Charlotte's parents viewed Merrick as little better than the man who came to their house twice a week to take the garbage away.

And now that she was gone, the weight of guilt that rested on his shoulders was almost unbearable. He had brought her to this place and it had killed her. Granted, she could've caught the series of colds and flu that had caused her death when she had been living anywhere, but the fact was she had caught them while she was living here.

So the sight of the men gathering to collectively assist one of their number lifted Merrick's heart ever so slightly. Perhaps the world wasn't a dark pit of despair after all.

Yesterday the council had determined that they would appropriate an abandoned ship that was roughly the same size as Sully's, although it was without an engine. The good news, of course, was that they had recovered Sully's engine from the bottom of the lake. There had been questions about the legality of taking over this ship; its owner was reputed to be exploring the far north. Who knew when he'd be back. Mayor Billy had insisted that they would deal with that problem should it arise in the future.

At the present moment the town was in desperate need of a way to get goods and people back and forth from the larger commercial centers in the southern part of the lake. Business owners, like Betty and Christopher Mitchell with their general store, depended almost entirely on Sully's ability to bring freight up from the south. They received a large delivery from him at least once a week, and this delivery in turn kept the town fed.

More men began to arrive at the lakefront and by eight o'clock the ship that they were planning to give to Sully had been pulled out of the old boathouse where it had been abandoned and brought with much effort up onto shore. It was propped up with a complicated arrangement of planks that held it upright so the men could work on repairing and repainting the hull.

Merrick still didn't sleep much these days and the night before, he had lain awake in the jail cell thinking about the *Mary Elizabeth* and wondering if perhaps her burning was an accident after all. He had yet to come across anyone who had been down at the lake in the middle of the night. The people who seemed to have motive, including Sully's brother Clarence, all had alibis. Although sleeping wasn't much of an alibi, one had to assume that whoever had burned the ship would ensure that they could account for their whereabouts at the time.

Merrick was scraping old paint off a section of the ship's hull when Walt found him. It was going to be another hot day, and both men had their shirts off. Merrick was enjoying very much the feeling of the sun on his back as he worked.

As though reading his mind, Walt asked, "Any progress on solving the mystery of how the *Mary Elizabeth* got burned?"

Merrick shook his head and continued scraping. "None. I'm beginning to think it was an accident."

"What kind of an accident?" Walt furrowed his brow. "How does a boat accidentally get burned up?"

"No idea. But anyone and everyone that I've talked to has an alibi for the night the ship was burned, or they don't have one, which seems to me to make them even more likely to be innocent. And with no evidence it's a little hard to make the assumption that the burning was deliberate."

"Could Sully have done it himself accidentally?"

"He was in the cell with me. Sleeping off his drunk that night. Besides, what would be his motive?"

Walt shrugged. "You're the expert."

The work progressed smoothly and more quickly than Merrick had imagined it would. The many hands of the men from all over town made light work of the big job of sanding, repairing, and repainting the hull. Merrick noticed that there were several ranchers who had come in from out of town to assist as well. This was the most exciting community activity that had happened in months.

Merrick stood up from his bent over position, stretching his back, which was tightening up a little. He dropped his scraper tool into Walt's tool bag and went to find Betty, who had set up a little table with jars of lemonade and freshly baked scones from Mrs. Thoreson. He grabbed his undershirt from the pile of clothes he had set at the edge of the dock and pulled it on over his head while he walked toward the table. It wouldn't do to stand in front of Betty and Mrs. Thoreson shirtless. He chatted with the ladies for a few moments, although his thoughts were elsewhere. As ever, most of his brain was in a fog of grief. But today he was also working on the puzzle of the lost ship.

Betty broke into his thoughts. "Did you hear what I said?"

Merrick brought his eyes back to Betty's, slightly embarrassed. He finished chewing the delicious warm scone and shook his head. "I'm sorry, Betty."

"I said did you see that young man who's been hanging around this morning?"

Merrick shook his head again. "What young man?"

Betty glanced around her, looking up and down the beach, her eyes scanning the men working on the ship. "I don't see him right now. But he's young; not a child but not a man, either. Skinny as a rail. I don't think he's from here. He's got a small rucksack with him and a little bed roll. He looks like he's traveling."

Merrick followed her gaze but didn't see anyone he didn't recognize. "Why do you mention him?"

"He was hanging around for a while, watching you fellows work. I offered him a scone and some lemonade and he took it very gratefully."

"And also the second scone that you didn't offer him," Mrs. Thoreson said, but with a smile. "I do think he's quite hungry."

Betty nodded and went back to her story. "And there was just something about the way he was watching you fellows. He glanced out at the lake a couple of times." Betty shrugged lightly and looked back at Merrick. "It's probably nothing. I'm probably making up a story that isn't there. He's probably just a young drifter. Looking for work."

"Thanks anyway, Betty. I'll keep my eye open for him."

From behind and to his right Merrick heard a shout and then some more yelling. He turned and saw two men scuffling, kicking up sand and throwing wild punches at one another.

Sully and Clarence were at it again.

MERRICK RAN to where the men were mostly shoving one another back and forth. Walt and Dr. Parker had pulled the two apart, though they were still shouting obscenities and making rude gestures at one another.

"Sully, for Christ's sake. Can you not behave in a civilized way around your brother for one minute?" Merrick had a more exasperated and frustrated tone than he normally did. He noticed Walt glance at him with questions in his eyes, but he didn't have the patience to think about how he should be handling this differently at the moment.

"He started it," Sully said, like a nine-year-old boy.

Clarence responded in kind. "I did not. You're the jackass who made the rude comment about Louise."

Merrick then noticed that the lady who had possibly been insulted was standing off to the side. She was watching Clarence and Sully, and the expression on her face surprised Merrick. If he had to guess, he'd say it reflected pleasure.

"I never said nothing," Sully said, and spat a stream of tobacco juice into the sand to emphasize his point. "I was only speaking the truth."

"The truth about what?" Clarence shouted. The skin around his eye sockets had progressed to a deep, bruised blue, though the tufts of cotton were gone from his nose. "The truth that Louise knew she had latched herself onto a loser and she wisely sent you packing?"

Merrick looked back and forth from Sully to Clarence, trying to catch up to what was going on.

Sully retorted, "Or do I mean that she wasn't good enough for me and she had to downgrade, and you were the closest thing she could find?"

Dr. Parker had loosened his grip on Clarence while this conversation was going on, and that proved to be a mistake. Clarence launched himself once more at Sully, but Walt had a good hold on Sully's arms. Clarence was able to land one solid punch on the side of Sully's head before Merrick and Dr. Parker grabbed Clarence once more and wrestled him to the ground.

"Alright, you two. That's it." Merrick said, brushing sand off his trousers. "You're both coming with me."

WITH WALT'S assistance Merrick marched Sully and Clarence through town and into his office. The two men sat on the opposite side of his desk while he sat in his new swivel chair. Merrick asked Walt to stay in case he needed to separate the two men once again.

Merrick leaned forward in his chair and laid his forearms on his desk. He took a deep breath and eyed both men. "You two idiots need to settle down and tell me what the hell is going on."

Both men looked at him solemnly and refused to speak. They were truly like nine-year-old boys.

"No? Nothing?" Merrick sat up straight again. "Alright. Lemme tell you what I see. I see some sort of bad blood between the two of you that seems to involve your wife," he looked at Clarence, "who, I'm guessing, was at one point involved in a relationship with you, Sully. How am I doing so far?"

Sully gave a small nod of his chin that Merrick would have missed if he hadn't been looking straight at him. Clarence was completely still.

Merrick continued. "Here's what else I see. Mr. Horan, it seems to me that you might have some sort of emotional motive for setting fire to the *Mary Elizabeth*." He had Clarence's attention now. The man sat up straighter in his chair and started to object, but Merrick held up one of his large hands, palm facing Horan. "I'll let you know when it's your turn to speak. Here's the police perspective on that situation. One: you arrive in town the day before the *Mary Elizabeth* goes up in flames. Two: on your first night here the *Mary Elizabeth* goes up in flames. Three: you have some sort of a grudge or bad blood against your brother here."

"Half-brother," Sully muttered.

Merrick's eyes flicked over to Sully and then back to Clarence. "And as far as I can see, that's as close as I can get to a motive for destroying Sully's boat and his livelihood. Now either you two are going to tell me the truth about what's going on or I'm going to lock you both up in that little cage over there," he pointed to the small cell in the back corner of the room, "and leave you there. If you want to fight it out to the death, that's fine with me."

He stopped talking and waited. Merrick noted that Walt, from his position leaning against the wall, had a sly grin on his face. He seemed to be enjoying the rattled Merrick show.

Sully spoke up first. "I bet he has done it, Merrick. I'm sure you're right. He is the one. He always hated me for dating his wife first."

Clarence glared at his half-brother. "That is bullshit and you know it. Louise was smarter than hell to get rid of you when she could. She could see you were a ne'er-do-well. Turns out she was right. Smart lady." Clarence nodded once, sharply, and was clearly going to continue on this rant, but Merrick knew he'd have them at each other's throats again any minute if he allowed it.

"Enough. Enough from you Mr. Horan, thank you. Sully, if you can keep your tone civil, I want you to give me the facts and only the facts about this business with Mrs. Horan."

Sully heaved a deep sigh, full of exhaustion. "It's true. Louise and I courted years ago. But it didn't last very long. I was on the move. You know me, Merrick. I can't be tied down." Merrick thought this self-assessment of Sully's was insightful. "So yeah, we were courting for a while and then I left and went on up to Barkerville."

"And that was it?" Merrick looked at the two men.

Sully answered. "Aye."

Merrick could see Clarence wanting to get his two cents in, but before he could, Merrick looked him straight in the eye and said in a very calm tone, "Mr. Horan, it's your turn now to tell me your version of the story. But I want to remind you, I need you to stay very calm and just give me the facts. Keep your emotions out of this while we figure this thing out."

Clarence nodded, his lips pursed. "It's true what Arthur says. He was courting Louise before I met her. In fact, I met her because of Arthur. But what he did was leave her behind."

Sully made an objecting noise, but Merrick shushed him with a look and Clarence continued.

"He left without saying a word, to either Louise or myself. She was devastated. She had thought they were going to get married."

Sully turned in his chair and opened his mouth. Merrick pointed a finger at him and gave him a stone-cold stare. "Sully, not one word. You had your turn." Merrick had never been a parent but he was starting to feel like one. "Continue please, Mr. Horan."

"Well, that's about it. Louise and I have been together ever since. She came to me after Sully abandoned her, trying to find out where he went. But I had no more information than she did." Clarence shrugged his shoulders, looking pleased with himself now. "We took a shine to each other. And we've been together ever since. We got married three months later."

Merrick nodded, thinking. He eased into the business at hand, "What about the *Mary Elizabeth*?" He looked directly at Clarence. "Mr. Horan, you don't have an alibi for that evening, other than the one given to you by your wife, that you two were both in your hotel room. Is there anything else you can tell me about that night? Did you happen to go down to the dining room late at night to have a nightcap or anything? Is there anyone who would've seen you between ten PM and three AM?"

Merrick could see Clarence thinking about this. But he shook his head. "Alls I can tell you, Constable Merrick, is that Louise and I had dinner in the dining room at about eight o'clock. And I would say we finished at around nine thirty. We had a nice leisurely meal, and a good chinwag with Edgar Finnegan there. And then we retired to her room. That was it. I can't tell you any more. The first I heard of the boat burning was the next morning when we made our way down to the waterfront. Someone in the dining room at breakfast that morning told us what was going on, and I realized pretty quickly it was Arthur's boat that was burning. And that's when we went down to the lakefront."

Merrick would check this, but he had a gut feeling that Edgar Finnegan would confirm everything that Clarence had said. He wasn't quite sure where to go from here. "I suggest you fellows go your separate ways this morning. Sully, I want you to stay away from your brother as much as possible. If you two can't prevent yourselves from getting into fisticuffs, then I think you should just stay apart."

Both men nodded somewhat reluctantly and Merrick

wondered fleetingly if the fighting was a way for the two men to reconnect.

Clarence stood up. "That's fine. I need to go back to the hotel for a wash and a rest anyway."

Merrick looked up at him from his swivel chair. "I will let your wife know that's where she'll be able to find you, Mr. Horan."

Horan nodded. "I'd be obliged."

The door to Merrick's office opened then, and much to Merrick's surprise, Mrs. Thoreson, the pastor's wife, poked her head across the threshold. She glanced around at each of the men in the room until her eyes found Merrick's. "Pardon me, Constable. I'm sorry to bother you. But I think I've found something you might want to see."

CHAPTER ELEVEN

The boy said that he was nineteen, but Merrick didn't think he was a day over fifteen. He was scrawny and in desperate need of a wash. He had light brown eyes and a dark mole high on his left cheek. His hair was an unusual combination of light blond and red.

He had returned to Betty and Mrs. Thoreson's table asking if he could have another scone. Of course, the two women, being the softhearted nurturers that they were, had insisted on feeding the boy.

After Walt, Sully, and Clarence Horan had left Merrick's office, she had explained to Merrick that she had told the boy that he might want to speak to him.

"I thought he might have information for you about what he might've seen down at the beach two nights ago, since that seems to be where he's spending much of his time."

"Good thinking." Merrick took his hat off the rack near the door.

"I told him that you'd likely feed him lunch in exchange," she said, with a twinkle in her eye.

So Merrick and the boy, whose name was Howard Patterson –

at least that's what he told Merrick – were now sitting in Finnegan's restaurant, waiting for Caroline to bring them some lunch. The boy's eyes darted around continually, taking in the surroundings and never staying for very long in one place.

"What brings you to Horse, son?"

Howard's eyes landed on Merrick briefly and then flitted away again. "I'm on my way up to the goldfields."

Merrick frowned. "The goldfields? Do you mean Barkerville?"

The boy shook his head. "No. I'm not that dumb. I know that Barkerville's all tapped out. But I heard that there was other places north of here where a man could make his fortune."

At least once a month throughout his adult life Merrick had run into someone who was headed somewhere to 'make his fortune.' Merrick had yet to meet the man who was on his way back from that journey having done so. The men he knew who were of great wealth had mostly been born into that position. Merrick supposed it was possible to make one's fortune in an unlikely gamble; however, he was a little more practical about life and about making a living.

He had been adventuresome when he was just a little bit older than the young man seated across from him. He had left the farm where he'd grown up and traveled all the way across the country over several years, having adventures and getting into scrapes. But it was never because he was seeking his fortune. He was seeking freedom, though he would not have described it as such and had never used that word, even to himself. But he imagined that much of what he'd felt was similar to what this young man was feeling now. A need to prove himself. Perhaps a need to prove himself to someone else back wherever he came from.

The food arrived and the young man tucked in almost before Caroline had set the plate down in front of him. She gave Merrick his bowl and a sleeve of beer that was Edgar's specialty. She also set down a basket of rolls on the table. She gave Merrick a meaningful glance. "There are seconds if you want." She winked at Merrick as she walked away.

Merrick let the boy finish eating and chewed thoughtfully on his own lunch, thinking about what questions he wanted to ask. When the young man was finished his meal he glanced around, and Merrick thought he was probably looking for Caroline, wanting to take her up on that offer of seconds.

"Why don't you let that first bowl settle in for a few minutes, son? And then we'll get Caroline to bring you some more."

The boy nodded and reached for another roll. He tore a large piece off and shoved it into his mouth.

"How did you get here?"

The boy looked at Merrick. Merrick didn't think it was a very tough question, but he let him take his time.

"I've been walking mostly, and catching the occasional ride. I didn't have money for the stagecoach or the steamship."

Merrick nodded. That much was obvious.

The boy's eyes flicked to the basket. The second roll was already gone, though Merrick hadn't noticed Howard eating it. He must have inhaled it. Now, he was clearly wondering if it would be impolite to reach for a third. Merrick leaned across the table and pushed the basket a little closer to him. Without hesitation the boy grabbed another one.

"Have you been in town long?" Merrick tried to keep his voice as casual as he possibly could. He had the sense it would be very easy to spook this young man.

"About three or four days, I think. Someone told me that one of the ranchers would be heading up toward Pattern Creek next week and he said that I could likely get a ride. So I thought I'd hang around and see if that was true."

Merrick nodded, remembering what it was like to have almost no money and to rely on others for transportation. Merrick had spent many a day searching around for a kind stranger who would take him in the direction that he was going, which was always west.

"And where have you been staying?"

"Down by the beach. It's nice and cool down there at night and I can wash in the lake in the morning."

Merrick wasn't entirely sure that the boy had been taking full advantage of the lake in that regard, but he kept his thoughts to himself.

"Here's why I wanted to talk to you today, Howard. You may have noticed that two nights ago the steamship that runs back and forth to Kelowna burned up."

The boy nodded and Merrick continued.

"And I'll confess to you, man to man, that even though I'm the local police constable, I'm having a hell of a time figuring out if that fire was an accident or if it was set on purpose."

He watched the boy closely, and Howard's expression remained neutral, listening, and as ever, chewing.

Merrick proceeded again cautiously. "So what I was wondering was if you had seen anything suspicious down there on the beach?"

With an instinct for poor timing, Caroline Finnegan brought a new bowl of stew over and set it down in front of the boy, taking his dirty bowl away. Howard had used his rolls to sop up every drop from the bowl and it looked as though it had already been washed. Merrick waited, impatiently now, for the boy to eat once more. When Howard was about halfway through the meal, Merrick ran out of patience and repeated his question. "Did you see anything at all down there two nights ago?"

The boy looked up and wiped his mouth on the sleeve of his coat. He nodded once sharply. "Sure I did. I saw the man start the fire on the boat."

CHAPTER TWELVE

Sand had crept under Merrick's shirt and was scratching at his back where the waistband of his trousers was. He reached around and wrestled with the hem of his jacket and his shirt, trying to swipe the sand away, but after a lot of struggling and grumbling he realized he had just made the situation worse.

"Ants in your pants?"

"Sand."

It was pitch black, and out of the side of his eye Merrick felt more than saw Walt nod his head. "Me too."

He and Walt were lying in wait, and the ironic thing was that they were actually lying down. They had positioned themselves under the dock. Merrick's theory was that the shadows were deepest under there, and it was also unlikely that their suspect would be looking in the shallow gap, hidden by the top of the dock, where the sand of the beach met the lake.

Howard Peterson had proved, once he had some food in his stomach, to be a fair witness. He had indeed been staying at the beach his entire time in Horse. And he was very clear about what he had seen two nights earlier, given the full moon that had shone that night, and the clear summer skies that didn't inhibit the moon's light at all. Why the boy hadn't reported what he'd seen was a question for another day. Merrick was just grateful to have a break in the case, and even just to have it confirmed that the fire was not an accident and had in fact been deliberately set.

"I seen a man come down quiet and all stealthy like," the boy had said in between bites of his second bowl of stew. "It was late, but I was awake. The mosquitoes were bothering me that night, and I couldn't sleep. Plus it was awful goddamned bright with the moon shining."

When Howard said the swear word, his eyes flicked over to Merrick. Merrick could vividly remember those liminal days when one is not a boy but not quite a man. A time in life when swearing seemed to be one way to advance the maturing process.

He had asked the boy to describe the man he had seen.

"Not very tall," he said. "He had a hat on."

That was about as much description as Merrick was able to get out of the boy. He waited a few beats but nothing more was forthcoming. He prodded a little. "Was he fat? Thin? Did he walk with a limp? Anything else you noticed about the man?"

"Not fat for sure," the boy said. "Pretty average, I'd say. No limp." He had obviously taken Merrick's suggestions concerning detail at face value.

This seemed to be all the description that Merrick was going to get, so he had moved on, asking about what had happened.

"Well, for the longest time I couldn't figure out what he was doing. He didn't have a lantern with him, and he was just walking around. For a while it looked like he was searching for something. I was lying a ways down the shoreline – you know, where that crooked tree is." He made a swooping movement with his hand.

Merrick nodded, picturing the shoreline. There was a fir tree that the children had been climbing the day of the boat restoration. It had a big dog-leg curve in its trunk, close to the ground, which enabled even the smaller children to climb it. He estimated that the tree was situated about thirty yards from the dock where the *Mary Elizabeth* had been berthed.

Howard had continued. "He kinda skulked around for a while, walking up and down the shoreline. I thought maybe he was thinking about going for a swim. And then he spent a long time with his back to the lake, which I didn't really understand. And then finally he just hopped up on the dock. And when he did that it was very purposeful. He didn't hesitate or do any of the skulking that he been doing before." Howard had stopped at that point and looked at Merrick, seeming to want confirmation that what he was saying made sense. Merrick had nodded and the boy continued. "He just walked straight out to the very end of the dock and for a while I kinda lost him. A cloud came over the moon, I expect. Then in the blackness there was a flare, like a flame from a match. And then it caught on something larger that I couldn't see. And then the flame moved in an arc and it was afterwards that I realized that he'd thrown it onto the boat. And then he did that twice more."

"He did what twice more?"

"He lit two more things. I don't know what they were, and they flared up and then he tossed them into different places on the boat."

Merrick had nodded, picturing the scene. Whoever had set fire to the *Mary Elizabeth* had not taken any chances.

AFTER MERRICK HAD ASSURED himself that Howard didn't have any more information, he gave the boy five dollars and told him that he should spend that night in the hotel. He would be Merrick's guest until he could find a ride to where he was headed. But the boy had shaken his head. "Honestly, sir, I'd rather have the cash and sleep on the beach. Cash is more useful to me. I can buy food and supplies with it for my journey."

Merrick had left the hotel and walked over to the blacksmith shop where he found his normal sounding board, Walt Sheehan, hard at work, as usual.

Together they had hatched a plan. Late in the day, they had spread word around town that the young man, Howard Patterson, had found pieces of evidence at the beach, dropped by whoever had set the fire. And when the next day dawned, Merrick would be following up and collecting the evidence.

It was an easy plan to set into motion. Rumors always flew around Horse faster than a buttered bullet. The thing that concerned Merrick was whether or not their culprit would take the bait.

Merrick's guess was that they would find Frank Moore combing the beach sometime that night. He fit the description Howard had given; not too tall, neither fat nor thin. Clarence Horan, Merrick's other prime suspect, had a pot belly. Howard hadn't been certain, but he'd seemed fairly confident that the silhouette he'd seen wasn't shaped like a man with extra weight around his middle.

Howard was thrilled to be involved with the plan. Merrick imagined that it must feel good to have a sense of purpose after weeks or months of traveling alone. Now, from his uncomfortable reclining position under the dock, he could look down the beach and see the boy smoking, the end of his cigarette glowing red in the night. The moon was waning, and was not as bright as it had been three nights ago. But there was still enough light for Merrick to keep an eye on Howard's shape, and hope that the culprit would show up and present himself for arresting.

Meanwhile, they likely had hours to kill.

Walt surprised Merrick by starting a conversation. "I saw some mail there in your office the other day when I was babysitting Sully."

Merrick glanced over at his friend, not sure what he was getting at. "Yep," he said. "I'm the mailman along with everything else."

"I mean some specific mail. Addressed to you."

For a second, Merrick wasn't sure what Walt was getting at. And then he remembered the pile of mail from his mother that he'd been ignoring for close to half a year. He grunted.

For a few moments all Merrick could hear was the lapping of the lake on the sand.

Then Walt spoke up again. "Your mother needs to know."

He knew exactly what Walt was referring to, but he feigned ignorance, trying to buy some time. "Know what?"

"She needs to know that Charlotte has died."

Merrick was silent, gobsmacked. "How do you know I haven't told her?"

Walt shifted his position slightly. "I know you're the detective and all, but it doesn't take a genius to figure out that all that unopened mail from your mother means that it's unlikely that you've written to her. And based on the dates that were on the envelopes, which started right around the time Charlotte got sick, I took a wild-ass guess that maybe you hadn't been able to tell her." Walt's voice was quieter than usual.

"Do you want my job? You seem to be pretty good at it." There was bitterness in Merrick's voice and he knew it.

Walt didn't answer. The two men continued to keep watch from their positions under the dock. Walt's task was to watch the street that ran parallel to the shoreline, keeping an eye out for any movement. Merrick's job was to watch Howard's position, in case Walt missed seeing their culprit come down from the town onto the beach.

Finally, Merrick spoke again. "It's awful hard news to break."

Walt swatted something close to his face. "It would be."

They were quiet for several moments, and Merrick reluctantly contemplated what Walt had said. It was true what he had discovered. But Merrick didn't like to admit it.

"I don't know what to say."

Merrick felt as much as saw Walt turn his head to look at him.

"Don't look at me. Keep your eyes on the street." Merrick heard a little chuckle from Walt.

"She must be some kind of worried about you if she hasn't heard from you for several months."

Merrick was quiet again for several moments. He watched the

section of beach that he was assigned to. For a second he thought he detected some movement, but it could've just been shadows thrown by the trees that bordered the beach.

"It's hard to tell your family that you failed."

"Failed?" Walt sounded puzzled. "Failed at what?"

Merrick was at a loss for how to explain what he was feeling. He groped around inside himself for a moment and almost gave up. "It was my job to protect Charlotte."

Walt made a little grunt but didn't speak. Merrick waited, more anxious than he cared to admit to himself. "Everybody dies, Merrick. It's not your fault Charlotte got the flu and then two colds back to back. You turned yourself inside out caring for her."

Keeping his eyes on the beach, Merrick took a deep inhale and then exhaled through his mouth. He was surprisingly close to tears, and this fact alone was annoying him. He was cursing Walt inside himself for bringing the subject up. Finally he said, "I should have been able to save her."

Walt started to speak again, but Merrick saw the shadow on the section of beach that he was watching move again. This time he didn't think it was a tree. He touched Walt's forearm. Walt turned his head, and Merrick pointed and whispered, "I think somebody might be down there. Let me know what you see."

The two men held their breath and watched and waited. The shadows on the beach were moving. A cloud passed over part of the moon and dimmed the light that Merrick and Walt had been using to see.

Walt whispered, "I don't see anything."

"Just wait."

A shadow became more solid and its movement gradually formed the pattern of someone walking, very slowly, down the beach.

"I see it now." Walt was still whispering.

Merrick turned his head away from what he was seeing and whispered very quietly into Walt's ear. "You head that way," he jerked his head down the lakefront beach in the opposite direction from where they'd been looking, "and go up onto the street and then circle back. I'll wait three or four minutes and then I'll head down the beach toward that man."

Walt nodded. Without a sound he rolled to his right, until he was clear of the dock, and then stood and disappeared into the blackness of the night.

Now all Merrick had to do was be patient and wait until Walt could do as he'd instructed. He hoped that the figure that they'd seen would continue to comb the beach away from the dock. All thought left his head, which was a relief. All that he was aware of was the sound of the lapping water and the shape of the moving shadow roughly twenty yards away. He would lose sight of it for moments at a time, and then it would reappear. Sometimes he doubted himself about whether or not it was a human being. And then it would step out of the shadows briefly and he was certain that it was someone searching around in the sand.

He wondered how long Walt had been gone and whether it was time for him to start creeping his way down the beach. He began squiggle out from under the dock, trying to keep his grunting to a bare minimum. He pushed up onto his knees, brushing sand away from the front of his jacket.

It was then that he heard an audible click: the safety being taken off a revolver. A metallic click that sounded in Merrick's ears as loud as the gong of a church bell on this silent, dark night.

A female voice said, "Stay right there, Constable. Do not move."

CHAPTER THIRTEEN

Without being asked, Merrick brought his hands up in an automatic and universal gesture of surrender. He glanced up and over his shoulder and saw Louise Horan's face, underneath the wide brim of a felt hat.

She was dressed in a man's jacket that was several sizes too large for her, a pair of men's pants, and, incongruously, a tiny pair of women's button-up leather boots.

"Where's your partner?" she asked.

"I'm here on my own."

"No, you're not. I saw you and that blacksmith arrive earlier tonight. Where is he?"

Merrick hoped that if he kept Louise talking perhaps he could distract her. "He was here with me earlier. But then he left. He gave up, thinking we were barking up the wrong tree and that the arsonist would never show up."

Louise looked as though she half-believed him. She glanced around the beach, and while she did Merrick carefully did as well, hoping that if Walt was approaching her from behind she wouldn't see him and shoot.

Their eyes swiveled back and met once again. Merrick was still on his knees and he reflected that it was unusual for him to be looking up at someone.

"Why did you do it?" he asked.

"Revenge."

Merrick thought back to what he had learned about Louise's early relationship with Sully. "You're angry because he left you years ago without saying good-bye."

She nodded and surprised Merrick by elaborating. "He ruined my reputation. We had been courting for over a year, and when he left I couldn't catch the eye of any other men. Any decent men, anyway. I was spoiled goods. Clarence was the only person who would pay me any attention." She made a face of disgust when she used her husband's name.

"Did you come to Horse deliberately to do this?" The sand was digging into his kneecaps, but he was not about to mention that to his captor. His ears were opened as wide as he could get them, hoping to hear Walt creeping up behind Louise.

"No, that was just a happy coincidence. I had really just wanted to see Sully and show him how happy I am with his brother. Even though it's not true." Even in the dark of night, Merrick could see contempt in Louise's eyes. "The man's a disgusting pig."

Merrick tried to keep her talking. "How did you know about the *Mary Elizabeth*?"

"We came down to the lakeshore late the night we got here." This was a detail that Merrick was unaware of. So Clarence had lied to him. Louise continued. "We saw the *Mary Elizabeth* sitting there, and there wasn't another soul around. And it just came to me in a flash: I could ruin Arthur's life the way he ruined mine."

"But you didn't set fire to it right then."

"No. I wanted to do it on my own. To show those two men that women are not completely helpless and useless. I made sure that Clarence had more than his share of whiskey that night, and topped it off with some port just before we went to bed. He always sleeps like the dead when he's been drinking. And then it was easy.

I just dressed in his clothes," she motioned with her free hand to her outfit, "and came down here."

Merrick thought for a moment. "What did you use to set the fire?"

Louise shrugged. "I found some old rags in the kitchen at the hotel. I poured kerosene on them and brought a package of matches with me. Easy." She was pleased with herself, and smiled briefly at Merrick.

For God's sake, Merrick thought, *where are you, Sheehan?* There had been plenty of time for Walt to have gone down to the other end of the beach and then double back.

Louise jerked the gun at Merrick. "Come on, then. Let's go."

Merrick stood, keeping his hands in the air. "Where to?"

"I don't know yet."

She turned, motioning Merrick to walk ahead of her. Emerging out of the darkness came Walt. Merrick was flooded with relief. In an instant he considered taking advantage of the surprise that he saw in Louise's eyes and grabbing her gun. Except immediately out from behind Walt emerged Clarence, holding another gun.

"Where did you come from?" This from Louise to her husband.

"I poured a lot of whiskey down the drain tonight, my darling. I had been wondering why you'd got me all liquored up the other night. When you did it again tonight, I wanted to see what you were up to."

"Where did you find this one?" Louise jerked her head toward Walt while still keeping her gun aimed at Merrick's chest.

"He was sneaking about, trying to get the jump on you, up on the street there."

Now that the pretense of being innocent bystanders had been dropped, the energy between Louise and Clarence was one of mutual disdain, rather than the adoration between husband and wife that they had displayed earlier. Clarence had obviously suspected his wife of being involved with the fire and had covered for her by acting the perfect husband.

"What do we do now?" Louise said.

"This wasn't a part of your plan, was it?" Clarence said, sneering at his wife. "Didn't you know they would be setting a trap for you here?"

"Of course I did," she snapped back. "Why do you think I brought the gun? But I was hoping they'd be together when I got the jump on them."

"Come on, then," Clarence said. "I'll show you what to do."

Merrick and Walt had exchanged a few glances, but Merrick hadn't come up with a plan yet to disarm the couple. He knew that the longer they were in custody the shorter the odds got that they would make it out of the situation alive. He was suddenly acutely aware of having dragged Walt, who was not a law enforcement officer but just a friend who was often willing to help out, into this predicament.

Louise and Clarence, one at each of their backs, instructed Merrick and Walt to head down the beach away from the town.

"There's an old cabin down here that I saw the other day. We can leave the bodies there," Clarence said.

A chill ran up Merrick's spine and he wasn't afraid to admit that he was frightened. The moon had disappeared almost entirely, covered again by cloud, and the darkness was nearly absolute. On their right the lake continued to whisper against the shore. On their left, where the beach met the closest road, the few little houses and buildings disappeared. They were moving out past the town limits.

Merrick was calculating the odds of Walt getting hurt if he simply whirled around and surprised Clarence and Louise. Unfortunately, without being able to communicate this idea to Walt, he thought that it would be especially endangering. Even if he did that and overpowered Louise, there was every chance that in that split second Clarence would be able to shoot Walt. So Merrick kept walking and kept thinking.

Sure enough, after about fifteen minutes of slogging through the sand they came to a small cabin that Merrick hadn't known existed. It was clearly abandoned; the glass in the one window at the front of the building was broken, jagged shards like sharp teeth protruding upward from the bottom of the frame. The front door was hanging off its bottom hinge, the top one having pulled away from the door frame.

Clarence and Louise had been silent on the journey. Clarence now spoke up, "Okay, you two. Inside."

Merrick and Walt both hesitated. Merrick assumed that Walt knew, just as well as he did, that once they stepped over that threshold, it was likely game over. They glanced at one another, and Merrick could see this thought in Walt's eyes. They continued to hesitate until Clarence got irritated with them.

"Come on, now! I said get in there. Don't make me shoot you out here and then have to drag you inside. You two are both monsters and I don't want to get my new suit all sweaty this early in the day."

"What if we let you go?" Merrick asked with faint hope. "What if we said that we waited down at the shoreline and nobody showed up? You two could just disappear into the night."

From behind them Louise said, "You would actually do that?"

Clarence made a small, rueful laugh. "Don't be an idiot, Louise. Of course they won't. He's just saying that to save his life. There would be a warrant out for us as soon as the sun came up."

Louise lowered her voice and whispered to her husband, though why she bothered Merrick didn't know. He could hear her as well as if she'd shouted. "I'm not comfortable shooting them. I was only going to use this gun as a threat."

Clarence spoke in a normal voice, and it seemed to Merrick that he enunciated his words a little better than usual. "That's all right, honey. I'm happy to shoot them both."

Merrick glanced at Walt again and the big blacksmith simply raised one eyebrow.

"Come on, now," Clarence said again to the two men. "Inside. I'm not going to say it again. I will shoot you here and drag you inside if I have to."

There was nothing for it. Merrick hadn't come up with a brilliant idea about how to overwhelm the two behind them.

He was just about to take the first step forward when there was a shriek from Louise and a loud thud. A shot rang out, nearly deafening Merrick. He and Walt spun just as a huge piece of driftwood connected with Clarence's forehead. The man dropped like a sack of potatoes, joining his wife, who was lying unconscious on the sand.

Instinctively and reflexively Walt and Merrick both lunged for the revolvers, which had dropped to the ground as well, picking them up in case their captors regained consciousness.

All this happened in a few short seconds, though to Merrick the time seemed to stretch out into minutes. When he rose up again from grabbing Louise's gun he saw Sully standing there, holding a piece of wood in one hand, staring down at his ex-girlfriend and his half-brother.

Sully looked up at Walt and Merrick and grinned. "I assume you're not going to throw me in jail for assault this time, are you, Merrick?" he said, his tobacco-stained teeth gleaming dully in the moonlight.

CHAPTER FOURTEEN

There had been a rainstorm the night before, loud and long, with thunder and lightning. Merrick had watched it from his office, standing in the open door, watching the wind buffet the few lonely trees that had been left standing on the main street when the storefronts had started being built. The street itself had turned to a muddy swamp, as it always did. But he knew that the next day the sun would rise again and dry out the mud, as it always did. Nature had a way of taking care of these things.

He loved summer rainstorms. It was something he remembered from his childhood in the Ottawa Valley. There, the humidity was such that a thunderstorm was always a huge relief, and he and his brothers would often go out into the yard, strip down to their underwear, and play in the rain. It was so warm that it was like swimming in a tropical lake.

Here in British Columbia, it was not quite that way. When it rained the temperature dropped. And besides, he figured he was too old to dance in his underwear.

Now he checked the lock on the cell in his office, rattling the door to make sure it was firmly closed. Louise and Clarence looked at him with disdain plainly written on their faces.

"I'll be back in a while," Merrick said to them. "Don't go anywhere."

He locked the office door as well on his way out and headed over to the smithy to find Walt.

As he arrived, the three mixed-breed dogs that were always hanging around Walt woke up from their naps in the sun. They stood, bleary-eyed, and shook themselves, heads rolling side to side, ears flapping, and then the shake moved through shoulders, torsos, and finally hindquarters. After this, two of the dogs extended their front legs and lifted their rear ends to the sky, stretching and yawning. Merrick greeted each of them in turn, ruffling the fur on their shoulders and backs, as they leaned against his knees.

When the blacksmith saw Merrick, he put down his tools, took off his apron, and grabbed his hat from the hook at the front of the shop. He also picked up his fiddle and bow from the work table near the front door. Without a word, he came outside and the two men headed down to the waterfront. The dogs preceded them, tails high, eyes bright.

When the group reached the waterfront, the man of the hour was there, dressed in a suit that he probably considered to be his finest, though it had food stains down the front. And he was still wearing his tattered bowler hat. Sully was grinning from ear to ear, clapping all the men on the back and making elaborate bows to the women.

The town's few musicians were setting up near the dock. Walt peeled off to join them.

Merrick stopped for a moment, watching the scene unfold. The refurbished ship that would take the place of the *Mary Eliza-beth* was sitting proudly at the end of the dock, her new paint gleaming in the sun. She was slightly smaller than her predecessor, but would likely be able to carry very close to the amount of cargo and passengers that the previous ship had. Merrick could see the steam engine from where he stood, its brass shining brightly. Not quite as brightly as Sully's smile, but close.

"Merrick. Good. You're here," said Mayor Billy, taking a puff on his cigar. "We can begin."

The mayor waddled down the sand and stepped awkwardly onto the end of the dock. He waved his arms and called out, gathering everyone's attention. The crowd gathered, murmuring, and then fell quiet.

"As you all know, we're here to launch this brand-new ship, the SS *Katherine Grace*. On behalf of the town counselors and the business owners' association, we want to recognize the contribution Arthur Sullivan makes to our community. We hope that this new vessel will continue to aid in our growth and prosperity."

Billy continued, expressing his thanks to just about everyone in town, making sure he wedged in a few plugs for the bank where he worked. The crowd stood patiently, used to Mayor Billy's long speeches. The man really did like to hear the sound of his own voice. Eventually, though, someone shouted out from the crowd, "Enough talk, Jones. Let's get this boat launched."

The mayor chuckled, never offended when someone spoke plainly, and said, "You're right, you're right. Come on up here, Sully, and do the honors."

Edgar Finnegan handed Sully a bottle of beer and the captain hopped up onto the dock to join the mayor. The two men walked down to the end where the ship was waiting, and Sully turned and addressed the crowd.

"I want to thank everyone who chipped in to help replace the *Mary Elizabeth*. She will always have a fond place in my heart. But I hope that this new ship will provide as much service to Horse as she did." He turned toward the ship and raised his voice. "Here is the SS *Katherine Grace*. May God bless her and all who sail in her."

He pulled his right arm back and brought it forward with force. The bottle of beer thunked against the hull, but didn't break.

"Try again, Sullivan. Put your back into it," someone yelled from the crowd.

Sully did as instructed but once more the brown bottle refused to break. After three more tries, and with the crowd getting restless and shouting jeers, Sully changed strategies. He pulled open the bottle top and splashed beer on the ship's hull. It wasn't as dramatic as the smashing of a bottle, but it did the trick of christening the ship.

The crowd cheered, clapping and whistling. Sully looked back down the length of the dock, holding the now empty bottle in his hand and grinning like a child on Christmas morning.

For the rest of the day the town celebrated there on the beach. Walt and his musician friends played an endless number of jigs and reels. Betty Mitchell, Mrs. Thoreson, and the other ladies of the town kept everyone well fed, while Edgar Finnegan kept them well lubricated. Once again, the two or three children from the town ran shrieking up and down the beach, enjoying themselves enormously.

At one point Merrick glanced over and saw Howard Peterson watching them shyly from several yards down the beach. He went and collected the boy and brought him in to join the celebration.

"Oh no, sir, I couldn't."

"Don't be silly," Merrick said. "If it weren't for you, we wouldn't have caught the culprits."

Howard had obviously heard the story. He looked up at Merrick and said, "If it weren't for me, you and Mr. Sheehan might not have almost been killed. I'm sorry I fell asleep at my post. I was so full from all that good food. That's the best I've eaten in weeks."

"Don't worry about that, son," Merrick said. "You did what you should've by telling me the truth. And none of what happened after that was your fault." He led the boy to Mrs. Thoreson's picnic table, knowing she would take good care of him.

Later, after several bottles of beer and one too many sausages roasted on the bonfire, Merrick was sitting on the edge of the dock talking to Dr. Parker about news of a railway crash in Ireland. Frank Moore approached them, a glass of what looked like lemonade in his hand. He nodded to both men.

"Lovely day for a boat launch, gentlemen."

"It is, Mr. Moore." Merrick reflected that his suspicions about Moore's guilt in the burning of the *Mary Elizabeth* had ultimately been unfounded. Even so, the man still gave him the creeps. "Will you be with us much longer?"

"I'm not sure. I'm waiting for instruction from head office. I've sent them my thoughts on the lake's suitability for a large passenger and freight ship. I expect that very soon your own version of that service," Moore motioned with his head to the newly christened *Katherine Grace*, "will reach its maximum capacity."

"It's possible," Dr. Parker responded, "but until then commerce can continue in our little town."

"Very true, doctor. Very true." Moore smiled weakly at both Parker and Merrick and then excused himself. "I think I'll get another of those delicious sugar cookies before they're gone."

"What do you think, Merrick?" Dr. Parker took a final swig of his beer. "Will Horse be better off being served by a large corporation like CRC?"

"Doctor, I think progress is coming whether we want it or not."

CHAPTER FIFTEEN

Now it was just after dusk, and the day, which had gone by in a whirlwind, had also included a telegraph message from the traveling judge saying he would be in Horse in two weeks to oversee the trial for Clarence and Louise Horan.

Walt and Merrick were sitting outside the livery, as they so often did on a summer's evening. The dogs had gone home, as they did every evening at dusk. Walt had handed Merrick a bottle of beer as he arrived and they both sat sipping, although Merrick already felt a little affected by the beer he had imbibed during the celebration.

He turned and looked at Walt. "Thanks for helping me out on the beach the other night. I'm sorry I nearly got you killed."

"No problem," Walt said. "It's all part of the blacksmith service."

Merrick smiled to himself. "What's it going to cost me the next time Earl needs a new set of shoes?"

"More than you can afford."

Without looking Merrick could hear the smile in Walt's voice.

The two men were quiet for some time, and then Walt spoke

up. "Were you surprised it was Louise Horan who burned the boat?"

"Completely," Merrick nodded. "I was fairly sure that it was either Clarence Horan or Moore that we were waiting for at the beach. Horan and his wife had alibied each other and he didn't fit Howard's description exactly, so I was leaning toward it being Moore. But after Howard came forward, I remembered that I'd smelled something akin to kerosene when I'd interviewed the Horans at Finnegan's. I made the assumption the smell was coming from Clarence."

"You mean from lighting the rags on fire?"

"Aye. It's a hard smell to get out of clothes, and even harder to get off your skin. It was faint, but persistent. It was only when Louise ambushed me that I realized that the smell had come from her, not her husband."

A mosquito buzzed in Merrick's ear and he swatted at it. He stood up. "Time to go in, I think. The bugs are out."

Walt stood as well and picked up his chair. As the two men walked through the wide livery doors, Walt asked, "Have you written to your mother?"

Merrick proceeded in silence. He set his chair down just inside the doors and walked through the building to Earl's stall. The big gray gelding came to the half-door and stuck his head over it, bumping his nose into Merrick's chest. Walt followed and stood at Nelson's stall. The two men were about twelve feet apart. The perfect distance for having a conversation that strayed into emotional territory.

"I haven't," Merrick finally said, rubbing his hand along Earl's neck. "But I will."

the end

THE HORSE YOU RODE IN ON

A Town Called Horse Short Mystery

CHAPTER ONE

Saturday, November 8, 1890

It was partly the horse that was clomping up the wooden steps to the Stratford Hotel that caught Julia Thom's attention. The two men aboard, one of whom was facing backwards and clinging to the horse's tail, also caught her eye.

"Good morning, Miss Julia!" Captain Arthur 'Sully' Sullivan, the backwards-facing passenger, attempted to doff his battered bowler hat as she stopped and stared at him from the middle of the main street. He grinned at her, but his courteous attempt to tip his hat was his downfall. He had let go of the horse's tail and now, as the horse finished its ascent up the staircase and proceeded through the open doors of the restaurant, Sully began to tilt to his right.

"Watch out, Mr. Sullivan," Julia called.

Unfortunately, Sully, completely oblivious to his predicament, raised his other arm and cupped it to his ear. "What's that?"

She began to call back to him, "I said—"

But the man's eyes opened wide and he held Julia's gaze as, ever so slowly, he began to slide down the animal's flank.

"Oh, dear," was all he said. He didn't try to correct his course—not that he could have. There was nothing to grab onto. He put his hat back on his head, all the while gently descending toward the porch deck. He landed with a surprisingly quiet thud, a small "Oof!" escaping his lips.

The horse and its remaining rider continued, unperturbed, into the restaurant.

Julia trotted across the street, stepping around the slush and puddles. She raced up the steps and crouched down beside Sully.

"Mr. Sullivan, are you quite all right?"

Sully stayed where he was, not moving, his eyes closed. Julia took one of his bare hands in her own and patted it with her gloved fingers.

"Mr. Sullivan? Sully? Are you quite alright?" She could see that he was breathing, and she could smell the alcohol from where she knelt.

Julia leaned forward to whisper to him, trying to see if he was conscious. In addition to smelling like alcohol, Sully had his usual aura of tobacco, lake water, and stale clothing. He was never the sweetest-smelling creature in town.

"Mr. Sullivan. Can you hear me?"

One of Sully's eyes opened and Julia suddenly realized just how close she had put her face to his in an effort to try to assist him.

"Give us a kiss, would you?" Sully said, pursing his lips and lurching upwards, trying to tag Julia with his dirty mouth.

CHAPTER TWO

Caroline Finnegan's shriek from the dining room was probably heard as far away as Kamloops. It was actually more of a roar than a shriek, rattling the windows of the hotel dining room and no doubt waking those in town who were still in bed.

Now that Julia knew Sully was conscious, she averted his kiss, patted him on the shoulder and instructed him to rest for a moment. She stood and dashed into the hotel dining room to see if she could help Caroline.

The horse was a deep chestnut color with a black mane and tail that reminded Julia of blacksmith Walter Sheehan's horse, Nelson, although this animal was more petite than Nelson. It had the finely boned legs and delicate head that suggested impeccable breeding. The horse looked around itself at the unfamiliar surroundings of the hotel dining room. Its ears were perked but it appeared calm, though alert. It had no saddle, just a bridle. The headpiece was not properly secured around the horse's right ear and Julia could see that the whole rig was about to slide off the horse's face.

Julia ran around to the front of the horse instinctively as she came in through the restaurant doors. She came to a stop beside the end of the bar, behind which hotel proprietor Caroline Finnegan stood, a broom in her hand and a look of thunder on her face.

"Edgar!" she roared, calling for her husband. "Get in here. Now."

Julia, meanwhile, took in the scene before her. If she hadn't been so worried about Caroline bursting a blood vessel, it would've been quite comical.

The tables around the dining room had just two occupants. On the far side of the room, near some of the windows that looked out onto the wide porch at the side of the building, sat what looked to be a couple of drovers. They had on work clothes and boots, and their sun-wrinkled faces told Julia immediately that they were outside workers. Probably part of a large influx of people coming to work in the area on the new ranches and orchards that were springing up. At another table off to Julia's right, in a quieter corner of the room, sat a man by himself in a dark suit, white shirt, and dark tie.

The drovers looked amused and had settled deeply into their chairs, leaning back with smiles on their faces, watching the proceedings. By contrast, the gentleman in the suit looked ill at ease. He stared out from behind his newspaper at the scene unfolding before him. Julia immediately assessed him as a city dweller.

Julia transferred her attention to the man astride the horse. He was obviously just as inebriated as his recently departed companion. He was riding bareback and appeared to have only one boot on. And though he was fully dressed in a suit and an overcoat, the overcoat itself appeared to be on inside out, the silk lining facing outward. He had a bowler hat on, which looked like it had been slept on. The man was someone she recognized vaguely. He had a pleasant-looking face, with wide dark eyebrows, dark eyes, and a strong jaw.

The man's head swam around a little bit, and Julia imagined

that he was trying to focus. The horse stood patiently, obviously much more collected than his passenger.

Julia glanced over at Caroline, who was now gripping the edge of the bar with both hands and staring at her unwelcome guests. Her eyes darted over quickly, met Julia's and then returned to the wobbly figure and the big brown animal. "Bloody Edgar," she said through gritted teeth. "Where the hell is that man when I need him?" She looked back up at the horse and rider, then weakly raised one arm and flapped it lightly. "Shoo," she said.

Julia knew that wasn't going to do the trick.

The man astride the horse raised his own arm and searched around in the region of his head to find his hat. His brain and his arm clearly weren't communicating with one another, but he was finally able to make contact with the brim. He lifted it up slightly off his crown and then set it back down gently, more askew than it had been before.

"Good morning," he said. "Might you have such a thing as a cup of coffee about you?"

To Julia's left, Caroline Finnegan made little huffing sound and stood up a little straighter. Caroline was not comfortable with horses, but she was a woman in command of her hotel and her restaurant. Julia could see Caroline's fear of large animals and her natural leadership ability battling with one another and was just about to offer to lead the horse back out of the restaurant when Caroline held up her palm toward Julia in a 'not right now' gesture. The hotel proprietress took a deep breath and began to walk toward Julia so that she could round the end of the bar.

Keeping a wary eye on the horse, Caroline passed around Julia and stood with one hand resting gently on the back of a dining room chair, possibly providing her with some stability. She looked up directly into the face of the rider, giving him her very best bartender's 'This is your last call' stare.

"Now listen here, Coinneach Dalton. You are going to back that beast up and get it the hell out of my restaurant before I send someone to get Constable Merrick." Caroline hesitated for a second and then she planted both closed fists on her hips in a pose of authority and defiance.

The horse stretched his neck out, reaching toward Caroline with his nose, and made a little wuffling sound. The hotel proprietress took half a step back.

"You won't serve a manna cuppa coffee?" the rider asked. He thrust his lower lip out in a faux gesture of sadness and petulance.

Outside, through the propped open front doors, Julia could see Sully, still lying on his back, pull one arm up over his face. She heard him let out a contented sigh.

The rider continued. "All's I'm wanting," he whispered conspiratorially, as though that would help, his words mushing together, "issa strong cup of coffee. Once I've got that I'll be on my way, Miss Finnegan."

Caroline's hands had remained on her hips but Julia could see her deep discomfort. Despite the cool temperature, thanks to the open door, Julia could see beads of sweat breaking out on Caroline's face. She stepped forward now.

"Caroline, let me lead him outside," she said, and began moving towards the horse.

The rider had righted himself and was muttering quietly while he straightened his hat.

Caroline Finnegan never like to admit defeat, or even to ask for help, but she glanced at Julia, her expression one of anger mixed with relief. "Would you?"

"Of course." Julia began to move toward the animal, who turned his head slightly to look at her. She made of soft clucking noise, like the one she always used with her pinto horse, Stanley. The horse's ears flicked towards her, and his body language told her he wasn't frightened or agitated. She thought she would spend a couple of minutes getting to know him and then hopefully get his bridle settled on his head properly. This done, she should be able to turn him around and lead him out of the restaurant without too much danger to himself, his rider, or the guests in the restaurant.

She took one step closer toward the horse, and then out of the corner of her eye she noticed the animal raise his tail in an unmistakable gesture.

She pulled her hand back down to her side and whirled around to face Caroline. Their eyes met.

Caroline's eyebrows went up. "What is it? What's wrong now?"

From off to Julia's left, and from the rear end of the horse, there was a loud and long toot of flatulence and then the horse's bowels let go. The distinctive plopping sound of manure hitting the wide-planked wooden floors filled the room. Caroline's eyes stayed frozen on Julia and opened so wide Julia thought her eyeballs might pop out.

Con Dalton swiveled around on the horse's back and regarded the deposit with fascination. When the horse's tail lowered, his toilet break over, Con turned back to Julia and Caroline. "Good heavens," he said, starting to laugh. "How rude."

CHAPTER THREE

There was a bank of clouds peeking over the hills on the horizon, and that worried Jack Merrick. Horse had not yet received its first major snowfall of the year. There had been a couple of light dustings recently, but he knew from experience that these were just teases, gentle prologues to the storms that would arrive in a few weeks. As he walked toward his Main Street office, his eyes kept darting to the horizon just beyond the hills that surrounded the town. Horse was cupped in a little bowl valley and surrounded by low hills on every side but one. Lake Okanagan, which lay several blocks to his left, just beyond his vision, was where his eyes were trained now.

When Merrick and his wife Charlotte had arrived in Horse, she had been thrilled to be so close to a body of water. It had made Merrick very happy to watch her spend time on the lakeshore during the first and only summer that they had spent together in this town. Charlotte had grown up in Victoria and had had an almost obsessive interest in being close to water. In her childhood, her family had often gone out in their small sailboat around the harbor and islands close to Victoria. Charlotte's father had been an avid sailor and he had imbued his only daughter with a love of the sea. When Merrick had transferred to this remote place in the interior of British Columbia, very soon after he and Charlotte were married, he knew that the one thing that bothered Charlotte only slightly less than being far away from her parents was being separated from the sea. So when they had realized that the town was set on the shores of an enormous lake, Charlotte had been thrilled, and Merrick had been relieved.

Charlotte's parents, her father especially, had done everything they could to dissuade their daughter from marrying the farmer's son turned police constable. Merrick had been deeply in love with Charlotte, whom he had met at a local dance in Victoria, where he was serving in his first post as a police officer. But at the same time, he was a young man who whose parents had instilled in him a deep respect for his elders. He had worked up the courage to ask the petite blonde to attend a picnic with him, but after Charlotte had arrived at several of their outings obviously upset from arguing with her parents, Merrick had understood that they would never let her marry him with their blessing.

The job in Horse had come available, and Merrick had made the difficult decision to leave Victoria and move to Horse without letting Charlotte know. It would be cruel, but he couldn't bring himself to defy Charlotte's father, whom he had come to respect. Mr. Porter had only had Charlotte's best interests at heart and, wise beyond his years, Merrick had understood this.

And then in a surprising turn of events, Mr. Porter had come over to Merrick's side.

"She'll never forgive me if we don't give her our blessing," he had told Merrick gruffly, "and I can't have that."

Charlotte had missed her parents terribly once they'd moved to Horse, as Merrick was sure she would. But she had done her very best to create a beautiful home for her new husband and to get involved in the small community where they'd landed. Merrick had taken Charlotte out on the lake every chance he could get in the fair weather, and nothing made him happier than rowing her along the shoreline to a picnic spot where they could sit and watch the water.

Charlotte had had only had one summer season in Horse, and then she was gone. Her parents had come up to Horse for the funeral, and any warmth that Mr. Porter had begun to feel for Merrick had disappeared by the time they arrived. Merrick knew that Mrs. Porter didn't blame him for Charlotte's death, but he was pretty sure that Mr. Porter did. The hostility and dismissiveness that had gradually faded from Mr. Porter's demeanor when Merrick had lived in Victoria now returned in full force. The couple had arrived the day before Charlotte's funeral and had left town just after the service, barely taking time to shake Pastor Thoreson's hand. Merrick had not heard from them since and had no idea how they were doing. He had disappeared into a dark hole of grief that was made worse by the fact that Charlotte's family had been against the match from the beginning.

Mr. Porter had not spoken to Merrick during the slightly less than twenty-four hours they were in Horse, but Merrick had overheard him say to his wife that it was no wonder Charlotte had lost her will to live in such a backwater place. This had hurt Merrick more than Mr. Porter could ever know, for Merrick knew how fond Charlotte had become of the small, growing town. She had told him many times that she loved being at the beginning of something, as she put it. Merrick suspected that she had written to her mother about this feeling, and he wondered if Mrs. Porter had passed the letter along to her husband. If she had, it obviously hadn't registered with him. Or, perhaps more likely, he didn't want it to register.

It was thoughts and memories like these that Merrick actively tried to stay away from. After the dark months immediately following Charlotte's death, when he had spent most of his time riding aimlessly through the hills, he had kept himself busy all summer and usually worked until he could no longer stand up in his boots. He found that living this way helped him to deal with what seemed like the bottomless grief that he felt about losing his wife, his soulmate. In addition to all the things he was responsible for as the town constable, he helped his friend Walter Sheehan at the livery whenever he could, cleaning stalls and making repairs when the building needed it. There was a nearly endless demand for his time and attention, and for this he was very grateful.

However, lately his life had been a little quiet and he was less exhausted than usual. As a result, Merrick's thoughts and feelings about Charlotte had been awake and taunting him. Her birthday was coming up and he suspected that this had something to do with his increasing discomfort. His grief felt like a rider he had been trying to outrun. For a while he tricked himself into believing he had done that. Now it felt like he was losing ground, the rider catching up once more.

As he stepped up on to the sidewalk outside the block where his office lay, Merrick mentally shook himself, like a dog shaking itself free of water after a swim. He unlocked the door to his office, one of the few buildings in town that used a lock, and let himself in to the place where he could lose himself in the solace of busyness. He did consider it a mark of progress that he was no longer sleeping in the small jail cell and was once again able to spend his nights in the house he had shared with Charlotte.

His office was cold when he opened the door. The hinges creaked a little as he stepped inside. Without taking his coat off, Merrick walked over to the wood stove in the center of the room.

Other than the small cell, the rest of the large square space was dedicated to Merrick's job as local constable and general dogsbody. There was a table against one wall that held the telegraph machine, which was Horse's connection to the outside world and Merrick's connection to his superior officers in Victoria. Separate from this, Merrick's oak desk stood to the right of the office doorway. The desk was large and imposing, and almost too big for the space and, as such, was a perfect metaphor for the man who occupied the office. There was a coat rack in one corner where, once Merrick had the fire going and the room warming up, he would hang his thick woolen coat and his black, wide-brimmed hat. Charlotte had bought him the coat rack for their first wedding anniversary. Until then, Merrick had always hung his coat on the back of his chair, and any townsfolk who came to speak to him had simply kept their coats on. Charlotte had been much more refined, and the coat rack was only one of the many ways in which, during their life together, she had gently but firmly softened Merrick's rough edges.

The fire crackled and popped as Merrick added slivers of kindling wood to the little pyramid of crumpled pages of the *Horse Herald* he'd made. As the wood caught he added some larger sticks and waited, crouched down in front of the cast-iron door, watching the flames, lost in thought.

He had never been able to figure out what it was that Charlotte had seen in him. He could still remember very clearly the way she'd looked at him, with a devotion and affection in her eyes that had surprised him every time he saw it, even though he had seen it every day while they were married. She had been a beautiful girl, so pretty that it had almost pained Merrick at times to look at her.

They should never have met, he reflected again. He had been a young man in his very early twenties who had spent a couple of years traveling across the wild Dominion of Canada. He had landed in Victoria unsure of what to do with himself next, but had made the acquaintance of a man who worked as a police officer in that small port town. Merrick's trip across the country had gifted him with skills for reading people's character and understanding the motivations behind behaviors and actions that few young men of his age possessed. In the late 1880s in British Columbia, police officers were not so much trained as appointed. The officer who had befriended Merrick had recommended his new friend to his superior officer as someone who might make a good police constable, and Merrick, when offered, had taken the job gladly.

Charlotte's father was a businessman who owned several shops around Victoria, successful clothing stores that catered to the landed gentry who were flooding into the city. Mr. Porter happened to know the local police commissioner, and it was at a dance that Merrick had first laid eyes on his future wife.

Charlotte and her mother had volunteered to serve refreshments. Merrick had drunk so much iced tea that night that he'd felt swollen and bloated for two days following. Charlotte was clearly used to men flirting with her; she was a deft hand at keeping the conversation going when the young man standing before her was at a loss for words. Merrick had reflected later that she'd made him feel at ease.

He had known, of course, who she was and where her family lived, but it had taken him three weeks to work up the nerve to call on her. Nearly everything in his body had been shouting at him to leave her alone, that she was too good for him, and that she could never have anything more than fondness for someone like him, a farm boy from the Ottawa Valley who had yet to find his place in the world. But she had received him at the door with a warmth that had encouraged him. By the time he'd realized Charlotte felt the same way about him, and how much her father objected to this fact, it was too late.

The sticks in the wood stove had taken a good hold now, and Merrick placed a larger log onto the fire. He watched it while it caught and then added another piece perpendicular to it, leaving space between them so that air could flow and feed the flames. He stood up and swung the stove door nearly closed, leaving it open a crack. He knew from experience that the room would warm up quickly; the stove was a good one. He took his coat off and hung it on the coat rack along with his hat, and then started to make himself a cup of coffee from the little stash that he kept in a small cupboard at the back of the office.

Behind him, Merrick heard the door of the office open. He turned and found Caroline Finnegan standing on the threshold, her face red with rage, and behind her, Julia Thom.

He knew from experience that the best way to deal with the hotel owner when she wore this expression was to remain calm and casual. "Good morning, Caroline. Julia. Cup of coffee?" He held his cup aloft.

Julia was grinning from ear to ear, but Caroline's face was rigid with anger. "Don't try to charm me, Jack Merrick. I need you to come to the hotel right now."

The two women stepped inside and closed the door. Merrick sighed inwardly and set the cup down, his hopes for a quiet morning of catching up on paperwork dashed. "What's happened?"

"I'll tell you what. That condescending leech Con Dalton rode his—"

The door to the office was flung fully open behind Caroline and Julia. They both startled and hopped out of the way, the leading edge of the door nearly knocking them over.

A young woman barely out of her teens stumbled into the room, out of breath and red faced. Her eyes roamed around the room wildly, like frightened birds unsure where to land. They passed by Caroline, swept over Merrick's desk, flew back to the little cell at the back of the room and then finally came to rest on the constable.

Merrick didn't recognize the girl. She was petite and wore a patterned cotton dress with long sleeves. There was a crisp white apron tied around her waist. She had no coat on and had obviously been running. She gulped in air, her corseted chest straining with every breath. Her hair was tied in a long braid that was hanging over one of her shoulders, and a halo of stray hairs framed her face. Her cheeks were two bright red spots on a clear white complexion. She was upset, that much was clear. Her eyes were rimmed red, and she unconsciously wiped her nose on one of her sleeves. Merrick stood still, waiting patiently for the girl to catch her breath.

Caroline Finnegan didn't have the time for such courtesies. Being interrupted was not improving her already strained mood. She waited a fraction of a second and then barked, "Speak up, child. We don't have all day."

The girl nodded, took another gulp of air, and said, "You're Constable Merrick?"

Merrick nodded. "How can I help?"

"Miss Marie sent me. She said for you to come right away. Please," she added as an afterthought.

"Of course. What's your name?"

"Bettina." The girl had a slight French accent.

"That's a beautiful name." Merrick was applying the skills his father had taught him for dealing with frightened animals: remain calm, speak in soothing tones, and don't rush. "What's happened, Bettina?"

The girl nodded, her eyes still wide. Her breath was returning to normal, though her face was no less inflamed. She looked at Caroline and Julia and then back to Merrick. Merrick was willing to wait, to let the girl arrive at the fence in her own time.

"Oh, for God's sake!" Caroline fairly shouted, her patience worn out. "Speak up, child, or go home." She crossed her arms under her bosom and glared at the girl.

Bettina startled and Merrick had to resist the urge to shoo Caroline out of his office.

"Marie asks for you to come. *S'il vous plaît.*"

Caroline groaned but Merrick ignored her, keeping his eyes on the girl. "Can you tell me what's happened?"

Bettina nodded, but didn't speak.

"Merrick, for the love of all that is holy. . ." Caroline uncrossed her arms and put her hands on her hips. "Can you help me first please? I was here before this girl and I've got a complaint to make. Obviously, whatever's going on with her can wait."

Merrick reflected, not for the first time, that the women in this town were awfully free with their opinions about how he should do his job. But it did seem as though Bettina needed some time to collect herself before she would be able to share whatever was going on. He spoke softly to her. "Why don't you have a seat?" He gestured toward the wooden guest chair in front of his desk. "I'll help Mrs. Finnegan and then I'll be able to help you. Is that alright?"

Bettina didn't say anything in return, but he stepped toward the chair. Merrick turned toward Caroline. "Now, Caroline, tell me what's on your mind."

"It's not what's on my mind that's the problem. It's what's on my dining room floor. Have you ever..."

Into the hotelier's tirade, Bettina was finally able to find her voice. "It's just that one of the girls is dead."

CHAPTER FOUR

The house on Findlay Street was not one that Julia had ever encountered before, and in fact she had not known this street existed until this morning. It was a three-story house and the tallest on the block, painted white with dark blue trim around the windows and doors.

Everything about the house was immaculate; the lawn was tidy despite the large oak tree at its center, shedding its leaves. The porch steps had been swept. The floral curtains seen on the other side of the living room window seemed to be standing at attention. There were two rocking chairs to one side of the front door with embroidered pillows propped up against their backs. Julia thought this a quaint touch. The house had a wide front porch that wrapped around the right-hand corner and lead all the way along that side of the house. As Julia and Merrick approached she could see that the front door was hanging open. Several townspeople stood on the dirt road in front of the house in small clusters, whispering to one another. On either side of the house there were smaller houses stretching up and down the block.

Merrick took the front steps two at a time. Julia followed, struggling to keep up with his long strides. Facing them beyond the open front door was a long hallway that ended at a dark wood door. Immediately to the left of the front door was a wide staircase climbing up to the second floor. Also on her left were a mirrored coat rack and an umbrella stand. On the right were two closed French doors. With a quick glance through the glass panes Julia could see several settees and wingback chairs placed around the elegant room, and a large stone fireplace on the far side.

Merrick hesitated for a moment, seeming to listen. Julia heard the sound of footfalls and voices coming from above. He glanced at Julia. "Are you sure you want to do this?"

She nodded without speaking and they began to climb the stairs.

Merrick hadn't been keen for Julia to accompany him.

Caroline Finnegan had been convinced to accompany Bettina over to Dr. Parker's office to rouse him, though she made Merrick promise to come to the restaurant to hear her complaint about her early morning visitors as soon as he could.

He had buttoned his coat and taken his hat off the coat rack. One glance at Julia had clearly communicated that she wanted to get involved with whatever was going on.

"You can't come with me, Julia," he had said as he buttoned his coat.

"Let me join you. You know how much I love to help."

"To interfere, you mean."

"I guess that depends on your definition of 'interfere'."

He shook his head. "Not this time. This is not a place for you."

"Because of the body, you mean?" Julia gave Merrick her best no-nonsense look. "I've seen a dead body before. In fact, when my father was—"

Merrick interrupted her, "It's not about the body, Julia. I know you're not squeamish about...well...about anything." He glanced at

Caroline, who raised her eyebrows at him. A look passed between the two that Julia didn't understand.

"I promise I'll be quiet, Merrick. I'll stand in the background. You won't even notice me."

"No, Julia. Not this time." He moved toward the open office door.

She stepped sideways to block him and tilted her head back slightly to hold his gaze. "I can just follow you, you know."

Merrick stared at her and she could see thoughts passing behind his eyes. "I don't have time for this," he finally said.

"Then stop arguing with me and let's go." She smiled.

The constable glanced once more at Caroline.

Julia looked back and forth from one of them to the other. "What is it? Why do you keep looking at each other like that?"

Merrick looked back at Julia and narrowed his eyes at her. "Fine. Come along. But when you lose your job over this, don't come crying to me." He stepped around her and walked out onto the wooden sidewalk.

"Lose my job? Over helping you with a crime?"

Over his shoulder, Merrick said, "It's not the crime. It's where it's taken place."

Julia exited the office behind him and had to trot to keep up with his long strides down the walkway. She was confused. "I don't understand. What do you mean? Is the body in an odd location? How did you gather that from what that girl said?"

Merrick came to a halt so fast Julia nearly caromed into his back. He turned and locked eyes with her once more. "The body is in a house of ill repute."

The stairs made a dogleg to the right after twelve steps or so. Julia and Merrick turned and continued up until they were in a long hallway, running directly above the one on the ground floor. This one, however, had several doors leading onto it. There was a long brightly patterned carpet runner stretching away in both directions. The hallway was bright from the light flowing in through a large stained-glass window on the staircase landing. Julia could hear voices and movement coming from her left. Merrick turned in that direction and they walked down the carpeted hallway until they found a door right at the very end that was open.

Merrick filled the doorway. Julia ducked her head to look through a tiny space between his right arm and the frame. She thought she could see two women sitting on the edge of a bed. Frustrated, she poked Merrick's arm. He glanced down and glared at her but did take half a step to his left.

Now Julia could see the whole room. There was an ornate oak dresser against one wall with a standing mirror above it. The jug and basin on the dresser were a beautiful porcelain of a type Julia had never seen before; the pattern looked European in style, and expensive. There was a large set of windows along the wall on the left side of the room, with delicate lace curtains covering the pane, while dark red velvet curtains hung on either side of the window frame, pulled back to allow in the daylight. A standing lamp stood sentry in one corner beside a wing-backed chair. The major feature was the large bed that took up most of the center of the room. It was covered with a fuchsia bedspread that appeared to be made of silk. The bed frame was brass and had both a headboard and a footboard with an intricate flourished design. Several large pillows decorated the head of the bed. The room smelled subtly of perfume and soap.

Julia glanced around, taking all this in. The two women on the bed were looking at Merrick. Another older woman stood near the window.

All three were alive, which was puzzling.

One of the women on the bed was sniffling into a handkerchief. She had dark hair and was wearing a pink silk dressing gown. One of the sleeves was torn at the shoulder.

"Good morning," Merrick said, nodding to all the women. "Bettina said you had found a deceased person."

One of the women stood up off the bed. "*Mon dieu*," she said. "I am so sorry, Constable. Bettina is excitable. I told her to run and find you and she has exaggerated our problems here. *S'excuser*."

The woman was tall and attractive in a way that almost took Julia's breath away. Her hair was palest yellow-blonde and was pulled up in a soft chignon at the base of her neck. She had high cheekbones and beautiful clear skin that Julia was immediately envious of. There was not a freckle or a mole to be seen. She had light brown eyebrows and Julia suspected their color had been aided with a pencil because the woman was obviously a natural blonde and had the fair skin and light eyelashes and eyebrows that came with that. Her dress was made of silk, something Julia had not seen since she left New Westminster. It was a dark blue color with pale gray trim and fit the woman like a glove. Julia was sure that it had been custom made, and not by any local tailor.

"I'm glad you're okay, Marie. What's happened?"

Just then, Julia felt someone at her back. She turned and found Dr. Parker squeezing past her into the room.

"Bettina came and found me." He sounded out of breath. "She said someone has died."

"No, Doctor. But we do need you." The tall blonde woman gestured to the younger, crying woman on the bed.

Dr. Parker stepped over to her and put his medical bag on the floor. He sat down beside her. "May I?"

The woman wiped her nose and nodded, turning her face to him for examination.

Merrick caught the eye of the tall woman he'd called Marie. "Can we speak in the hallway?"

She nodded once and Julia backed out of the room to make way for them.

Merrick and Marie emerged and were followed by the older woman, who had so far been silent. Merrick was about to speak when Julia thought she should introduce herself. She held her hand out to the tall blonde woman. "Good morning," she said. "I'm very sorry to see what's happened. I'm Julia Thom, the schoolteacher."

The woman Merrick had called Marie hesitated for a moment, but then extended her hand and shook Julia's briefly. "I'm Marie Bellanger. This is my mother, Esme."

The older woman had her hands clasped tightly in front of her. Julia decided not to try offering hers.

Esme was an older, but no less beautiful, version of her daughter. Her hair was dark, as were her eyes. She was a few inches shorter than her daughter but held herself in the same poised way. Her dress was also silk, a pale yellow with white accents.

Merrick stepped closer to Julia and tried to take her elbow. "I really don't think I'll need your help, Julia. Perhaps you should go home."

Julia was about to object and stress to Merrick that he would have a hard time getting rid of her, but before she could say anything there was a flurry of French from the two women. They had their heads bent together and spoke urgently, though in hushed tones. Julia caught a few of the words that they were saying, but not enough to fully understand the conversation. Her French was rusty.

The women seemed to be having an argument. Marie's forehead gradually became more creased, and though she tried to keep her composure, Julia could hear notes of disagreement and impatience. Julia watched the little flurry, her eyes pinging back and forth from one woman to the other. These two were obviously not unused to arguments.

There was suddenly one very clipped, sharp word from Esme and the conversation came to an abrupt halt. Marie took a deep breath and then shifted her eyes over toward Julia.

"Mama says that she would be grateful for your assistance. She's heard about you since you came to town, she says, though I don't know how or why, but she's decided that you will be our ally." Marie looked past Julia's shoulder at Merrick. "We'd like her to stay, Constable. Would you please grant your *authorisation?*"

Merrick gave a little flap of his hands, seeming to realize that he was outnumbered and outgunned by three strong-willed women. He looked to Julia. "Fine," he said. "But you need to know this is probably not going to go over very well with the school board."

CHAPTER SIX

Dr. Parker emerged from the room, his jacket off and his shirtsleeves rolled up. He looked at Marie Bellanger. "There are no broken bones. There's a lump on the side of her head where she was obviously struck with something or perhaps hit it on something if she fell. She needs rest and quiet." At these final words Dr. Parker raised his eyebrows.

"*Oui*, Doctor," Marie nodded. "*Merci*. She will rest until she is completely healed."

Julia had stood quietly all this time, watching the conversation but endeavoring not to interfere. Though he had agreed to let her stay, Julia knew she still walked a very fine line with Merrick.

After knowing Julia for only a few weeks, the local constable had realized he was not was going to be able to stop the schoolteacher from investigating when things went wrong. After several arguments that Merrick recognized as a power struggle, he had surrendered to the fact that he might as well use Julia's sharp mind and inquisitive nature to his advantage.

When Merrick had shared this with her, Julia had been extremely grateful. The passion that she had for justice, and the energy that she had wanted to channel into being a lawyer, had to go somewhere. But she also knew she shouldn't overstep her bounds.

Dr. Parker turned and went back into the room. Merrick looked at Marie. "Tell us what happened."

Marie turned to her mother. "Mama, will you please help Dr. Parker and give him anything he needs."

When the older woman had left them, Marie gestured to Merrick and Julia. "Come. Please." She led them down the hallway.

This room was as beautifully appointed as the previous one, though it did not hold a bed or dresser. It had originally been intended as a bedroom but was now set up as a small sitting room. Marie indicated a small sofa where Julia and Merrick could sit. She sat in an upholstered chair with a delicate floral pattern.

Marie placed her hands in her lap, folded neatly together. There were three inches between her spine and the back of the chair. She sat very still and looked at Merrick, waiting.

"Tell us what happened," the constable said again.

Marie nodded her head once, a tiny gesture. "I was downstairs in my office when I heard noises from up here. At first, I wasn't concerned. Sometimes the evening's activity can be..." she searched around for a word, "...*vigoreaux, oui?*" She looked at Merrick, who nodded.

Julia was working very hard at not reacting to Marie's description of the activity that occurred in the house. She could feel herself blushing, and hoped that the other two would not notice.

Marie continued. "But then the noises became louder and I became concerned. I came out of my office and found Celeste and Rose at the bottom of the stairs. They had heard the noises as well. Right away we heard a loud crash. The three of us came upstairs and found Alice in the room, just there. She was on the floor. She wasn't moving. I sent Rose to tell Bettina to fetch Dr. Parker." Marie stopped, as though unsure of herself for the first time. "I don't know why she went to your office first."

Merrick encouraged her. "Was Alice unconscious when you found her?"

"*Oui*. We tried to wake her but she would not. Celeste found a washcloth and we pressed that to Alice's head. After several minutes she began to revive. And then you arrived not long after."

"You were able to get her to sit up."

Marie nodded. "*Oui*. She began to wake up. I thought she should stay until Dr. Parker arrived, but she wanted to sit up. She didn't like being on the floor."

There was a clock somewhere in the room and Julia could hear it ticking, thought she couldn't see it. She glanced to the window and noticed it had begun snowing. Tiny, glittering flakes floated through the air, seemingly without any sense of purpose.

"And then what?" Merrick asked.

"I sat with Alice. She was confused. I don't think she knew who I was for a moment. Then I heard you coming up the stairs so I sent the other girls away. They were not dressed for company." Marie looked at Julia as she said this and gave her a weak smile.

"Your mother must have arrived at some point," Merrick said.

"*Excusez?*"

"You mentioned that Rose and Celeste had come upstairs with you, but when we arrived your mother was in the room. She must have joined you at some point."

"Ah, *oui*. I suppose so. I think she came into the room just after we found Alice. It is difficult to remember. It was *frénétique*."

"Did Alice have any customers last night?"

"*Oui*. A drover from one of the ranches."

"Do you know his name?"

"Risely, I think. Yes, Hugh Risely."

Dr. Parker appeared in the doorway. "I'm leaving now, Merrick. The girl is lying down. Esme is with her. She didn't need any stitches or anything, miraculously. Though that bump on her head is cause for concern. She seems confused." He turned to Marie. "I'll be back later this afternoon to look in on her."

Marie nodded. "*Merci*, Doctor."

Parker turned to leave but Merrick stopped him. "Did she say anything to you about what happened?"

The doctor turned back and shook his head. "She says the last thing she remembers is collecting eggs from the chickens yesterday."

"So no idea who attacked her."

"None." Parker looked as though he was about to leave again. But he turned back once more. "You might want to interview me, though."

"You?" Julia could hear the surprise in Merrick's voice. "Why?"

"Well, not just me, I suppose. Sully too, and Con Dalton. And Mayor Billy, for that matter." Parker could obviously see the questions in Merrick's eyes because he answered before being asked. "We were all here at the poker game last night."

CHAPTER SEVEN

errick left Julia at Marie's house to interview the girls who had been there last night. He hoped that the rapport that Julia seem to be building with the women of the house would encourage a flow of information.

It was a closed society, he reflected. The women who worked for Marie kept to themselves. They didn't socialize with the other members of the community. Neither did Marie or Esme. He imagined that it was a lonely life, partly because of their job, but partly because, from what he could determine, it seemed like the girls in the house were like a close-knit family, with Marie and Esme playing the role of parents.

Marie had always struck Merrick as a businesswoman first, and then a brothel owner. Certainly, she was beautiful, and had done a bit of 'hospitality' work in her youth. But from the few brief conversations that he'd had with her at times when there was a troublesome customer at the house, which happened occasionally, he was never left with even a hint of seductiveness or beguilement. She was a businesswoman, in business for herself and for her mother. This was a well-known fact about her, so much so that the brothel's nickname among the men of Horse was Lazy Mary's, because Marie was anything but.

He knew very little of her back story, but he did know that Esme had lost her husband when Marie was very young, back in Montreal and had had to work long hours in a factory for very little pay. Marie had once commented to Merrick that by the time she was seven years old she had known that she was going to find a way to make a living in the world that would keep her mother out of those dark, dank factories.

And she had done exactly that, and more. She owned several of the new buildings going up in town. And he had a vague memory of hearing that she also had an interest in a new ranch that was being started outside of town. She was a force to be reckoned with, and he really liked that about her. She was so self-contained that anytime he'd encountered her he was always left wanting to know more about her, but he had never had the opportunity to have that conversation with her.

Merrick guessed that he might find Sully still at the Stratford Hotel, unless Caroline had kicked him off the property. Before he'd even climbed the steps, he could hear snoring coming from the porch. He stood near the front door looking left and right; he could still hear the snoring but couldn't see the musician who was making the noise. He followed his ears down to the corner of the porch and turned right, and found Sully sprawled in a large wooden rocking chair, his head hanging down at an angle that, if he were conscious, would have been extremely uncomfortable.

Merrick was surprised that Caroline had let Sully sleep off his drunk here. He tapped the bottom of one of Sully's boots with his toe. "Sully, wake up."

Sully snorted and his head jerked back up into a vertical position. He cracked open his eyes and then stretched, sending both arms out wide, heaving a big yawn, showing all the spaces where many of his teeth used to be. His mouth was like a picket fence with many of the slats knocked out.

Stretch finished and yawn complete, Sully rubbed his face with his hands and mumbled through his fingers, "What can I do for you, Merrick?"

There was another rocking chair beside Sully's. Merrick pulled it a little closer and sat down, comforted by the curved embrace of the chair. He sat quietly for few minutes, not answering Sully's question. They were on the side of the hotel, facing a side street that didn't yet have a name but that locals called Hops Lane, because of its proximity to Finnegan's bar and his homemade beer. He could hear the noise of crockery and silverware clinking together in the dining room. A small brown bird landed on the porch railing. It hopped along few steps, eyeing Sully and Merrick, possibly checking them out for a source of food, and then it flitted away. Merrick could also hear the steady *chink chink* of Walt's blacksmith hammer, which, during daylight hours, was like the background music for the town.

"I understand you got into a bit of trouble with Caroline this morning." Merrick said at length.

It was good to sit this way, looking forward onto the street and the trees opposite. Sully was sometimes uncomfortable with being interrogated, though he should have been used to it by now. He was in trouble often enough.

The captain yawned again and began speaking just before as the yawn finished. "It were a bit of harmless fun. Although I'm pretty sure Caroline is not happy about the deposit Con's horse left on the dining room floor." There was amusement in Sully's voice, but Merrick thought that would be extinguished quickly the next time Caroline got a hold of him.

"You and Con were at Lazy Mary's last night?" Merrick asked, even though he knew the answer to this question.

"Aye. She has a regular poker game on Friday nights and I've gone the last couple weeks. Won a little bit of money too." Sully sounded pleased with himself. Merrick wondered if he measured those wins against the losses or just considered them to be a separate entity.

"Doc Parker says Mayor Billy were there too."

"Yep. The doc is a terrible poker player. It's always great to have him at the table."

"Worse than you?"

Sully chuckled. He turned his head and looked at Merrick out of the side of one eye, grinning. "Well. Maybe not that bad."

Merrick became a little more serious. "You probably didn't hear, seeing as how you were sleeping off your drunk, but there was a situation at the house this morning."

"What happened?"

"Alice, one of the girls from upstairs, was knocked out."

This got Sully's attention. He turned and looked at Merrick full on now, his eyes wide. "Who did it?"

"That's what I'm trying to find out. I wondered if you could help. Did you see anything or notice anything during the game that might have led to such a situation?"

Sully turned his head again and looked out onto the street. Merrick could see him thinking and he reflected that Sully was an interesting character. He was quite often flirting with the wrong side of the law. And from what Merrick understood, he tended to bounce from one business venture to the next, although the last year or so had found him in a period of stability, running a steamship business that took passengers and freight up and down Lake Okanagan.

His trouble-making tendencies were more about an impulse to have fun, a lack of foresight, perhaps a sense of mischievousness. They were never motivated by maliciousness. He had a good heart under the scruffy beard and tatty bowler hat, and most of the town tolerated him for that reason. Although Caroline Finnegan had a more difficult time than others. Caroline took life seriously, and Sully was the antithesis of that, which tended to rub her the wrong way.

Despite all this Merrick knew that he would get straight answers out of the man. If Sully had information to give him, he would give it. The two men were quiet for a few moments while Sully thought, and then he turned back to Merrick.

"There was a drover at the table who I think was her customer."

Merrick nodded. "Yes, Marie mentioned that. Although she escorted that gentleman out at about three AM. Where were you around that time? Were you guys still playing?"

"Three AM? Well. I don't think we were so much playing as drinking at that point. Dr. Parker had lost all his money so he went home at about midnight. The mayor left with him. It was just Con and me and a couple of other drovers from out of town. They had been trying to win enough money to spend some time with one of the girls upstairs. A couple of them did, like the guy who was with Alice. But a couple of them didn't." Sully was quiet again for a few moments, thinking. "I think I might've fallen asleep at some point. There's a small sofa in that room where Marie hosts the games. I woke up again before daylight and Con woke up as well. We had a few snorts, and that's when we got the idea to come over to the hotel for breakfast." Sully looked at Merrick and shrugged, a bashful look on his face.

Merrick imagined that this had been one of those times when Sully's idea seemed like a good one in the moment.

"You didn't hear anything from upstairs early in the morning, then?"

Sully shook his head.

"Anything else that you can think of that struck you as odd? Were any of the men feeling particularly aggrieved by their losses? You mentioned a couple of drovers—do you know who they were?"

Sully scratched his beard. "One of them was called Burton, I think. But the other two I didn't know. I recognize them, from seeing them around town, but that was all."

"That's okay," Merrick said. "Marie will have their names and no doubt she'll know where they work as well."

"It was a pretty quiet night, Merrick. Kind of dull, actually. Which is why I think Con and I got into the grog a little more than we should've. Just trying to put some excitement into the evening."

"It can't be cheap buying alcohol from Marie." Merrick knew that the food and drink at Marie's was complementary for customers, but he doubted it was the same for those at the poker table.

"She gives us the first drink for free but after that we have to pay. But in this case, Con smuggled in a bottle of whiskey. I'm sure she knew about it, but she let them get away with it, especially since his father was there flirting with her."

This got Merrick's attention. He sat up a little straighter in the rocking chair. "Lord Inverness was there?"

Sully must have heard the change in Merrick's tone. He turned his head and met the constable's eyes. "Aye. Did you not know that?"

"No. Marie didn't mention him. Was he there the whole night?"

"He and Con arrived together, about ten PM, I would say. I'd gotten there about half an hour earlier. The game was supposed to begin at eleven. I don't know when Lord Inverness left. He was gone when I woke up in the wee hours."

CHAPTER EIGHT

Esme made Julia breakfast, which rivaled any meal that Julia had ever had in a restaurant. A fluffy omelet, delicious coffee, some fried potatoes left over from the previous night's roast, which had an interesting tangy taste that Julia didn't recognize, and a blackberry scone straight out of the oven for dessert. Julia had never had breakfast dessert before. She wondered how Esme end Marie stayed so slender with food like this being cooked up every day. She complimented Esme on her cooking, and Esme nodded and smiled. She hadn't said two words to Julia through the entire meal.

Marie had left them alone in the kitchen while she went up to the girls' bedrooms and let them know that their presence was required. Julia imagined there would be quite a bit of grumbling, given that the girls had probably only had three or four hours' sleep at that point.

Every once in a while, it would come back to Julia with a jolt that she was actually sitting in a brothel. If her mother had known this was happening, she would have fainted dead away. Julia couldn't decide whether to be horrified or fascinated. She decided it would be more fun to be fascinated.

Just as she was buttering her scone, Marie reappeared through a doorway at the back of the kitchen. Julia glimpsed a stairwell behind her as she closed the door. Marie glided across the room and sat in the chair at the end of the table, the silk of her dress rustling prettily. She smiled at Julia, looking relaxed and as though everything was in order. "The girls will be down in a few minutes, Miss Thom."

"Please call me Julia. May I call you Marie?"

Marie nodded. "Of course," she said. "Before we are interrupted, do you have any questions for me?"

Julia was impressed already with this woman, and her respect was only growing. So far, Julia had been struck by Marie's calm and steady demeanor. There was nothing Julia abhorred more than a woman who played up her own delicacy in a dramatic situation. Growing up, her mother had had more than one friend like this— women who nearly fainted if someone used the word 'crinoline' or 'outhouse' in their vicinity. More than once, Julia's mother had sent her to fetch smelling salts for a woman in their front parlor who was having, in Julia's mind, an outsized reaction to a minor event. Marie was clearly not this type of woman, and that made her all right in Julia's books.

In fact, Julia noticed something within herself that was more than admiration. With a start, she realized that the feeling was jealousy. This astonished her and she filed the feeling away to be examined later.

She began her questions. "You mentioned that Alice had a drover who was her customer last night." Julia tried not to blush when she used the word 'customer.' "Had he been here before? Do you know him?"

"*Oui*. He has been here several times. He usually comes on a Friday night and plays poker for a while and then wins enough to spend some time with one of the girls."

"A different girl each time?" Julia didn't know why this question mattered; she was just following her nose.

Marie thought about this for a moment. "I think he has spent time with Alice on three occasions, and then perhaps a couple of the other girls once or twice. I'm not exactly sure, but I could look in the ledger if you like."

The word 'ledger' caught Julia's attention. "You track that kind of detail?"

"Of course." Marie nodded her head and gave Julia a small smile. She was on firmer ground now. "This is a business. I need to know about the patterns and practices that take place. I need to know which of the girls are more popular."

"How long have you been in business?"

Marie glanced over at her mother, who was washing up the dishes and the pan from Julia's breakfast. "How long have we been here, Mama? Two years?"

Esme nodded. *"Oui. Deux ans plus quelque mois."*

"And before that we had the same sort of business in Montreal."

"Why did you leave Montreal?" Julia asked. She realized this had absolutely nothing to do with the problem of Alice's assault, but she was infinitely curious.

To her surprise, Marie sat back a little further in her chair, relaxing. "I took a chance that this part of the world would be good for business."

Julia smiled at her, encouragingly.

"We were doing very well in Montreal," Julia went on, "and had a very good business. But I felt that there were opportunities available here that were not available to me in that city. For example, I wanted to get into real estate and couldn't quite afford to do so there. Here I have been able to invest in several properties, simply because land is cheaper and things are not as well established."

For Julia, someone who had been denied access to the education that she had so badly wanted, to hear a woman explain that she was doing just as she pleased was inciting in her both admiration and, she noticed again, a tiny bit of envy. Not, of course, that she would have chosen to run the same sort of business that Marie ran.

"And what brought you to Horse specifically?"

Marie held out both hands at her side in a regal gesture of embrace. "Just look around you, Miss Thom." She corrected herself. "Julia. I don't think I have ever seen a more beautiful place. The sunshine, the rolling hills, *l'étoiles de la nuit*. It is all so beautiful. The winter I could do without, but we are used to that, aren't we, Mama?"

From her spot at the sink, Esme nodded. *"Oui."*

Julia was filled with questions and wanted to know everything about Marie's life, but at that moment she heard chattering voices. The doorway at the back of the kitchen opened and four girls came into the room, some of them sleepy eyed. Each one of them went to the sink and kissed Esme on the cheek, and then they settled into chairs at the table. Esme wiped her hands on a dishtowel and took the clean pan back to the stove. Julia imagined that it would be pressed into service again right away, and sure enough, Esme began cracking eggs into a bowl.

The girls sat across from Julia, four in a row at the long table that filled the center of the room. Julia imagined that this was the heart of the house, and indeed, the girls seemed very comfortable here. There was now a feeling in the room of a family community.

Julia looked more closely at the young women, doing her best not to stare. Each had a brightly colored silk dressing gown on. They were like an Easter parade. They all had long hair that was piled loosely at the back of their heads, with tendrils falling down. Any makeup that they'd had on the previous night had been washed off. Sitting there freshly scrubbed, waiting for their breakfast to be served, they looked like children. No doubt a couple of them were just a year or two older than Julia's oldest pupils at the school.

"Miss Thom, please allow me to introduce you to my girls." Marie gestured with her hand, beginning with the girl closest to her and moving down the table. "This is Adele, Celeste, Madeline, and Elise."

The girls each gave Julia a coquettish little wave and flutter of their eyelashes. She imagined that habits died hard. She was about to ask her first question when Marie gracefully took that job out of her hands. "*Petites*, you know that Alice has had an injury this morning. Miss Thom is assisting Constable Merrick to understand what happened. You will answer her truthfully and tell her whatever she wants to know." Marie said this without sounding cross, or even stern, and yet Julia could tell by the looks on the girls' faces that they would follow her instruction to the letter.

Julia began. "What do you know about what happened last night?"

Elise spoke up first. "Miss Bellanger just mentioned that Alice had fallen and hit her head and that someone had attacked her. That is all we know."

Julia nodded. "The attack seems to have happened very early this morning, after Alice's customer had left the house. We think perhaps it happened at around seven AM. Did any of you hear anything at that time?"

The girls shook their heads and remained quiet. Esme placed a plate of omelet and potatoes in front of Adele. She picked up her knife and fork and began tucking in. Julia heard the cracking of some more eggs.

"Did each of you have a customer last night?" Once again Julia felt like she wasn't confident about whether or not her line of questioning had to do with the attack or her own curiosity. Celeste and Elise both said yes.

"Were they regular customers?"

It was Marie who answered this question. "Yes. Alfred Brown and..." Marie hesitated. She looked at Celeste. "Armstrong?"

Celeste nodded. "David Armstrong."

Marie nodded and continued. "They are drovers from the O'Brien ranch. They tend to come into town on Friday nights for the poker game."

Julia had been to the O'Brien ranch a few weeks earlier, searching for answers related to another beating that had taken place. The ranch manager was a good man named Cobbs, but the other cattle hands and workers there had frightened Julia. They were coarse and rude. A small shiver ran up Julia's back as she remembered her encounter with them. She didn't recall the two names Marie had just spoken, but, according to Merrick and Walt, the turnover at that spread was regular. The men were paid poorly and treated worse, and they never lasted long.

Julia looked back at the girls. "Did anything unusual happen during the evening? Did you notice Alice looking uncomfortable at any point? I understand that she was with a drover as well. Were there any arguments going on?"

Once more the girls shook their heads.

"What about Alice's personal life? Does she have any family nearby? Does she have any friends in Horse?"

Marie took the lead once more. "Alice has a sister who lives in Montreal, and they correspond regularly, but that's her only family. Like the rest of us, she didn't know anybody here when we came out." Marie gave Julia a small mischievous smile. "And the girls don't tend to socialize in town very much. We tend to keep each other company."

Julia found Merrick at the livery, saddling Earl. She had checked for him at his office and, when he wasn't there, she knew that it was likely she'd find him with Walt.

Walt was nearby, saddling his horse, Nelson. The two giant animals stood in the cross ties at the front of the building, their ears pricked forward, anticipating an adventure.

Walt looked at Julia as she came through the door, and a wide grin spread across his face. "I hear you've been having an interesting day. How did the interviews at Lazy Mary's go?"

Julia could see that Walt was amused by the situation. She wondered if he thought she would be offended by the business that she was investigating. She had to admit that she was working very hard to be objective and to ignore her mother's voice in her head, screaming at her that her reputation was now ruined, and her life was ruined, and she had fallen from grace simply by having a conversation with Marie and the girls at the bawdy house.

Inside Julia, the refined young woman who was the daughter of a judge and had been brought up in cultured society in New Westminster was waging a battle, as ever, with the independent, thoughtful Julia who believed that so many of the laws of the land and cultural expectations of women were unfair.

Marie Belanger was a businesswoman just the same as Walt was a businessman. She admired them both for that reason. They contributed to the economy, each in their own ways, and Julia wished very much that she could do the same. Working for the school was fulfilling to her in some ways, but there was an entrepreneurial part of her spirit that was suffocated by not being able to do what she wanted to do and run her own law practice.

She deflected Walt's mischievousness right back at him. "It was a very productive meeting; thank you for asking, Walt. I'm sure you are well acquainted with the beautiful insides of that house and with Marie's hospitality."

Walt laughed, knowing that he had met his match, in this conversation anyway. Julia even thought she saw him blush slightly. He managed to move sideways along Nelson's flank and disappear behind the horse's great head.

From the other side of the aisle, Merrick asked, "What did you find out?"

Julia sighed gently. "Not a lot, actually. The other girls in the house didn't hear or see anything. They were all asleep. Esme does make a really good omelet, though." Julia took a second to absorb the scene in front of her—the saddles being lifted onto horses' backs, bridles jingling. "Where are you two headed?"

"Eden Water Ranch," Merrick said tugging on Earl's girth.

Julia furled her brow, puzzled. "Why? I thought we were focused on figuring out what happened to Alice."

"We are," Merrick said. He finished securing Earl's saddle and lifted the bridle off the hook on the wall beside him. With the bridle looped over one shoulder he undid the halter. The horse shook his head gently, his mane fluffing. Merrick slipped the bridle over Earl's ears and guided the bit into his mouth. He gathered the reins in one hand. "We've got some questions for the people at Eden Water."

"Why? Because Con was at the poker game?"

"Yes, that." Merrick hung Earl's halter up on the wall. He turned and faced Julia. "Also, Lord Inverness was there."

Julia couldn't prevent her mouth from falling open slightly. "Lord Inverness? At Lazy Mary's?"

"Yep," Merrick said. He looked pleased with himself.

From across the aisle Walt said, "Saddle up, Miss, if you'd like to join us."

Julia grinned at her two friends. "I wouldn't miss it."

THE DAY WAS WARMING UP, though it would likely only hit 44 degrees, at best. Watery sunlight shone in Julia's eyes as she and the two men rode out of town and the horses began climbing the first of several hills on the way to Eden Water Ranch. The only sound was the creaking of the saddles, and the occasional birdcall Julia couldn't identify. Where she always preferred conversation to silence, Walt and Merrick were the opposite.

Julia had shared all the information she'd gathered from Lazy Mary's within the first few minutes after they'd left the livery. Now the quiet was making her slightly uncomfortable.

She glanced over at Merrick. The wide brim of his hat was shading his eyes. He sat his horse in the languid way of someone who has spent lots of time in the saddle. He and Earl were perfectly matched in size and even temperament.

"You're from Upper Canada, right, Merrick?"

The constable glanced at her quizzically. "Yes. Why?"

"Just making conversation. And you grew up on a farm?"

"Yes."

"What are your mother and father's names?"

Merrick glanced at her again, and she wondered if he'd refuse to answer, but then she saw him make the decision to play along. "Callum and June."

"June. That's a lovely name. And you have brothers, correct?"

Merrick nodded, and before Julia could ask he supplied, "Daniel and Michael."

"Who were you named after?"

"My father's uncle Jack. I never met him, but he was, by reputation, quite a rapscallion."

Julia could see the corners of Merrick's mouth turn up. She assumed the memories of his family were good ones. "So they named you well."

The constable let out a soft snort. "Any trouble I've ever been in doesn't hold a candle to Uncle Jack. Or so I'm told."

"Tell me about some trouble." Julia's attention was now riveted and Merrick couldn't have peeled her away from this conversation with a sharp blade.

He tried to delay. "What do you mean?"

"You traveled alone all the way from home. Tell us a story. You must have had some adventures."

"Oh, I don't know," the constable demurred, and Julia thought he looked adorable doing it. "I was mostly just working my way along. I'd take a job and earn enough to take a train or a stagecoach to the next stop."

"I'm not having it," she pressed. "One story. We promise we won't tell a soul, right, Walt?" She glanced at the blacksmith, who was on her other side.

"I'm not making any promises," he said, but he winked at Julia when he said it.

Merrick stayed silent.

"One story," Julia continued to cajole. "Make your old Uncle Jack proud." Merrick turned his head slightly and looked at her, smiling. She surprised herself by taking Walt's lead and winking at him. Her mother would have called her a flirt and likely slapped Julia's cheek for it, but she enjoyed seeing Merrick's reaction to her boldness. His eyes lingered on hers for a moment longer than necessary and then he grinned. "Alright. I've got one story that's clean enough to tell you."

Julia laughed out loud at this and raised her hands, reins still twined around her fingers, and clapped twice. "Excellent."

"I had been traveling for several days with this fellow called Gilly. I don't think that was his real name, but I never knew what that was. I suspected he was on the run from the law—just a gut feeling I had when I met him. He never spent a dime if he could take food from your plate or steal a newspaper. But he was good fun and always had stories to tell that would leave you gasping with laughter."

Julia was enjoying this side of Merrick. The expression on his face was different than she'd seen before; his eyes were alight with the memories coming to him, and his normally stern expression was suddenly more fluid. She listened and watched him, rapt.

"He was forever bumming tobacco off me, which annoyed me. For example, I had the very last bit of some nice stuff Father had given me and I didn't want to give it up, but Gilly just laughed at me and snatched the bag outta my hand." Julia could see this still rankled Merrick. But then he let out a short bark of laughter.

"One day, when we were leaving Fort Garry, we were rushing to catch the train. We had been asleep in a little field beside the station and nearly missed the train we'd been waiting two days for. During that time Gilly had used my tobacco and eaten most of the food I'd bought. So when we were waiting for the train, I..." He chuckled at the memory and then continued, "I tied his boots together. I distracted him until the last minute when we had to run for the station. He tried to put his boots on—and couldn't, of course. He had to run for that train in his bare feet, across rocks and through brambles." Merrick laughed out loud and then sighed. "I haven't thought about that in years. He was so angry with me I thought his head would burst." He glanced over at Julia again. "But I tell you what. He never took any tobacco from me again."

Julia laughed as well, more from the delight of seeing Merrick come out of his shell than because of the story. She had been hoping for something a little more salacious. Surely a man who had traveled nearly 1500 miles over several years had more dangerous stories to tell than tying someone's bootlaces together. She resolved to ask him again for more stories and pry the juicier ones out of him as soon as she could.

THE HORSES and their riders were now following the road that led up to the long driveway into Eden Water. They had come over land, which was quicker than following the road all the way from town. They joined the drive about a third of the way along its length and guided the horses onto its path. On either side was fenced land, though Julia couldn't see any of the famous Eden Water cattle. Nor could she see any of the more recently famous fruit trees. But up ahead she could see the house where the Invernesses lived. And she could hear the sound of hammering.

It had been rumored that the Invernesses were adding to the ranch house, to make it grander in scale and more befitting their positions in the community. The house was three stories tall and looked about as wide as it was deep. The carpentry noises came from the left side of the house, where an addition was being built, almost as large again as the house itself. The house was painted a bright cornflower blue, with crisp white trim around the windows and doors. There were numerous decorative touches on the building, of a type that Julia had not seen since she left New Westminster, including intricate scrollwork along the eaves and ornately carved spindles for the porch railing. There was a wide, shaded porch that seemed to encircle the entire house, which was held up at intervals by double sets of pillars. At one corner of the porch, the roofline changed into a triangular turret and the porch formed an attached gazebo. Several sets of the double pillars encircled this feature as well. The house was an anachronism out here in the still largely unsettled Okanagan Valley. But it gave Julia some ideas about what the people within its walls would be like. She looked forward to getting to know more about Lord and Lady Inverness.

Merrick led the way and they rode their horses directly up to the front of the house. They dismounted and tied the animals to the hitching rail that was set off to one side. Julia waited while Merrick ascended the front steps and knocked on the door. A young woman in a black dress with a white apron opened the door and chatted with Merrick. After a moment he motioned Julia to follow him. She glanced back at Walt, happily sitting on a wooden bench at the side of the house, his face turned up toward the weak November sunlight.

Lord Inverness, First Marquess of Torrish and Lairg, stood like a mountain in his front hallway. He was reputed to be as large in personality as he was in stature. He easily stood a couple of inches over six feet in his stocking feet, and was the only person other than Walt who could look Merrick square in the eye. Everything about him was oversized. He had large gray eyes that were expressive and seemed to absorb and refract light in a way that other people's eyes didn't.

A true Scotsman, he had a shock of red hair on the top of his head that was tousled and unkempt. Julia guessed that he probably thought combs and brushes were for sissy men. He combined this Highland cattle tuft with a generous red beard and mustaches, and had a crackling of laugh lines beside his eyes. Julia had always been partial to a man with laugh lines. To her it signaled someone who was unafraid of life. His left canine tooth was turned at an odd angle in his mouth, which gave him a somewhat wolfish appearance.

He engulfed Julia's hand in both of his own and grinned at her. "Welcome, Miss Thom. What are you doing hanging about with this rascal?"

"There's another one outside," Julia said, smiling at her host. "They are often the ones keeping me out of trouble, though."

"I believe it," Inverness said with flirtatious eyes. He let go of Julia's hand and stood up to his full height. "What can we do for you, Merrick? I assume this is not a social call."

Merrick had taken his hat off and was holding it in his left hand, tapping it gently against his leg. "You are correct, sir. I wonder if I might have a word with you and your son-in-law."

Inverness's eyes narrowed slightly. "What's this about?"

"I'd rather not stay out here in the hallway. Perhaps we could speak somewhere private. And Miss Thom," Merrick glanced at Julia, "would like to speak to Lady Inverness and your daughter."

"Good *God*," Inverness boomed. "What is this? The Spanish Inquisition?"

"No, sir, but we do need..."

"All right. All right." He waved a meaty hand. "No need to fuss. Let me find Frances." He glanced at Julia. "Miss Thom, follow me. I'm sure my wife will want to see you in the parlor."

CHAPTER TEN

With a sweep of silk skirts and a slightly chilly greeting, Lady Inverness arrived in the small parlor at the side of the house where her husband had placed Julia. The lady of the house was known throughout the valley as a champion gardener, and Julia noticed that the windows here would face the beautiful garden in the summertime. Back in England, Lady Inverness's gardens had been award winning, as she'd been heard explaining at many dinner parties and local gatherings in her new community.

The Invernesses had given up a life of splendid luxury and comfort to come to the Dominion of Canada and start anew with the Eden Water Ranch. It was understood that this venture was Lord Inverness's brainchild. Julia had met Lady Inverness only once or twice, but it was very clear that this was a woman who had started this new life under duress. On those few occasions, Lady Inverness had not been reluctant to complain about the absence of amenities and the lack of what she called civilized company. The fact that she was insulting those around her when she said this seemed to escape her understanding.

She and Julia were joined now by Lord and Lady Inverness's daughter Clara, who was married to Con Dalton, the man whose horse had left the deposit of manure at the Finnegans' restaurant that morning.

On the way out to the ranch, Merrick and Julia had discussed their strategy and had decided, given the nature of the troubles that they were investigating, that it might be wise to separate the men and the women, and for Julia to interview the ladies of the household while Merrick interviewed the men. It was doubtful that in mixed company they would be able to get anything resembling the truth out of the people involved.

So Julia sat now with Clara and Lady Inverness. They made small talk about local events in the coming winter, about the harvest dance that had just gone by and the plans that Lord Inverness had to grow fruit trees. A servant brought them tea on a sterling silver tray and Lady Inverness made a fussy production of pouring out and serving Julia finger sandwiches and tiny pieces of cake. Lady Inverness kept the conversation going on topics that were obviously comfortable for her, and Julia could tell that the woman was stalling, delaying the time when they would have to move on to the indelicate subject of Lazy Mary's brothel.

Julia let Lady Inverness have her head for a little while, but then it was time to get down to business. Lady Inverness took a sip of tea and Julia leapt in at the opportunity. "Lady Inverness and Clara, I'm very sorry to have to ask you these indelicate questions. There was an incident at Marie Bellanger's ... establishment this morning and we're trying to find out what happened."

Clara Dalton set her cup down on the coffee table in front of her with enough force that it rattled in the in the saucer. "There's really nothing to tell, Miss Thom," she said. There was a tone of derision in her voice. "Con and my father like to play poker. That's the end of the story. They tend to go on Friday nights. Mother and I are perfectly aware of it. And frankly, it gives them something to do with other men. They're often stuck in the house here with us during the week, unless they're out managing the ranch. And I'm sure they get very tired of not having more male company."

Julia felt like a schoolgirl who had been reprimanded. She

looked over at Lady Inverness. "Do you agree with that assessment, ma'am?"

Lady Inverness took a bite of her finger sandwich, clearly a delaying tactic. She chewed and swallowed and then dabbed at her mouth with a napkin. "I do agree with what Clara said. And I trust my husband, and my son-in-law, implicitly. I know that there was nothing untoward going on last night."

"You mentioned that they go to this poker game regularly. Would you say that they go every week?"

Clara spoke again. "I should correct myself. They've been to the game once or twice. But that's it."

"So they're not regulars at the game, then?" Julia said, not believing Clara's correction.

"That's correct."

Lady Inverness spoke up. "The location of the game is deeply unfortunate, and I've had that conversation with my husband several times. But as there are so few opportunities for men to socialize, I made an allowance for Bertie. He and Con both know that they are threading a delicate social needle by attending the game at that house. They assured us that because the game starts late, no one will see them arriving. They also leave several hours later, which would be the middle of the night, when most people are asleep. I'm aggrieved that, because of whatever happened last night, their attendance has come to light, but there's nothing we can do about that now." She set down her teacup and folded her hands in her lap with an air that said this was the end of the matter.

"That didn't exactly happen last night, or rather this morning, did it?" Julia looked at Clara. "Con left the house just after first light today."

Clara pursed her lips and Julia could see her thinking. She thought Clara would reply, but instead the woman just gave a sharp nod of her head and kept silent. "When Con arrived home," she pressed, "did he explain why he'd left early this morning, allowing himself to be seen in town?"

Lady Inverness glanced at her daughter and when Clara didn't say anything, she stepped in for her. "Con is a young man, Miss Thom. He doesn't have the maturity that he will eventually have. We have to make allowances for that. Clara understands and she's willing to give him some leeway during these years when he's young and perhaps a little bit foolish."

Clara made a little shift in her seat, and when she looked at Julia her expression changed in a way that was almost theatrical. A stiff smile spread across her face, though it didn't reach her eyes. "Con's lack of maturity is about to come to an end, I'm happy to say."

Julia looked back and forth from Clara to Lady Inverness. Clara looked like she had a secret that she wanted to share, but also as though she wanted to be asked to do so. Julia played along, "Is there a reason for that upcoming change?"

"There is." Clara looked over at her mother and a more genuine look of joy spread across her face. She looked back at Julia. "We're going to have a baby."

CHAPTER ELEVEN

"I hope you don't think we had anything to do with this, Constable."

Inverness had brought Merrick into the formal dining room, which had a door at either end. He closed the door from the hallway firmly and stood facing Merrick with a glower on his flushed face.

"With what, sir?"

"With whatever you're about to ask me!" Inverness's deep voice began to sound more like a roar.

"I don't know much of anything yet, sir. I'm just trying to get the lay of the land. I understand that you and Con were at Marie Bellanger's brothel last night and therefore you may be witnesses to something that has happened."

Inverness was quiet for a moment, meeting Merrick's eyes. Merrick could see the large man thinking and wondered if he was about to be thrown out on his ear. Inverness was not known for having patience with any matters that did not benefit him in some way. He was one of the, if not the, most powerful men in the valley. Why he had chosen to uproot his family from the comfortable conditions they must have had in the old country and move them all the way across Canada to the outer edges of the frontier was something that Merrick still hadn't figured out. He suspected that the big man had a thirst for adventure.

That was one possible explanation, anyway. In Merrick's experience, nearly everyone in Horse was either running toward something, like new opportunities, or away from something troubling. He wondered which description fit Lord Inverness.

After the moment's pause, during which he didn't flinch from meeting Merrick's eyes, Inverness said, "Have a seat. Let me go and find Con."

The big Scotsman exited the room through a swinging door kitty-corner from where they'd entered, and Merrick heard his growling voice enquiring after Con's whereabouts. For the next few minutes there were noises of feet traveling quickly over the hardwood floors and carpets. He heard doors in the floor above open and then close again quickly.

After about ten minutes Inverness came back through the swinging door, pushing it so that it nearly slammed into the wall. He pulled out the large wooden dining chair at the end of the table, turned it on an angle and sat down facing Merrick.

"Con will be here in a minute. Someone's gone to fetch him."

Lord Inverness didn't seem inclined to chat with Merrick while they waited. All the genial warmth he'd shown him and Julia in the front hallway had evaporated. The big man sat and stared out of one of the dining room windows, occasionally drumming his fingers on his knee. Merrick was more than happy to sit in silence and quietly observe his host.

The hammering continued from the far side of the house.

Merrick wondered if Inverness's grouchy response to the visit was because he was unhappy knowing others were aware of his visits to Lazy Mary's or simply because he wasn't in charge at the moment. Merrick imagined that the instances when Inverness was not in control of a conversation or a situation were few and far between.

The front door to the house opened and a few seconds later the same door Merrick had come through from the hallway opened.

Con Dalton looked as though he'd slept in his clothes, which, upon reflection, Merrick realized he probably had. His brown hair was sticking out at odd angles and, in Merrick's opinion, was sorely in need of a cut. A strong smell of whisky followed him into the room.

Lord Inverness made a motion with one of his meaty hands toward another chair at the table. "Good morning," he said sarcastically. According to the mantel clock opposite Merrick, it was nearly 2:30 in the afternoon. "Glad you could join us," Inverness said. He didn't sound glad at all. Inverness wasted no time. He turned toward Merrick. "All right. Give us your questions."

Merrick nodded at Con and then began. "I'm not sure if you both have heard, but one of Marie Bellanger's girls received a blow to her head early this morning, one that knocked her unconscious. I understand that you were both at the house last night, and I wanted to ask for your help. I wondered if you noticed anything that caught your attention or seemed to be different or unusual about last night's poker game."

Inverness's eyes flicked briefly over to Con, then back to Merrick. "Who says we were at the poker game last night?"

You silly bastard, Merrick thought. *I have about six witnesses who place you at the scene. Why would you begin on the defensive?*

He tried to keep impatience out of his voice. "Well, sir, I have several witnesses who place you there last night, including Marie Bellanger. Also, Con's little stunt with Captain Sullivan in the Finnegans' restaurant this morning did not go unnoticed either. Shall we discuss that first? I believe Caroline is looking for some reparation."

Inverness leaned back in his chair and took a deep breath. "Finnegans' restaurant?" He looked over at Con. "I don't know that part of the story. Do you want to tell me about that, son?"

Con had an interesting expression on his face. It was a mix of cockiness and subservience. Merrick hadn't seen such a combination on someone's face since he'd arrested a nine-year-old boy in Victoria for stealing tobacco.

Con began to explain himself. "It was just a small bit of nonsense that Sully and I got up to. We were looking for some breakfast and so I rode my horse into the restaurant on a bit of a lark."

Inverness waited for more explanation but there was none forthcoming. "Why, then, is Caroline looking for reparation?"

Con fidgeted with a napkin that was on the table in front of him. "Well, the gelding took the opportunity once we'd arrived in the restaurant to take a shit."

Merrick had only encountered Con Dalton twice before today. Both times it was in the hotel bar. He knew that Con had been working as a carpenter before he'd become engaged to Clara. He had felt on the two occasions their paths had crossed, and felt it again today, that Con was a man who was only ever interested in his own well-being. There was also an air about him that life owed him a favor, an attitude that never failed to put Merrick's back up. What young Clara saw in Con, Merrick couldn't fathom.

Inverness closed his eyes briefly, an extended blink, and then opened them again and looked over at Merrick. "I'll talk to Finnegan about that as soon as I can, Merrick." Inverness seemed to be familiar with the task of cleaning up Con's messes. "We'll make it right."

"I'd appreciate that, sir. And then in the meantime, could you answer my question about the poker game?"

Lord Inverness's eyebrows crashed together and his eyes narrowed. "Why are you asking us? What does the girl herself say happened?"

"She has no memory of the event. That's why I'm trying to piece together what happened."

Inverness made a small growling noise and shifted in his seat. He was quiet, and Merrick wondered if he was going to refuse to cooperate. Merrick waited, watching the man. Waiting patiently for answers was a skill he'd developed early on in his law-enforcement career. Most people were uncomfortable with silence, a fact that Merrick often used to his advantage.

Eventually, Inverness stepped into the space Merrick had left for him. "We do go to the Friday poker game fairly regularly. But I had assumed that Marie Bellanger was being discreet and that no one knew about our presence there. I wouldn't want word to get around town and back to my wife. Not that I avail myself of the other services available at the house." Inverness shifted in his seat again as he said this, and Merrick wondered if he was being fed another line. "But still. It wouldn't do to have Lady Inverness questioning my whereabouts." He said this last bit as though it was a direct order, and Merrick had to work to stay calm and not speak with a defensive note in his voice.

"Marie Bellanger is the epitome of discretion. Until this morning I had no idea the poker game even existed, which is quite something considering that both Captain Sullivan, who I consider something of a friend, and our own mayor are often regular guests at the game. What brought it to my attention was the assault on, as I said, one of Marie's girls. Without that event I would still be in the dark."

Inverness nodded his head, seeming satisfied but also troubled. He glanced over at Con again, whose eyes were downcast as he fiddled with the napkin. Inverness's eyes then flitted over the to the doorway to the room. Merrick had a sense that the big Scotsman was concerned about his wife entering unannounced and hearing their conversation. He looked back to Merrick. "Are you asking if we noticed any arguments or upset in the house that last night?"

Merrick nodded. "It could be that. Or it could be something more subtle. Some tension that you noticed between one of the players and the girl who was assaulted. Her name is Alice, by the way. Are either of you familiar with her?" Merrick wasn't sure if the word *familiar* would connote what he was asking.

"What does she look like?" Inverness seemed to be working

himself into a state of mind where he was willing to be cooperative.

"Dark brown hair. Not very tall. Dark eyebrows. Brown eyes."

Inverness shook his head. "Doesn't ring a bell with me. What about you, Con?"

Con looked up at the other two men. He had a slight look of bewilderment on his face. Merrick got the sense that he hadn't been following the conversation, which was interesting considering that the events of the day were clearly so troubling to his father-in-law. "Sorry? Who?"

"The young woman's name is Alice," Merrick said. "Dark brown hair and dark eyes. She was wearing a pink dressing gown."

Some sort of awareness flitted briefly through Con's eyes. If Merrick hadn't been looking straight at him he would have missed it. But the young man shook his head. "No, I wasn't really paying attention to the girls. I was more focused on the game."

"And the drinking," Lord Inverness said, with sarcasm.

"Con, you were there early this morning, before you left with Sully," Merrick said. "The assault seems to have happened in the early hours of the morning, around the time you and Sully were headed out for breakfast. Do you recall seeing or hearing anything at that time?"

Con shook his head slowly but Merrick could see in his eyes that he was thinking back, which was gratifying. At least the young man was making a small effort. "No, nothing that I can recall. It was pretty early and Sully and I were trying to be quiet, even though we bumped into a fair bit of the furniture on the way out." He smiled for the first time since entering the room. "We may have been into our cups a bit."

Lord Inverness leaned forward and thumped his open palms loudly on the mahogany dining room table, startling both Merrick and Con. "Don't you dare sound pleased with yourself, son. These kinds of antics are fine for a single man, but you have no business carrying on in such a way. Especially not when you're married to my daughter." He pushed his chair back and stood up, towering like a red buffalo at the end of the table. "I'll tell you this right now. If you hadn't knocked her up, by God, you'd be packing your bags today and leaving this house."

CHAPTER TWELVE

Julia took a deep breath of the crisp autumn air as she rode and tilted her face toward the sun. She knew that soon the valley would be covered in a blanket of snow, and the lake frozen over. She wasn't looking forward to the winter in this part of the world. She was used to a mild winter. The coastal town of New Westminster, where she had grown up, occasionally experienced a snowfall, but it rarely lasted more than a day or two. Here in the North Okanagan, though, they would start receiving snowfall very soon, if what the locals had told her was true. And once it started, they likely wouldn't see the ground again until April.

Riding with Merrick and Walt had become one of her very favorite things to do. It was so different riding out here in the hills compared to the riding arenas and paddocks where she had grown up on horseback. Stanley always seemed to enjoy himself as well. No matter how long or how far they rode, he always seemed ready for more.

As they rode back to town, Julia and Merrick shared information from their individual conversations with the women and the men at the Invernesses' house. They quickly realized that the stories they'd received contradicted one another.

"So Lady Inverness *is* aware that her husband plays poker at the bawdy house?"

Julia nodded. "She and Clara reluctantly acknowledged that Lord Inverness and Con join the game. At first, Clara said they did that regularly but then she changed that to 'occasionally.' Oh, and Clara is going to have a baby."

"Yes. Inverness mentioned that."

Julia nodded. "So that made me wonder if it wasn't one of the women at the house who attacked Alice."

Merrick glanced over at Julia, his eyebrows raised. "Do you actually think Clara or Lady Inverness would have gone into town in the wee hours this morning and attacked Alice? That seems a bit farfetched."

"I'm grasping at straws, I know. But it's possible."

"I suppose. Did you ask them where they were last night?"

"Yes. They are each other's alibi. In bed by eleven, up at eight for breakfast, they said. That's it." Julia was disappointed by how little she'd found out.

The three riders were quiet for a few moments, the only sound the jingling of bits and the creak of leather.

It was Walt who spoke up first. "I've only seen them in town once or twice, but do Clara and Con seem like a good match?" He looked across Merrick to Julia. "I'm not an expert on these things, but Con seems a little rough around the edges for the likes of a lord's daughter."

"I wondered about that too." Julia leaned back in her saddle while Stanley navigated a little fold in the hillside. "Lady Inverness was defensive of Con. And Clara seems a little, shall we say, spoiled. I wonder if Con was her choice and the Invernesses went along with it to appease her. And now they're all stuck with him. Clara does seem to have affection for him. And she's certainly excited about the baby. But you're right, it is an odd match."

The group was quiet while the horses navigated a small creek, crossing from one pebbly bank to the other. It wasn't much of a hazard; the water at its deepest point barely reached up to the horses' hocks. But Stanley decided to treat the obstacle as though it was a fire-breathing dragon. He danced around on the bank for a little while until Julia could get him settled. Once he decided the water wasn't going to swallow him whole, he seemed to enjoy the journey across. She suspected his antics were simply the result of enjoying the day out.

The two men on their large horses waited on the far side of the bank for Julia, and then together the three riders continued down a gentle slope toward the town. Below, they could see it laid out as though it were on a map. The sunlight glinted off the windows in the storefronts on Main Street and Julia could even see Christopher Mitchell sweeping the sidewalk out in front of his general store.

It suddenly occurred to her that somehow in the past few days she had gone from feeling like a stranger in Horse to feeling like this was her place in the world. The town's other inhabitants had become dear to her. Betty Mitchell was fast becoming one of the best friends that Julia had ever had. And much to her surprise, she realized she would also consider the two men beside her to be her close friends.

Her decision to move to Horse had been a knee-jerk reaction to an argument she had had with her father. For several weeks after she'd arrived, she had second-guessed her decision, wondering if she'd overreacted or damaged her life irrevocably. But now it seemed things were settling. She enjoyed her job and the independence that it afforded her. Being a schoolteacher didn't tax her mind as much as she might have liked, but surprisingly, Jack Merrick had conceded to her offer of help with the little mysteries that happened around town. She admired him for this. It couldn't have been easy for a man in his position to admit that he was willing to receive assistance from a woman. It had taken him a while to come around to this but he had done it. Something most men, Julia thought, wouldn't have.

She glanced over at him sitting easily in his saddle, his long legs stretching down to the stirrups. She could see that he was thinking about the situation with Alice and Marie at the brothel. He had his concentrating face on.

Merrick must have felt Julia watching him. He lifted his chin, turned his head and met her eyes.

A little flutter rippled through the bottom of Julia's stomach, surprising her. She pulled her eyes away from his, suddenly embarrassed.

Beside her, he spoke up. "Did you think of something else?"

Julia shook her head without speaking, unsure she would be able to find her voice.

CHAPTER THIRTEEN

Once the horses were bedded down and munching contentedly on their oats, Julia made a hasty retreat out of the livery. Mercifully, Merrick and Walt were absorbed in fixing a saddle tree that had come away from the wall in the tack room and only grunted their goodbyes.

Julia walked down the street in a daze. Until now her relationship with Jack Merrick had been a combative one. He was nearly as strong-willed and stubborn as she was, and that combination had resulted in a lot of head-butting and fireworks in the early days of her time in Horse. She'd often thought of him as an obstacle in her way, and though there were feelings of friendship that had begun to underlie that, she still sometimes felt on edge around the man. Sometimes, though not always, she was conscious of the fact that she was stepping on his toes. This hadn't stopped her, naturally, but it had colored the way that she saw him.

Almost without realizing where she was, Julia walked through the front door of the general store. Betty and Christopher Mitchell both looked up from behind the counter that ran around the store in a U shape. They smiled at her.

"Good morning, Julia," Christopher said. "We were just

discussing this beautiful new fabric that came in." Christopher was stocking cans on the shelves behind the counter but he indicated with his chin where Betty was standing over a bolt of cornflower-blue fabric.

Julia walked over and examined it more closely, fully aware that she was just going through the motions. Her mind was entirely distracted. She pulled off her riding gloves but left her wide-brimmed hat in place. When she stopped on the opposite side of the counter from Betty, she said, "It's beautiful."

Betty looked up at Julia and then seemed to make a decision. She turned to her husband. "Christopher? Would you be a dear and go into the back and sort out that box of suspenders that arrived, please?"

"I thought I'd do that after I finish here."

Betty walked over to where her husband stood and took the cans that he held in each of his hands. She put them back in the box at his feet and then gently guided him away from the shelves and through the doorway that led into the back storeroom. Julia heard them murmuring quietly, but she couldn't hear what they were saying. When Betty returned, Julia asked, "What was that all about?"

"I can see there's something on your mind."

Julia's eyes opened wider. Was she really that transparent? "What do you mean?"

Betty smiled a sly grin. "Come, now. You're not the only observant person in town. Tell me what's happened." Betty moved to her right, away from the bolt of fabric that they had been pretending to discuss, then reached down and lifted up a box and placed it on the counter. "Where have you come from?"

"Jack and Walt and I went out to Eden Water Ranch to talk to Lord and Lady Inverness. And to Clara, their daughter, and their son-in-law."

"Is this about what happened to Alice last night?"

Once more, Julia was surprised. "Do you know about that? Do

you know about the…" she lowered her voice to a whisper, "brothel?"

Betty cast a quick glance toward the doorway into the storeroom and then looked back at Julia. She nodded her head with sort of an eager shake up and down, her eyes bright. Lowering her voice, she said, "Christopher doesn't know that I know. But people in this town talk. I've known about the brothel since before the paint was dry on the house. Esme comes in here nearly every day to do their shopping. She's a lovely woman, by the way."

"They both are. I met them at the house."

Now it was Betty's turn to be shocked. "No! When?"

"This morning. Bettina is one of the…"

Betty filled in for her. "The kitchen girl from the house."

Julia nodded. "I was in Merrick's office when she arrived to tell Merrick… well, initially she said was that someone was dead. But that turned out to be not to be the case, thankfully. So I went with him to see what was going on."

"He let you?"

"He tried not to," Julia grinned, "but I made him take me."

Betty grinned as well. "I bet you did. Have you found out any more about who attacked Alice?"

Julia shook her head. "We're getting nowhere. I spoke to Lady Inverness and Clara and they reluctantly acknowledge the existence of the brothel. But they swear that Con and Lord Inverness only go there to play poker. And even then, only occasionally."

At this, Betty gave Julia a skeptical look.

"We haven't come up with any other suspects. The drovers who were at the house that night had all left by the time the attack happened. Merrick's about to go over to talk to Dr. Parker. He was at the game and Merrick wants to get his observations. Sully and Con left together, as I'm sure you know, and the attack seems to have happened after they left."

Betty leaned forward a little bit over the counter and adopted her conspiratorial whisper again. "You know that Alice is engaged to Clement Small?"

Julia's jaw dropped. "The tailor? What do you mean, engaged?"

Betty stood up tall again and picked a linen napkin out of the box in front of her and began folding it. "You know the definition of engaged, Julia Thom. They're going to be married. In the spring." Betty had a twinkle in her eye. She had adopted a teasing tone that said this was a completely normal circumstance.

Julia's mind was whirling from this new information. "Does he know what she does for a living?"

Betty nodded. "Apparently."

"How do you know this?"

"Esme told me. About three weeks ago she was in placing her order, and I could tell she had something she wanted to share. She was all giggly. Most different from her usual mood when she's in here. She's usually quiet and businesslike. Just points to the things she wants and I make a list. She's very efficient. It's amazing how she runs that household with all those girls to feed, not to mention the snacks they feed the men."

Julia could tell this story was building to a long digression. "Alice. Engaged," she prompted.

Betty shook another napkin out. "Oh, right. Well. Esme hardly speaks any English, but I speak a bit of French. We had a nanny when I was a child who was from a town near Bourges in France. Or was it Toulouse? What's the town just south of Paris with the river that runs though it?"

"So you speak some French..." Julia encouraged.

"Yes. Right. So, between Esme's broken English and my broken French she was able to get the message across. She's very happy for Alice." Betty's story jerked to a halt so fast, Julia felt disoriented.

"I'm not sure I... How does that... Did you say they're getting married in the spring?"

Betty nodded again.

"And until then Alice will continue to..."

Betty scrunched up her nose and whispered, "Take customers? Yes."

While this was difficult for Julia to wrap her mind around, she did realize that it gave her another suspect to speak to. "I need to go tell Merrick about this. I'm pretty sure he doesn't know."

"I bet he doesn't." Betty glanced down and folded the napkin in her hands in half and then in half again. "I don't think Alice or Mr. Small have told anyone. From what I understand, I think they're planning to move away and start over once they get married. The tailor is aiming to save up a certain amount of money. That's why the wedding won't be until the spring. And then he's going to take Alice away and, from what I gather, start a new life elsewhere."

Julia filled in. "Where no one will know about her past."

Betty nodded.

Now Julia's mind was full of all sorts of questions and her stomach had a little frisson of excitement about having what could potentially be a break in the case. She didn't know the tailor well at all. He had just moved to town around about the same time that she had. She knew he was on the town council, which surprised her given how new he was. But then the town was so small that finding volunteers for the councilor positions wasn't easy.

Thoughts whirling, Julia backed away from the counter and started putting her gloves on again. "Thank you so much for this. I'm going to go see if I can find Merrick and let him know." She turned and stepped around the small wood stove in the center of the room. When she reached the door, Betty called out, "Wait!"

Julia turned back.

"Tell me what was on your mind when you came in. What was that face you had on?"

Julia's stomach did another little flip. She had momentarily forgotten about her strange reaction to looking into Merrick's eyes earlier. She made a face of innocence at Betty. "Not sure. Maybe I was thinking about Alice. Bye!"

She whipped open the door, the bell jingling wildly, and quickly closed it behind her.

CHAPTER FOURTEEN

Julia was deep in thought walking towards Merrick's office when she realized someone was calling her name. She stopped, turned, and saw the constable himself trotting down the street toward her.

"Didn't you hear me calling you?" He pulled up beside her, his breathing slightly puffed. There was a slight red flush to his face, she assumed from the exertion. She took this in and then glanced away quickly. "Were you calling me?"

"A few times. What were you thinking about?"

She turned back, all business now. "Did you know Alice from Marie's house is engaged?"

It took Merrick a few seconds to absorb this information. Julia watched his expression, often so stoic, now transparent with thoughts: first confused, then surprised. "Engaged. As in, to be married."

Julia nodded.

"To whom?"

"Clement Small."

Merrick thought about this for a moment. "We should go talk to him."

"We should."

~

CLEMENT SMALL'S shop was two blocks down from Merrick's office, almost at the current edge of the main street. There was another block of buildings going up just past the cross street. Julia had never had occasion to visit Mr. Small. The dresses and other clothes that she had brought with her so far had been sufficient, though she imagined that come spring she would feel a familiar desire for something new.

As they approached, Julia could see that the shop had windows almost as large as those of Betty's general store. Standing in the window were two tailor's busts. The one on the left was wearing a man's suit, including shirt and tie. The figure on the right had on a dress with a little cape over its shoulders. The cape had a fur ruff that looked like rabbit to Julia's inexpert eye.

Merrick pushed the door open and held it for Julia. The shop smelled faintly of tea and dust. Immediately on their left was an oak desk, liberally covered with sheets of paper. Beyond this, along the walls, was a rack filled with suits on wooden hangers. At the very back of the store was a large wooden table, almost the same width as the shop, covered in pieces of fabric. Perpendicular to the table was a push-pedal sewing machine.

As they entered, the proprietor looked up. Clement Small suited his name. At first glance, Julia thought he probably weighed half of what Merrick did. He was likely just an inch or two taller than Julia and she thought his waist might be smaller than her own. He was wearing, naturally, a beautifully made suit with a faint pinstripe. Looping over his vest was a gold watch chain, and over his shoulders looped a soft measuring tape. He wore round spectacles and peered at Merrick and Julia through them with a squint, as though they weren't strong enough for him.

He came around the table with a smile on his face. "Good morning, Constable. May I help you?"

Julia held out her hand and introduced herself. "I don't think we've met, Mr. Small."

Small shook her hand with a surprisingly firm grip. "It's a pleasure. How may I help you?" He looked confused.

Merrick waded in delicately. "Mr. Small, I don't know if you've heard that there was an incident at Marie Bellanger's house early this morning."

Small nodded and looked grave. "I did. Marie sent Bettina over to tell me. My poor Alice." He looked as though he might start to cry.

"That's actually what we wanted to ask you about. I understand that you and Miss ..." Merrick stalled and Julia realized he didn't know Alice's last name.

Small came to his rescue. "Miss Cholet. Yes, we're engaged. We plan to be married in the spring."

Julia noticed that Small said this without any defensiveness or embarrassment. He sounded pleased.

"I wonder if we might ask you about that and whether you have any idea who might have wanted to hurt her," Merrick said.

"Of course. Of course. I'm happy to help. Let me get some chairs."

Small disappeared through a doorway at the back of the shop and returned quickly holding a wooden chair in each hand. He set these down in the middle of the shop, close to where Merrick and Julia stood, and then brought a third chair from in front of the sewing machine and set it close. As he sat, Small folded one leg delicately over the other and clasped his hands in his lap, reminding Julia of her grandmother, which surprised her.

"I don't know how much I can help," Small said, leaping in before Merrick could start. "Alice is a dear girl and I don't know who could possibly want to hurt her."

"When did you last see Miss Cholet?" Merrick asked.

"Tuesday evening." Small nodded, very sure of himself. "We have a standing date on Tuesdays. In the summer, we would go on a picnic, by the lake perhaps, or up onto that little ridge south of town that overlooks the valley. At this time of year, though, we often just have dinner together and go for a short walk, if it's warm enough."

"Was that the case this past week? Did you go for a walk?"

"Yes, yes indeed." Small picked a piece of lint off his knee. "We had a walk around town before it got too dark and then we had a lovely meal at Finnegans'."

"And you didn't see Alice again for the rest of the week?"

"That's correct. Tuesday is her day off so that's when we see each other."

Merrick was quiet after this. Small looked from him to Julia, his large blue eyes magnified by the lenses of his spectacles. He had long, dark eyelashes that Julia began to envy.

She decided to ask a question of her own. "Mr. Small, how did you meet Alice?"

"Oh, it's a funny story." Small smiled and gave a little awkward snorting chuckle. "And a little embarrassing. I was carrying bolts of fabric in from my wagon. It was June, this past year. I was in a rush and picked up too many bolts at one time. As I climbed up the steps to the shop they began to slide. I was trying to catch them— I didn't want them to land on the ground, you see, and get all dirty before they'd even been made into clothes. Miss Cholet came to my rescue." He smiled again at the memory. "She happened to be walking by and she came over and took the two bolts that were slipping off the top of the pile and carried them inside for me. And that was it. We've been friends ever since."

"Friends?" Merrick asked, looking slightly puzzled.

"Well, yes, I should say, friends at first. And then it blossomed into something else."

"When did you become engaged?" Julia asked.

"Just last month."

Julia wasn't sure how to ask the next question. "And you've known this whole time..."

Small's expression changed from one of amusement to slight

irritation. "Did I know that Miss Cholet was a working girl? Yes, I did. It was one of the first things she told me. When she came inside the shop, right away she was concerned that I might not want her here, in case it gave the shop a reputation. I said balderdash to that. I could see right away what a lovely girl she was and the fact that she would be worried about me just proves it. I was proud to have her as my friend and I am proud now that she is my betrothed." Small snapped his jaw shut, as though that was the last word on the matter.

Merrick took up the thread. "Thank you for being so honest with us, Mr. Small." He sounded like he was trying to soothe Small's ruffled feathers. "You probably know Miss Cholet better than anyone in town, other than Miss Bellanger and the others at the house. Can you think of anyone who would want to harm her?"

Without pausing to think, Small shook his head vigorously from side to side. "No. Who could harm such a darling creature? She is innocence personified."

Strange choice of words, Julia thought. She imagined that the last thing the girls at Lazy Mary's were was innocent.

"Has she ever mentioned having any difficulty with any of the men who visit the house?"

This time, Small thought for a few moments before he spoke. "None that I can recall. Though she doesn't share much about her work with me. We tend to discuss other things. Current events and such."

I'll bet, Julia thought.

Merrick's long fingers played with the brim of his hat in his lap. "And you can't recall if she's made mention of any strange events at the house or anything she was concerned about?"

Small shook his head again. "No, I'm sorry, Constable. She's never mentioned anything that gave me pause."

"What about from her past? Has she mentioned anything or anyone she knew from her days in Montreal that concerns her?"

This question seemed to surprise the tailor. He was still for a moment and then uncrossed and recrossed his legs, thinking. "I'm sorry," he said finally. "I can't think of anything. Her mother died when she was very young, and she never speaks of her father. I confess I don't know much else about her life before she came to Horse."

CHAPTER FIFTEEN

"Well, that was odd," Merrick said as they closed the shop door behind them. He looked more confused that Julia had ever seen him.

They walked down the length of the sidewalk, heading toward Merrick's office. Julia stayed quiet, thinking.

Merrick did the same until eventually he turned his head toward her. "Didn't you think that seemed odd? That whole conversation has left me with a funny feeling and yet I don't think he's the one who hurt Alice, do you?"

"Unless we're both very wrong, no, I don't think he did it. He doesn't seem to have an angry bone in his body."

"He had no alibi, though." Merrick sounded as though he was trying to convince himself of something.

"Neither does anyone else. Being asleep and alone in the wee hours of the morning is perfectly normal."

"True." The constable was quiet again.

The distinctive jingle of a horse and cart caught Julia's attention and she glanced up the street, where she saw a little two-seat wagon pulling up to the hitching rail outside the shops opposite.

To her surprise, she saw that the wagon carried Con Dalton and his wife, Clara.

Con climbed down out of the cart and tied the horse to the hitching rail. Then he ducked under the horse's neck and went around to Clara's side and helped her down from the front seat. Together, with Clara's arm wound around Con's, the couple went up the steps onto the sidewalk and turned to walk toward the new furniture store that had opened up just weeks before. Just as Con was about to grab the doorknob, the door opened and out of the shop came Marie Belanger.

Each person paused for a moment and then Julia was surprised to hear Clara say good afternoon to Marie. Was Clara really that open-minded that she would greet the madam? This thought was followed immediately by another: maybe Clara didn't know who Marie was. Perhaps Clara assumed she was saying hello to just another townsperson. Living out on the ranch, it could be that Clara wasn't as familiar with every face and name in town. Julia's thoughts ran around in circles, chasing one another. She tried to remember back to her conversation with Clara and Lady Inverness: had Clara referred to meeting Marie? Julia didn't think so.

Marie nodded and smiled at the young woman. Her eyes passed over Con as she stepped across the threshold and out onto the sidewalk. Con ushered his wife through the door and it closed with the jingle of a bell behind them. Marie turned and walked away in the direction of her home.

Julia continued to mull over this little interaction while she and Merrick continued toward his office. The day had warmed up enough that after Merrick let them inside he left the door open. He hung his hat and coat on the rack and made a motion to take Julia's coat.

"No, I'll keep mine, thanks." She sat in a chair opposite the desk.

Merrick didn't sit, though. He went over to the telegraph table first, checked the machine, and then paced slowly over to the window that looked out over the street. "What is it that's bothering me?" he said to the glass. Julia smiled to herself and left him to his puzzling. She had her own thoughts that she was chasing. Eventually he turned and faced her. "I keep running over that conversation with Small in my head and I can't figure out why it felt so strange. On the surface he was helpful and seemingly had nothing to hide. And yet, underneath that it was like there was something else going on. I don't know if ..."

Julia looked Merrick directly in the eye, took a small breath and interrupted his monologue. "He's a homosexual, Merrick."

The constable froze, his eyes on hers. He didn't even blink. "A... No."

Julia nodded. "Yes."

Now Merrick stepped away from the window. He grasped the back of his desk chair with both hands, staring at her but not speaking.

"That's why you felt an undercurrent of untruth." Julia could see the wheels turning behind Merrick's eyes.

He glanced away from her, thinking, and then glanced back. "But he's marrying Alice."

"Yes, and I think the arrangement will work out very well for both of them."

Merrick's eyes opened a little wider. Julia could see him putting the pieces together. "She'll be able to leave her work. She gets a husband and some respectability. And he gets a wife and some..."

"Camouflage."

"I'll be damned," Merrick breathed. He walked over to the window again, looking out. Julia imagined he was adjusting his perception of Mr. Small and their conversation. And perhaps his worldview. After a few moments, he said, without turning, "How did you know?"

"Know that Mr. Small is ..."

Merrick wouldn't let her speak the word again. "Yes," he interrupted. "How did you know that?"

Julia shrugged, though Merrick didn't see it. He wasn't looking at her. "Process of elimination, I think. The relationship didn't add up. Plus, my mother has an uncle who is that way. It was never spoken about, but this fellow, my great-uncle, was very matter-of-fact with me when I was almost grown. He saw himself as completely normal and felt no shame about who he was."

Merrick turned from the window once more. "Did your mother feel the same way?"

Julia gave a most unladylike bark of laughter. "She most certainly did not."

CHAPTER SIXTEEN

"By the way," she continued. "What did Dr. Parker say?"

Parker hadn't had much, if any, information to add to what they already knew. "He left the game early. Just like Sully said; he's not a great player, and he tends to lose whatever he's brought with him fairly early on in the night."

"And he didn't notice anything that gave him pause?"

Merrick shook his head.

"Here's something I've been wondering about. What about the back door to the house?" Julia said.

Merrick seemed distracted but he turned once more and focused his eyes on her. "What back door?"

"When I was talking to Marie and Esme this morning, I noticed that they and the girls tend to use a back stairwell that goes off the kitchen when they go up to the second floor. Did you know about that?"

Now Merrick had questions in his eyes. "No, I didn't. The stairwell is off the kitchen?"

Julia nodded. "There's another door at the very back of the kitchen. When I first went in there I assumed it led outside, and it does eventually. I could see when the girls were opening and closing it that there is a small foyer and then there is another door that leads to the backyard. But in the foyer there's also a stairwell that leads up to the second floor. When the girls came down from their bedrooms this morning to talk to me, they arrived via that stairwell. I wonder if we should ask Marie who has a key to that back door, and if she even locks the door at night. I wonder how many other people know about that stairwell? Do any of the customers know about it? Because if they do, someone could've accessed the house without anyone else knowing."

MERRICK KNOCKED at Marie's front door. He and Julia had decided that they might as well ask Marie now about the stairwell, rather than let it sit. Esme answered the door and ushered them into the parlor that was immediately to the right at the front of the house. She disappeared without a word and Merrick and Julia had to assume that she was going to fetch Marie. Sure enough, a few minutes later the lady of the house arrived, walking into the parlor and greeting Merrick and Julia with as much professional reserve as ever.

When Julia had seen Marie on the main street half an hour earlier she'd had a full-length wool coat on, with a fur hat, collar and cuffs. Now she was dressed as splendidly as she had been earlier in the day, but wearing a different dress. This one was made of pale green silk. It had a high neck and long sleeves and a slight bustle at the back. When Marie turned and gestured toward the sofa for Merrick and Julia to have seat, Julia noticed a long line of silk-covered buttons all the way down her back. Julia reflected that being a madam must be a lot more financially lucrative than being schoolteacher was.

Julia let Merrick take the lead about the staircase at the back of the house, and the door to the backyard, even though it had been her observation. Just as he was about to begin, Esme arrived with a silver tray and a tea service. This delayed things while she set it down and poured the tea. There were more fresh-baked scones on a plate, which Esme passed around. Merrick took one and bit it half.

Julia waved her hand at the plate when it arrived at her, declining a scone, and looked over at Marie. "How do you stay so slender, Marie, with your mother's delicious fresh-baked goodies around all the time?"

Marie waved her mother's plate away as well, saying, "Take another one, Constable Merrick." Then she looked over at Julia and smiled. "I stay slim by offering the baked goods to the men in the house and never touching them myself."

"Wise," Julia said. The two women exchanged a look of mutual understanding.

Pleasantries out of the way, Merrick began his questions. "Marie, Julia pointed out to me just now that there is a stairwell at the back of the house just off the kitchen."

Marie nodded, but looked slightly confused. "*Oui.*"

"You didn't mention that when we were here asking about the details of the attack on Alice."

"I also didn't mention the chicken coop in the backyard," Marie said. "Or the pantry cupboard in the kitchen. Or the new wardrobe that I had brought into my room two weeks ago. Should I have mentioned all these things?"

Julia noticed that her mild French accent had gotten a little thicker in her irritation.

"Miss Bellanger, none of those other things you mentioned has a direct bearing on the case at hand." Julia could tell that Merrick himself was irritated; he began to speak more formally than usual. "Whereas the stairwell at the back of the house could have a direct effect on our investigation."

Marie sat very still in her chair, her back as straight as a rod. Julia's mother had raised her to have impeccable posture, and it was something that Julia was quite proud of. However, she didn't hold a candle to Marie in that regard.

"*Excusé*, Constable. It's been a long day and I shouldn't have been so flippant with you. What can I do to help?"

Julia saw Merrick give an almost imperceptible nod of his head. "Do you lock the back door at night or at any time during the day?"

Marie shook her head. "No, we don't. The girls are required to use that door when they enter and exit the house. I don't want them going out the front door at all hours of the day and night. It would be improper." Julia thought this was a quaint requirement considering what the business of the house was.

Marie continued. "So *non*, that door is never locked. I think it does have a key but I have no idea where it is. When I had this house built, I specifically requested such a stairwell. We had a similar one in Montreal." Marie met her mother's eyes and then turned her focus back to Merrick. "It is most useful not only for the girls but also for deliveries. Christopher Mitchell delivers our groceries there. It is most convenient to have that doorway straight off the kitchen. There's a little yard at the back and Christopher pulls his cart around to unload."

Merrick nodded, and Julia could see him thinking. "How many people other than those in the house and Christopher Mitchell do you think know about the back door and the stairwell?"

Marie took a deep breath and let it out slowly. "I have no idea, Constable."

Merrick tried again. "In other words, do any of the men who are customers here enter or exit through that door?"

"Oh, I see." Marie glanced away again and looked through the wide windows in the front of the house. The sun was shining through the branches of the oak tree that was now bereft of about half its leaves. The rest would come down in no time at all, the tree closing up shop for the winter. Marie looked back at Merrick. "I've instructed the girls to always escort their gentlemen to the front door to say goodbye. However, I do know of a few cases when men requested to leave through the back for reasons of discretion."

Understandable, Julia thought.

"But I'd have to think back and make a list of who might know about it, and then we would have to also ask the girls who specifically has requested to leave by the back door."

Julia was about to interrupt and say that a comprehensive list of who knew about the back door might not be necessary; it might only matter who was in the house the night before who knew about it. But then she realized that if Alice's attacker knew about the back stairwell, he wasn't necessarily in the house earlier in the evening. He could have entered the house and gone upstairs at any time.

Suddenly it occurred to her that their suspect list had just been enlarged to encompass anyone who might know about the back door and the back stairwell.

Julia glanced at Merrick and expected that the same thought had occurred to him.

He was quiet for a few moments and then spoke again. "Was Con Dalton ever a regular customer of Alice's?"

This question surprised Julia. It seemed to surprise Marie as well. She took a little breath and Julia could almost see her deciding whether to answer truthfully or not. Eventually she did. "Yes. He was. For a time, before he got married. Why?"

"I got the sense he was lying to me at Eden Water. He said he didn't know who she was. It makes me wonder why."

Marie looked from Merrick to Julia and back again. "I don't know. Maybe to protect the Inverness family." She took a deeper breath and seemed to come to a decision. "Normally I do not discuss the customers of this house. They are as entitled to their privacy as anyone. But in this case, I will make an exception. Lord Inverness has never been a customer of this house, except for his attendance at the poker games. I just want to make that clear." She held Merrick's gaze, making sure she got her point across.

Merrick nodded, understanding. "But Con was."

"*Oui*. He was working here, doing some carpentry for us. He saw Alice several times over a period of months. This was before he became engaged to Clara."

"Do you have any idea how he met Clara?"

"*Non*." Marie shook her head. "No idea."

CHAPTER SEVENTEEN

"We need to talk to Sully." Merrick was striding down the walkway leading away from Marie's house. Normally he made allowances for Julia's shorter legs, but now she could tell he was distracted. She walked as quickly as her legs, and corset, would allow her.

"Why Sully?"

"It's too late in the day now to ride out to Eden Water again."

"No, I mean, what do you want to ask him?"

"I want to know which door he and Con used when they left the house this morning."

"Why does that matter?"

"Now that we know he used to avail himself of Alice's services, I'm wondering if they had a disagreement or if she wanted the relationship to continue. What if Con snuck up the stairs and attacked Alice just as he and Sully were leaving the house?"

THEY FOUND the captain sitting on old milking stool at the back of his house, whittling a stick, the shavings scattered around his feet. The back of the house faced south and Julia could understand why he was here. It was warm against the back wall of the little cabin, though the sun would set very soon.

When they rounded the corner into the yard Sully glanced up from his work and smiled his gap-toothed smile. "Constable Merrick. And Miss Thom. To what do I owe this honor?"

If Sully remembered that he had tried to kiss Julia earlier in the day, he didn't show it.

Merrick got right to the point. "When you and Con woke up this morning, how did you leave Lazy Mary's house?"

Sully's knife paused over his work for a moment and then he continued running the sharp blade down the piece of wood. "What you mean, how did we leave? We left in the usual way." A little smirk appeared at the corner of Sully's mouth. "We opened the door and stepped through it and then closed it behind us."

"I mean which door did you use?"

"Which door?" Sully looked up at Merrick, squinting in the light. "The one at the back. Con had left his horse in the yard back there."

Merrick nodded and then, as much to himself as to Sully, said, "So Con knows about the back door and the stairwell there."

A curled shaving of wood flew off Sully's knife and landed at Julia's foot. "Everyone knows about that door. How's a feller supposed to get in and out without all the neighbors seeing?"

Merrick sighed. "And you and Con left together?"

Sully nodded.

Now it was Julia's turn for a question. "Sully, did Con tell you to meet him in the yard? You didn't go out the door separately, did you?"

Sully shook his head. "Nope. We both woke up in the parlor at about the same time. And when Con realized what time it was, he hot-footed it out of there. I tagged along and he said he'd give me a ride back to the center of town. So that's what he did." Sully grinned widely at the memory. "Except he took things a little further than I thought he would. I didn't expect him to take us right into Finnegans' restaurant."

CHAPTER EIGHTEEN

By the time Julia and Merrick had finished talking to Sully the twilight was deepening.

"I think we've spent the day creating a larger suspect list, not a smaller one," Merrick said as they walked through Sully's front yard and out onto the street.

Julia was hungry and realized she hadn't eaten anything since Esme's delicious breakfast.

Merrick walked her home. "We'll tackle it again tomorrow," he said, sounding more confident than he looked, and then strode away.

Julia watched his back disappear into the shadows and remembered the thrill of feeling she'd experienced earlier in the day while looking at him. She pushed the memory away and opened her front door.

After a supper of sliced bread and leftover stew, she drifted around the house for the rest of the evening, unable to settle down. Her mind was troubled by the day's events, and also by something she had seen or heard. Her mind had picked up on a clue that had disappeared again instantly. She was frustrated, and finally gave up and went to bed an hour earlier than usual.

~

Hᴇʀ ᴇʏᴇs ᴏᴘᴇɴᴇᴅ hours later in her darkened bedroom. She listened for a moment, wondering if a noise had woken her up.

All was quiet except for a faint crackle from the wood stove in the living room.

She let her mind drift, trying to fall asleep again. And then it came to her. She knew what it was that had jolted her awake.

~

A ᴡɪɴᴅ ʜᴀᴅ ᴘɪᴄᴋᴇᴅ up and fat, swirling flakes of snow flew into and out of the beam thrown by Julia's lantern. She had dressed hastily and had neglected to bring her scarf, so her neck was cold. She tried to snuggle her chin down into her coat collar. The snow was piling up surprisingly fast and her boots were soaked through by the time she'd gone three blocks.

The house she was aiming for was glowing from its indoor lanterns, as she knew it would be. The occupants would not be sleeping now, though the rest of the town was.

Julia took the track down the side of the house and turned right at the back. She found the door that had been the cause of so much speculation hours earlier, and let herself in. The back door closed quietly behind her. She set her lantern down and brushed off her shoulders and the front of her coat. She took off her wide-brimmed hat and shook it, and then hung in on the banister knob at the bottom of the stairs.

Light was filtering down from above. Julia blew out her lantern and left it beside the back door. She opened the door to the kitchen and was met with warmth and the smell of apple pie.

Marie Bellanger looked up from where she sat at the long kitchen table. Her eyes were tired and worried. But her courtesy didn't fail her. "Miss Thom. This is an unexpected surprise. *Entrez.* You must be chilled. It is snowing, *non?*"

"*Oui,*" Julia said, smiling self-consciously.

"Let me take your coat." Marie did just that and hung it on a set of hooks beside the door. "*S'il vous plaît*, have a seat. May I give you a cup of tea? I just poured one for myself."

"That would be lovely. Thank you."

Marie brought the teapot over from the counter and set a mug in front of Julia. No china teacups at this time of night. Julia wrapped her hands around the mug, grateful for its warmth.

Her hostess returned to the far side of the table and sat. She was still wearing the pale green dress, though it looked slightly wrinkled now. "You are here because of Alice, yes?"

Julia nodded.

"Have you figured out who hurt her?" Marie's expression was filled with worry.

"Yes," Julia said. "But I think you've known all along."

CHAPTER NINETEEN

"I saw you on the street this afternoon," Julia said, the steam from her tea rising to her face. "When you bumped into Clara and Con. It didn't occur to me until later—while I was asleep, actually—that what was odd about the meeting was that you and Con didn't acknowledge each other. Clara said good afternoon to you, which surprised me. But you and Con ignored one another. It came to me that one reason for that could be to cover up that you know each other. More than you wanted to admit in front of Clara."

Marie gave a chagrined smile. "Such a simple thing, *non*?"

"How long have you and Con been... seeing one another?"

"Oh," Marie sighed, sounding slightly defeated, "almost since my mother and I arrived here. We met Con while the house was being built. He was not married to Clara then. They were engaged. He has some experience with carpentry, and as I mentioned earlier we hired him to work on the banisters and things like that. He did an excellent job. And we..." Marie made a delicate motion with her hand, "became friends. And then lovers. He's a charming man.'

"But he was not a customer?"

"He was Alice's customer first. But, *non*, never mine." Marie shook her head vehemently. "I do not have customers any longer. And besides, I always had a rule about not falling in love with a customer."

"Our hearts often don't follow the rules."

"*Oui. C'est vrai.* Most often, wouldn't you say? They are unpredictable."

There was a quiet break while Julia, and perhaps Marie, thought about the nature of love. A feminine laugh filtered into the kitchen from the floor above.

Julia took a sip of her tea. "Tell me what happened last night. What was the event that sparked your argument with Alice?"

Marie's head lifted up sharply and she looked at Julia with wide eyes. Her expression was one of surprise laced with something else Julia couldn't decipher.

Julia prompted her. "Why don't you tell me what happened."

Marie shifted in her chair and for the first time that Julia had seen, she leaned into the chair's back, her body slouching as much as her corset would allow. "Alice is a good girl. You must understand. But she has ..." Marie waffled her head slightly. She seemed to be looking for a word. "She is getting married in the spring. You know this?"

Julia nodded.

"Since she became engaged to Monsieur Small something has changed in her. I'm not quite sure how to describe. You have an expression in English: 'taking on airs,' *non*?"

"Putting on airs?"

"*Ah, oui.* Well, Alice has been 'putting on airs' for months. Talking down to the other girls. Being superior. Acting as though she is too good for this business."

Julia wasn't sure what this had to do with Marie's relationship with Con Dalton, but she let the woman tell her story her way.

"She is counting the days until the spring when she and Monsieur Small move away and setting aside all her money to support their new life. She has become very 'thrifty,' as you say.

Last week, I had to reprimand Alice for berating Adele about buying a new hat. Adele loves pretty things and she spends her wages as fast as they come in on new clothes and that sort of thing. Suddenly Alice thinks everyone should behave as she does." Marie sighed. "She is a good girl, as I said, but she is young and lacks the maturity to see that we are all different. Suddenly she wants everyone to be married like her." Marie glanced away. "It is too bad. She is one of my most popular girls."

Julia smiled, appreciating Marie's eye toward business even in the face of her own impending arrest for battery. After a few moments, with Marie seemingly lost in thought, Julia prompted her. "How does this fit in with you hitting Alice?"

Marie's eye's returned to Julia's. Her face was grave and she hesitated for a moment. Julia got a sense Marie was going to lie to her, but when she began, the story she told fit in with what Julia had guessed. "Because Alice had been putting on these airs and talking down to everyone, she got it in her head that it was immoral for me to be seeing Monsieur Dalton. She confronted me about it. She wanted me to stop seeing him. Apparently, she ran into Madame Dalton at Monsieur Small's shop the other day. Clara was being fitted for larger dresses and Alice realized that she was pregnant. She came home directly and instructed me to break it off with Monsieur Dalton." Marie sat up straight again, the memory of the audacity of Alice's actions filling her up like a balloon. "I said I would not listen to such talk from her. I sent her to her room and cut her off from working until she promised to stay out of my business. She apologized the next day. But a few days after that I heard from one of the other girls that Alice was talking to all of them about my relationship with Monsieur Dalton. She would not let it go." Marie was quiet then and Julia could see her thinking.

"But yesterday morning...?"

Marie took a deep breath. "*Oui*. Yesterday. Well, Friday night, I suppose. Early in the evening, once more she came to me, imploring me to break off with Monsieur Dalton. Once more I told her to mind her own business. She refused and went one step further. She said she was going to tell Madame Dalton about the affair."

Julia nodded. She had guessed that somehow the attack on Alice had to do with preventing Clara Dalton from finding out about her husband's affair with Marie. She let her hostess continue.

"I sent her to her room again. I had half a head to fire her and send her packing."

Julia assumed Marie meant 'half a mind.'

"I was deciding about that and then..." Marie stuttered to a halt, seeming uncertain for the first time since she'd begun her story.

"You went upstairs and argued again?" Julia filled in the blank.

"*Oui. Oui*, that's what I did. She had made me so angry that I needed to speak to her again."

"Did you hit Alice deliberately?"

"*Non*. It was an accident. We were..." Again Marie hesitated, and then continued. "We were shouting and she was stomping around the room, all up in her airs. And then she tripped. That was all. She was moving around so quickly and she caught her toe on the carpet, which was bunched up. She fell and hit her head on the bed post." Having come to the end of the story, Marie gave a little sigh and took a sip of her now cold tea.

Julia thought about what Marie had told Merrick when he'd first questioned her. "But you said to Constable Merrick that you were downstairs when this happened."

Marie nodded, hesitating, fiddling with the handle of her mug. "*Oui*. Yes, that is true. I came downstairs, you see, to get help. And that was where I encountered Celeste and Rose. At that moment I decided to cover up what had happened. I didn't want m... I didn't want trouble to come to the house, you see."

Something tickled at Julia's mind. If Marie hadn't wanted trouble to come to the house, she had gone about it the wrong way. By covering up the accident, she'd shone more light on the event. Julia was turning this over, wondering what she was missing, when she heard the door to the stairwell open behind her. Jack Merrick stood in the frame, his hat and coat covered in melting flakes of snow. He registered shock at seeing Julia at the table, recovered, and then looked over at Marie.

"Where's your mother?" he said. "Where's Esme?"

"She is asleep, Constable. Why?" Marie rose slowly out of her chair.

Merrick stepped into the kitchen and closed the door behind him. He looked to his right and found the row of coat hooks. Placing his hat on one, he shook off his long overcoat and hung it up as well. Turning back to the table, he said, "Please go and wake her."

Julia looked up and saw that the facial expression she most associated with Marie, one of being in command and in control of herself and her environment, one of confidence and self-containment, had returned. "*Mais, non*," she said, looking directly at Merrick. "It is the middle of the night and the last two days have been very upsetting for her. She needs her rest."

"She can rest later, Marie. I need to speak to her now."

From her seat, Julia watched the two opponents square off and, if asked to place a bet on who would win this argument, she wouldn't have been sure where to put her money. Merrick and Marie continued to hold each other's gaze in silence. The only sound was the gentle ticking of the kitchen stove as it cooled.

Behind Marie, the swing door opened. Julia startled slightly as the subject of the debate stepped into the room.

"*Arête. Assez. Je suis là*," Esme said, moving toward the table beside the stove. "*S'il vous plaît*, have a seat, Constable. Would you like some pie?"

Julia was stunned now at the clarity of Esme's English.

"Maybe later, Esme," Merrick said, looking slightly startled himself. "Right now, I'd like to know why you covered up your involvement in Alice's injury."

CHAPTER TWENTY-ONE

Esme gave Merrick some pie anyway, which he didn't turn down a second time, Julia noticed. He sat at the head of the table and waited while he was served. It diminished his authority slightly that he was eating while he questioned Esme, but what kind of man would turn down fresh pie in the middle of a snowstorm?

It transpired that nearly everything Marie had told Julia was true. Alice had been threatening to tell Clara Dalton about the affair between her husband and Marie. And Marie had argued with her about this several times. But in the end, it had been Esme who had confronted the girl in her room. And it was Esme who saw her fall and hit her head.

"Why didn't you just tell us that at the beginning?" Merrick asked, wiping a pastry flake off his chin.

Esme sighed and sipped the cup of tea her daughter had poured for her. Her English was clear and crisp, with just a slight French accent. "Because Alice seemed to have no memory of what happened, and also because it seemed the fall had wiped out her knowledge of Marie's..." Esme glanced at her daughter with fondness, "...indiscretion. We wanted to keep things *simple*. There's no need for Clara Dalton to know what her husband has been up to. She is a *bonne fille* and we don't want to upset her. Do we, *cherie*?"

Marie nodded and smiled at her mother. "*Non*." She looked at Merrick and Julia. "Mama has made me promise to break off with Con. For her, I will do this."

Julia felt a little twinge of jealousy at the expression of love on Marie's face for her mother. The two women were business partners, family, and obviously friends. Suddenly Julia felt very alone. She gave herself a mental shake and turned to Merrick. "How did you know it was Esme and not Marie?"

Merrick set his fork on his now empty plate and leaned back in his chair. "When we first interviewed Marie in the little sitting room upstairs," he turned to Marie, "I asked you where Esme was when you found Alice. You were vague about that and it was the only detail you seemed unsure of. Also, Esme's grasp of English seemed slightly better than she was letting on." He looked at Esme. "So that got me wondering why you were pretending to me, and to Julia, that you only spoke French. And the only reason I could think of was that you were covering up what had happened on Friday night."

Esme nodded. "*Oui*."

"Tell us what really happened."

Marie reached out and held onto her mother's hand while the older woman gave her explanation. It had happened almost exactly as Marie had related to Julia, except it had been Esme having the argument with Alice. Esme had threatened to fire Alice. Alice had retorted that if she did that, she, Alice, would definitely tell Clara Dalton what was going on between her husband and Marie. The argument had become very heated and Marie had been heading upstairs, following the raised voices, when Alice had tripped on the rug and struck her head against the bedpost.

They had revived Alice slowly and it was when Bettina was fetching Merrick that Marie and Esme had realized Alice had no memory of the past 24 hours. Or of Marie's affair with Con. Somehow that information had been wiped out. They decided then to cover up the cause of the injury in order to protect Clara Dalton and her unborn child.

Marie then asked Merrick a question. "Does Dr. Parker think Alice's memory will come back?"

"He doesn't know. It could. But it might not. There's no way to tell."

Esme pushed her kitchen chair back and stood up. "You can take me to the *guillotine*, Constable. I am ready to face the consequences for my actions."

Merrick sat forward in his chair. "This isn't a capital offense, Esme." He smiled at her. "I see no reason to cut your head off. I believe that it was an accident. And your motives for covering it up were admirable, though not entirely moral. There was no real harm done." He looked down at his plate and then back up again. "How about you give me another piece of pie and we call it even?"

CHAPTER TWENTY-TWO

The wind had dropped and it was snowing thicker and faster when Julia and Merrick stepped outside. He held her lantern aloft and they picked their way along the back of the house through two inches of fluffy snowfall.

When they reached the street in front of the house, the snow was no less thick underfoot, but the going was slightly easier. Uncharacteristically for her, Julia had been silent since they'd said goodbye to Marie and Esme.

Merrick glanced down at her as they walked, and in the yellow-orange glow of the lantern he could see Julia thinking hard about something.

"What led you to the conclusion that Marie was the one who had caused Alice's accident?"

"I was wrong, wasn't I?" She glanced up at him, the brim of her hat already white with snow. "I woke in the night and somehow my brain had come to that conclusion."

"You weren't entirely wrong. She was involved."

Julia nodded, her thoughts still seeming far away.

The world around them was utterly silent, the way it always was during and after a big snowfall. The powdery whiteness covered every tree branch, rhododendron bush, and roof. The fence posts at the front of a yard they passed looked like they were wearing tiny white hats. Merrick was comfortable with silence, so he let Julia have hers. He was enjoying the satisfying feeling of having figured out a puzzle. Ahead he could see a slight graying at the horizon, promising another sunrise, though he knew the day would likely be overcast and snowy. Perhaps for several days. Winter had begun.

Julia finally spoke. "I wonder what the attraction is for Marie."

"To Con?"

"Yes. They seem so opposite. She's so refined. From the very few encounters I've had with him, he seems rough around the edges, despite the family he's attached himself to."

"Maybe that's the draw."

Julia looked up at Merrick again, a puzzled expression on her face.

He explained. "Maybe it is Con's coarseness that attracts Marie to him."

"I dunno about that." Julia shook her head and Merrick could see her continue to think. Obviously, something about the relationship between Con and Marie was troubling her. They picked their way along the street, Merrick keeping his strides short so Julia wouldn't have to rush. "Ah!" she said suddenly and looked at him, her eyes alight.

"What?"

"They're outsiders." She grinned, pleased with herself. "That's what it might be. They're both outsiders. Marie lives here in Horse but she, and Esme and the girls, are invisible. I didn't even know they existed until yesterday. They can't mingle with polite society. They're part of the economy here, but at the same time, no one acknowledges them. And Con, I would bet, feels very out of place at Eden Water. Clara has chosen him, for whatever reason, but Lord and Lady Inverness probably treat him like the help. He's a stranger in a strange land."

Merrick nodded, considering Julia's hypothesis.

She continued, fueled now by her theory. "They both know what it's like to be living within a community but also outside it." She paused momentarily and then continued, keeping her eyes on the ground as she walked. "Do you think Marie will stop seeing Con?"

Merrick thought about this for a moment. "No. Do you?"

The schoolteacher shook her head. "It's a shame that the one person she seems to have fallen in love with is married. And to one of the most powerful families in the area. Messy," she said succinctly.

"Aye."

"One of the things I admire about Marie is her business sense." Now that Julia was speaking she didn't seem to want to stop. "She's got such a clever head on her shoulders."

"She does."

"I admire that she's the one who is in charge of her life, financially." She paused, hesitating. "I'm envious, actually."

"You're doing much the same." Merrick glanced down at her. She was holding the hem of her skirt up out of the snow, though it was doing little good. He was sure her feet and ankles must be wet and freezing. Luckily her house was a just another few blocks away. "You support yourself with your schoolteacher pay."

"Mmm," Julia affirmed, "though I doubt that salary will ever enable me to be a real estate mogul, like Marie."

"Maybe not. But she's had to make some pretty serious trade-offs for that money."

Julia nodded. "True. I don't think I could be in her line of work."

"I should hope not."

They were approaching Julia's street now. Merrick could see the houses more clearly in the muffled silver light. He lowered the lantern to his face and blew out the flame.

Julia stopped at the top of her walkway and turned to face him. He handed her the lantern.

"Thank you," she said.

"I'm glad you brought it along."

"No, I mean thank you once again for letting me be a part of your investigation."

Julia was holding his gaze. Even in the low pre-dawn light he could see something new in her eyes. Her expression was the same —direct, no-nonsense, intelligent—but she was different somehow. He couldn't place what he was seeing. He felt suddenly self-conscious.

"Well, good-night, Miss Thom."

Julia smiled at him, amused. "Good morning, Constable Merrick."

She turned and walked to her front door without looking back. She stepped inside, the door closed behind her and Merrick stood where she'd left him, wondering.

the end

A ONE HORSE OPEN SLEIGH

A Town Called Horse Short Mystery

CHAPTER ONE

December 1890

The first significant snowfall had happened the night before, and although it was a few inches deep on the hillsides that surrounded the town called Horse, under the cover of the trees it was sometimes barely a skiff.

A small rust-colored bird with white stripes on its wings that Julia didn't recognize landed on a low branch ahead of her. It made two short *jeet-jeet* calls and then flew off again, disappearing among the trees. Julia spotted another pinecone and bent over to add it to her basket.

She was collecting cones to take with her to school so the children in her classroom could make Christmas decorations from them. On Monday, Christmas would be three days away, and she knew the students would have a terrible time concentrating on their work. She was rapidly learning, in this her fourth month of teaching, that her best weapon when dealing with excitable young temperaments, was planning ahead and anticipating periods when no matter how fierce she was, the children would not be able to settle down. Better then to distract them in those moments with something fun like a crafts project.

Despite the snow and the subzero temperature, Julia's feet

were warm, which pleased her. No doubt this was due to the two layers of socks she had pulled on top of her stockings. The double layer was necessary because she was wearing the smallest pair of men's work boots she could find at Betty Mitchell's general store.

"You're not going to buy those, are you?" Betty had held one hand up in front of her mouth and gaped the day before when Julia sat down on a wooden chair in the middle of the store and pulled her skirt up over her ankles.

Julia had begun unlacing the pair of thin leather ladies boots she was wearing. "You bet I am. Have you ever tried to go for a walk in these things?" Julia pulled her left boot off and shook it at her friend. "They are a death trap on ice. Not to mention my feet are always cold."

Betty was Julia's closest friend in Horse. She crossed her arms in front of her chest and sighed. She knew it was better not to argue with Julia, but she couldn't help herself and said, "You'll be swimming in those, my dear. You have the tiniest feet I've ever seen."

Betty had been right, of course. As Julia took a turn around the store, trying the boots out, her feet flopped around so loosely in the men's size eights that they'd almost fallen off, no matter how tight she tied them.

"Never mind," she had said, looking up into Betty's laughing eyes, "I'll wear extra socks."

And indeed, she was wearing two pairs of the thickest woolen socks the store sold, overtop her usual wool stockings. The boots had stopped sliding off her feet, although walking was still a hazard. Julia had to make sure to be conscious of every step. Twice she'd caught the extended toe of a boot on a root or branch and nearly fallen.

Off in the distance, Julia could hear Walter Sheehan and Constable Jack Merrick having what her father would have called a 'spirited discussion'. Their voices reached her through the trees, though she couldn't see the men. They were choosing an evergreen tree to cut down to take back into Horse to put up in the schoolhouse. In addition to being the only classroom for miles around, the schoolhouse did extra duty as the local church and the community hall. It made sense as the holiday approached to have a little festive atmosphere in the building.

Julia's hands and cheeks were getting chilled. A breeze had picked up that she could feel even inside the little forest where she walked. She decided that perhaps it was time to go back and see how the men were making out with the tree. She followed the sound of their voices and could hear the rhythmic strikes of an axe on a tree trunk.

Until now Julia had been keeping thoughts about Christmas at bay. She had deliberately pushed them out of her mind when they had come up. It was to be her first Christmas ever away from her family, and she was preemptively anxious about all the feelings that she might have about that. Thankfully, she had been invited to join Betty and her husband Christopher for their Christmas dinner at mid-day, which would be a welcome distraction.

She stopped in her path and stood still. The landscape was quiet, the way it is after a snowfall. Julia took a deep breath and thought about what the weather might be on the coast where her parents were. She wondered if they were dealing with snow this morning as well.

Beginning when Julia was very young, she remembered Christmas as the time of year she and her mother got along the best. Throughout the rest of the year, Mrs. Thom had never seemed very keen on doing things with Julia. She tended to give out instructions and leave Julia to the tasks assigned to her. But throughout December, Julia's mother would invade Cook's kitchen, and spend time making cookies, fruitcake and other delicacies with her daughter.

She also decorated the house until one could hardly move in any of the rooms without bumping into a festive garnish. Late each November, she sent her husband to the small room tucked under the eaves of their house to retrieve all the boxes filled with baubles and wreaths, ribbons, bells, and candlesticks. It would take two full days of all hands on deck to trim the house just the way Mrs. Thom liked it.

Judge Thom, Julia's father, had never been a huge fan of Christmas. In hindsight, Julia reflected that he probably objected not just to the extra work involved in decorating, but mostly to all the socializing that happened in December. He was not a social man and preferred to spend his spare time reading up on case law in his study at home. But in December his wife dragged him to numerous parties and late afternoon teas and dinners. Julia smiled as she remembered that each year when the Christmas meal was over, the judge had pushed his chair back from the table, lit his pipe, and said, "Thank God that's over," meaning the season, not the meal. He loved plum pudding and Cook only made it at Christmas time.

As she stood among the trees, the silence broken only by Walt and Merrick's voices and the sound of the axe against a tree trunk, Julia took a deep breath and allowed herself these memories about her parents. Her chest tightened and she felt cold tears begin to slide down her cheeks. Not for the first time, she reflected that while she was loving living on her own in Horse, and having a job and her own life, the abrupt way she'd left her parents had created a rift in her relationship with them that she wasn't sure how to mend. She hadn't written to her parents since she'd left the coast in late August. Now, with the holidays approaching, Julia allowed herself to consider that it might be time to try to mend some fences.

She sniffed, something her mother would have hated, and this thought made her smile as she dug into her pocket for a handkerchief to wipe her eyes and nose. If repairs were to be made, Julia knew the first gesture would have to come from her. She had inherited her stubbornness from her mother, a woman for whom being right was a higher calling.

Julia was pulled out of her reflection when she noticed the conversation between Merrick and Walt drifting toward her through the trees had changed in tone. She started walking again, and as she crunched her way across the skiffs of snow, she could hear what sounded like a heightened argument.

"You've made the notch too deep." Walt's deep baritone sounded more aggrieved than Julia had ever heard it.

"I have not," Merrick shot back. She was familiar with this exasperated tone. It was often directed at her.

She peered through the trees but couldn't quite see where they were yet, even though she was easily able to follow their voices. She picked up her pace, surprised at the sound of the two men shouting at each other. She'd never heard them in such an argument. Still being careful to pick up her feet because of her large boots, she quietly moved through the forest, keeping her attention entirely focused on her agitated friends. The basket filled with pine cones bumped against her leg as she walked.

Suddenly, up ahead, Merrick appeared as though conjured in the space between two trees about 12 feet away. He called her name loudly and sharply. Julia froze where she stood, instinctively. Merrick was making sweeping motions with his arms across his body from left to right as though he was pushing water away from himself.

Julia furled her brow and cocked her head and couldn't figure out what he was motioning to her for.

"What?" She held both hands palms up at her waist, shrugging, trying to show him that she didn't understand what he was doing.

Through the forest one word reached her. "Move!"

Everything slowed down. Now she could hear the crackling, which she slowly identified as the noise a tree makes when the trunk begins to break and the tree starts to fall to earth.

She had glanced away from Merrick, trying to figure out what was going on, and then glanced back. She heard him call again, "Move, Julia! Get out of the way."

She took half a step to her left, and it was then that she could also see Walt, who until then had been obscured by the other trees between her and the two men. He was standing on the opposite side from Merrick of a beautifully shaped spruce tree that was trembling and was obviously the source of the crackling noise Julia had heard.

For a moment it felt like nothing moved. The sky above, peeking through the treetops, the trees themselves, everything was still. Even the birds had disappeared. Julia held her breath. The tree hovered where it was. Walt and Merrick stood frozen in their spots.

And then Julia understood what it was Merrick was trying to tell her. She was right in the path of where the tree was going to fall.

She turned without thinking, and began to run, holding tightly to the handle of her basket. Even in this dangerous situation, she was damned if she was going to go back to the school empty-handed without her arts and crafts project.

An athletic woman, under normal circumstances Julia would have had no trouble sprinting away from the path of the tree. However, in this instance, she only made it four steps before her man size boots caught both toes. She felt herself falling forward, and because she had been moving at such a pace, she knew there was no way to right herself. She did let go of the basket of pinecones then, throwing it off to one side in a Hail Mary gesture. She windmilled her arms to no avail. The white and brown earth came up to meet her faster than she could've imagined it would, and her chest and arms slammed into the ground. She landed with a thud and received a face full of snow mingled with pine needles.

Just as she landed, she felt a rush of cold air up under her skirt and over her back as the spruce tree landed with a soft *whump* behind her feet.

Seconds later, Merrick and Walt were both at her side grabbing her by the arms and trying to pull her upright.

"Are you all right?" Merrick held onto her left arm and instinctively reached to brush the snow away from the front of her coat. She was too stunned to stop him.

Walter Sheehan, seeing that she was fine, smiled at her reassuringly. He seemed to be enjoying both Merrick's fright of the situation and also the way that the constable was manhandling Julia, his large gloved hands sweeping away the snow and dirt and pine needles from the front of her body.

He winked at Julia and then said to Merrick. "I told you that notch was in the wrong spot."

CHAPTER TWO

The next hour was spent loading the tree onto the sleigh that the three friends had brought up into this wooded area above the town.

It proved to be no easy task because Merrick and Walt seemed to have chosen the largest possible spruce tree they could find.

"That will never fit in the schoolhouse," Julia said, staring down at the thing that had caused her so much trouble.

"I told Merrick that, but he wouldn't listen. Again." Walt said, still grinning.

"It will fit." Merrick sounded petulant.

She had assured him she was all right as soon as he had stopped fussing over her, but she could tell he was feeling guilty about nearly killing her.

Once they had realized that Julia was in one piece, the two men explained that the argument Julia had heard involved a misunderstanding about the way that the tree would fall. The two men had laid a bet and each, of course, had had their own way of going about felling the tree. In the end Walt had been correct, but accidentally attempting to crush the schoolteacher had not been in their plans.

The two men wrestled the tree onto the sleigh's flatbed of rough, wide wooden planks. They strapped the tree down with some rope, making sure it was secure, and then all three climbed onto the wooden bench at the front of the sleigh. Once they were settled, Merrick picked up the reins and clucked Earl, his enormous dappled grey gelding, into motion.

The surge of adrenaline that Julia had experienced while trying to avoid disaster was settling down. She hugged the basket of pinecones tightly in her lap. After her fall, while Merrick apologized, Walt had courteously gone about picking up all the scattered cones and putting them back in her basket for her. With one man on either side of her on the bench, Julia felt safe, but it would be a while before she would go tree felling with her two friends again.

The sleigh slid easily along in the couple of inches of fresh snow that had fallen the night before. Earl seemed to be thrilled with the adventure, tossing his head and snorting and picking his feet up higher into the air than entirely necessary. It always made Julia happy to see a happy animal.

They were on the far side of a hill and couldn't see the town yet, but Okanagan Lake below sparkled so brilliantly in the bright winter sunlight it was almost painful to look at. The lake was perfectly flat today with no breeze moving the water at all. In places near the shoreline, the lake had started to freeze. Soon the whole large body of water would be frozen over. Julia couldn't imagine that it would actually happen, but the locals had assured her it would.

After coming out of the forest they bumped along a sloped field, and then Earl turned without much instruction from Merrick onto a track that would lead them around the hillside and then down into town. Julia was already wondering what kind of arguments would ensue when Merrick had to finally admit that the tree would not, in fact, fit into the schoolhouse.

Julia was starting to shiver, partly as a result of sitting still in the cool air, but also partly because the rush of adrenaline was now leaving her body. She handed Walt her basket to hold, which he did without comment. She reached down onto the floorboards of the little bench and found the thick woolen blanket that she'd brought with them and pulled it up over her knees.

Julia glanced at Walt and wondered about his Christmas plans. In the past few weeks, she had come to know that though the tall burly Irishman looked like he could break saplings with his bare hands, he was, in fact, a very gentle soul. She thought she had heard him say at some point that his family was still all in Ireland.

She was just about to ask him this question when for once it occurred to her to think before she spoke. On her left, holding Earl's reins in his gloved hands and still looking guilty, was the local police constable, whose wife had passed away only a little over a year and a half ago. Julia wondered if the subject of Christmas would bother Merrick; this would only be his second one without Charlotte. She decided to hold her tongue.

While Julia was examining this new train of thought, and wondering how to broach the subject, she thought she heard a shout from somewhere up above them on the hillside. She glanced at Walt and then at Merrick. "Did you hear that?"

They both nodded.

Merrick murmured, "Whoa," to Earl and tightened the reins slightly. The horse slowed down from his trot and in a few steps had stopped. The big grey horse glanced over his left shoulder.

The three passengers in the sleigh all turned to their left as well and looked up and back to the hill from whence they came. There was a single figure riding toward them at a fast pace, snow spraying under his mount's feet. He raised one arm up in the air, hailing them, and they heard a shout again, though the word or words were indistinct.

"Who's that?" Julia said.

"No idea," Merrick said.

There was a pause, and the three friends waited while the figure approached them.

"I think it might be Ed Bence," Walt said. "From over at Mackenzie Ranch."

The man grew closer. Julia didn't recognize him. He was riding a tall chestnut horse with a white blaze down its face that ended in a diamond point at its nose. The man was dressed in what looked like bearskin coat. He had on a black hat with an oversized crown that looked slightly ridiculous to Julia, and he had a large graying mustache that was frosted from his breath. He pulled the horse up beside the sleigh, and Julia heard Earl nicker quietly at the chestnut gelding.

"Mr. Bence," Merrick said. Walt had obviously been right about who this man was. "What can I do for you this morning?"

"Thank God I found you, Constable." He was out of breath, and clouds of frosted air billowed around his face as he spoke. Julia could see there was worry around the man's eyes. "I've got a problem up at the house."

"What's that?" Merrick said.

"My boy's gone missing."

The house at Mackenzie Ranch was tall and imposing, with gabled windows at every elevation of the roof, and a wide railed porch that ran around its circumference. Brick chimneys poked out of the roof at several spots. Clearly this was a prosperous man, but even as Julia recognized that, she also recognized that, as ever, prosperity doesn't inoculate one against difficulties.

After they had turned the sleigh around and began following Bence back to his homestead, he had explained that he had been on his way into town to find Merrick. His younger child, Henry, had disappeared a couple of hours earlier. The house had been searched. And the gardens in the yard. But he had seemingly vanished without a trace. Mrs. Bence was frantic.

It was not a long journey back to the homestead. They went over land, rather than following the dirt roads and tracks, which was made easier by the snowfall and the sleigh. When they arrived at the house a young man in coveralls and a much stained fawn-colored hat met them at the front of the house and took Earl's reins from Merrick. He offered to give Earl rest, water, and oats in the Bence's barn. Merrick nodded at him in agreement but said nothing. Julia could see that he was busy absorbing all the details of the house in front of them and continuing to listen to Mr. Bence's narrative about the events of the day.

The quartet climbed the steps of the porch. Bence opened the front door and ushered his companions inside.

The welcoming warmth of the house met them. Mr. Bence began to take their coats and hats, and Julia looked down to see that without realizing it she'd brought the basket of pinecones into the house with her. She set it down on the floor near a mirrored coat stand and hoped it was out of the way.

Suddenly there was the sound of a door opening at the end of the hallway that Julia could just see past Merrick's shoulders. A woman burst into the hallway from the adjoining room and came running toward them, her shoes clicking on the hardwood floors.

"Oh my, Edwin, that was quick!" She jerked to a stop in front of Merrick and reached out to shake his hand. "You must be Constable Merrick," she said. "I'm Mrs. Bence."

"Pleased to meet you," Merrick said, "although I'm very sorry about the circumstances."

Julia had not yet met Mrs. Bence; the family's nanny always brought their daughter to the schoolhouse and picked her up at the end of the day. She was petite and pretty, in a severe sort of way, though Julia assumed her expression had much to do with the day's circumstances. "I'm sure this will all be cleared up in no time at all," she said. Her eyes were glassy and her quavering voice betrayed her. "I'm sure there is a very simple explanation for where Henry's gone and we will all be laughing about this any moment." She said this with a smile on her face, but it was forced and stiff, and as she finished she dabbed at the corner of her left eye with a handkerchief.

Mr. Bence finished taking their coats, and then began to usher his guests down the hall. Merrick, Walt, and Mr. Bence had all removed their boots, and now Julia bent down to do the same with hers.

The Bences led them to a large room that had sofas and chairs scattered around in conversational groupings. The central feature of the room was a large stone fireplace set against one wall, elegantly appointed with a large mantle.

"Constable, Mr. Sheehan, Miss Thom, you know my sister, Millie and her husband, of course." Mrs. Bence nodded toward the pair and then sat abruptly into one of the upholstered chairs as though her legs could no longer support her.

"Hello, Constable. Mr. Sheehan." Millie Jones bared her teeth at them in her best lupine smile, seemingly oblivious to her sister's condition. "The cavalry has arrived. And Julia Thom! Good heavens. All sorts of fuss over a silly little boy. Ruth, you know this is ridiculous." She threw a withering glance at her sister. "I'm sure Henry will come out when he's hungry. He's simply vying for attention, don't you think?"

That's the pot calling the kettle black, Julia thought.

Merrick glanced at Millie on his way to pick up a wooden desk chair from a small secretary tucked into a corner of the room. He took it over and sat in front of and slightly off to the side of Mrs. Bence. He began to gently ask her about the events of the day. Mr. Bence had told them his version of it on the ride back to the house, but Julia knew that Merrick would want to hear it from Henry's mother as well.

Julia felt a tug at her skirt and looked down to find Mildred Bence, the elder child of the house, and also one of Julia's students. Julia crouched down, bending deeply at the knees. "Hello, Mildred. I understand your brother is missing."

The child was dressed in a beautiful cornflower blue dress with delicate yellow flowers scattered throughout the fabric. Her hair was in particularly tight ringlets today, with sections of it tied back with silk ribbons that matched the dress exactly.

At school, Mildred was a social creature; always chattering with the other little girls in the class. Today, she was different. Subdued. She nodded but didn't speak an answer to Julia.

Julia looked into the girl's eyes, which, like the ribbons in her hair, matched her dress. She glanced over to where Merrick and

Mrs. Bence were talking. And then back at Mildred. "Any idea where your brother has gone, Mildred?"

The girl glanced down and shook her head side to side, indicating no. She looked back up at Julia and shrugged. "We were playing nurse and patient this morning. Then later I couldn't find him."

Julia began to say to Mildred that she was sure Constable Merrick would find the girl's little brother, but before she could do so the girl turned away and went and climbed onto her uncle Billy's lap.

Julia stood and looked over to where Merrick was interviewing Mrs. Bence. The woman was crying openly now and dabbing at her eyes and nose with a handkerchief. She was fighting to get words out and was taking gulping breaths. Julia could hear Merrick trying to soothe her. As gruff as he could sometimes be, he was very gentle with her.

Julia heard Mrs. Bence say, "Come, and I'll show you."

The woman stood up out of her chair, and Merrick followed suit. Julia was about to step out of the way to let them out of the room when suddenly Mrs. Bence's eyes rolled back in her head, her knees buckled, and she began to droop toward the floor. Merrick lurched forward and grabbed her around the waist just before she hit carpet.

From across the room, Julia heard Millie say, "Good grief, Ruth. Stop the theatrics. You're going to delay lunch."

CHAPTER FOUR

Julia went to the kitchen to get a cool cloth to put on Mrs. Bence's forehead. She found a clean dishtowel in a basket on a shelf in the pantry. She dunked it in a bucket of water beside the sink and then squeezed it out. When she turned to leave the kitchen, she noticed Mildred sitting on a chair in a corner of the room talking quietly to a cotton doll with brown woolen hair. The doll was wearing a dress that matched Mildred's own. Julia's gaze also caught a small round iced cake sitting high on a shelf in the pantry. She thought about Mildred's dress, which was definitely one meant for special occasions, and also about the presence of the girl's aunt and uncle. This, combined with the cake, and Mildred's demeanor, which was so different from what it usually was in the classroom, were clues that led Julia to a conclusion.

She walked over to where Mildred was sitting.

"Is it your birthday today?"

The girl looked up from her conversation with her doll, her eyes distracted and a little sad. She nodded. "Yes, Miss Thom."

"Oh dear," Julia said. She pulled out a chair that was at the table in the middle of the room and turned it so she could sit and face Mildred. "And now all this kerfuffle is going on and everyone's forgotten about you, haven't they?"

Mildred was silent but she nodded again. One crystalline tear spilled over the brim of her eyelid and rolled down her cheek.

"How old are you today?"

The child sniffed. "Nine."

Julia's heart broke for her. "Here's an idea." She leaned forward and lowered her voice, adopting a conspiratorial tone. "I'm going to be helping Constable Merrick with his search for your brother." This got a cold gaze from Mildred. Julia pressed on. "But what I really need is a detective's assistant. Someone who knows the layout of this house, and perhaps even knows all the places where a little boy could hide in it."

Julia could see the girl considering this offer. She twirled a bit of her doll's hair around her fingertip. Teaching a room full of children for the last couple of months had taught Julia a lot about their behavior and their way of seeing the world. It was amazing what one forgot when one became an adult. It was as though adults developed amnesia about what it was like to be a small person in a world filled with grown-ups who expected one to know the rules of life without ever having them explained. Julia still felt this way sometimes.

Finally, Mildred looked back up at her and pulled the doll in and hugged it to her chest. She didn't say anything, but she nodded once, decisively.

Julia sat up straight in her chair, still holding the damp cloth. "Excellent. I'm a stranger in these parts and I'm going to need your help." She stood up and transferred the cloth to her left hand and held her right hand out for Mildred. "Let's take this cloth to your mother and then you can show me around."

THE UPSTAIRS HALL on the third floor was dim, and it was hard to see the details of the architecture and how many doors there were leading off the hallway. There was a small dormer window at either end which allowed in some light. Julia could only imagine how dark it must get up here in the middle of the night.

"Now tell me, Assistant," she looked down at Mildred who had led her up to this part of the house, "what rooms are these? What goes on up here?"

Mildred was in her element showing Julia around, chattering to her and introducing her to all the nooks and crannies of the Bence home. She was acting more like the cheerful student Julia knew. She was a bright girl and before today Julia had enjoyed teaching her. Although the situation had started out as a ruse to help Mildred feel better, Julia was actually very grateful for her assistance.

"There are some storage rooms up here," Mildred said, gesturing with the hand that wasn't holding the doll. "Cook's bedroom is also up here. And there's a sewing room, but Mother doesn't use that very often. She says that sewing is for poor people."

Julia smiled inwardly at what was obviously a direct quote from Mrs. Bence. Mildred was young enough that she hadn't developed her social filter yet. At least once a day Julia had to keep herself from laughing out loud at something a younger child blurted out unselfconsciously in her classroom. This had become one of her favorite parts of the teaching job.

Mildred turned and opened the door immediately to their right. As they entered the smell of dust filled Julia's nostrils. It was not an unpleasant smell, just the specific scent of a room that has been closed up for a while. The roof was slanted which meant that at the far side of the room the one window was small and close to the floor. In the dim light, Julia could see that under white sheets were the shapes of chairs, a loveseat, and something rectangular that Julia guessed might be a desk or a dressing table.

"Let's check under all these dust sheets and under all the furniture to see if Henry is hiding here."

The child marched into the room purposefully. Together they

checked everywhere. There was a wardrobe standing sentry in the far corner, uncovered by a sheet. Mildred and Julia pulled the doors open and checked inside. No sign of Henry.

They proceeded down the hallway and performed the same operation in every room on the floor. Julia was meticulous about checking every tiny nook and cranny. At only four years old Henry was tiny and undoubtedly could squeeze into a small space that an adult might not even see, let alone be able to fit his or her head and torso into. In some dark corners she wished she had a lantern, but for now the natural light from the windows would have to suffice.

Mildred kept up a running commentary the entire time they performed their search. Julia learned about her tenuous relationship with one of the other younger students in Julia's classroom.

"Elsie Campbell says her father's ranch is larger than this one, but I don't believe that's true. Father says this is the largest spread in the valley. And Mary Baker agrees with me. We think Elsie is exaggerating. She does that. Makes up stories, you know. She once said her papa had rescued a man after he'd fallen down their well. I didn't believe that for a second and Mary said she didn't either. Elsie lives in town with her mother." Mildred made a scoffing sound. "How could she know how big their ranch is?"

Julia vividly remembered what relationships were like at this age; best friends became mortal enemies and then swung back to being inseparable, all in the span of half a school day. It was how she imagined being at French Court in the 1600s must have been, the constant maneuvering for position and power. In the classroom, she deliberately stayed completely removed from all the gossip, heartbreak, and make-ups. Today, she listened to Mildred with half an ear, which seemed to be all the girl needed. Julia was focused on finding Henry.

As the pair reached the end of the hallway and closed the door on the last room at that end, Mildred's chattering seemed to increase in intensity and volume, as though she was squeezing what she had to say into what she knew would be a limited amount of time together. They stood beside the window, each with their backs to one side of the hallway, facing one another. Mildred was telling Julia a story that seemed to involve a stray cat and someone's lost dress shoes, but she hadn't been paying full attention and was fuzzy on the details.

Julia glanced back down the hallway. *Where else could a little boy hide in a house like this?*

"And *then*..." Mildred's voice rose into the shrill pitch that only a nine year old girl's can reach, "Elsie said that Mary was just jealous of her. Although, I'm not sure I agreed with that..."

Julia smiled inwardly. Mildred sounded like a politician at work, winning over constituents. The girl was really wound up. She had her back pressed against the wood paneled wall, one hand whirling and gesturing as she told her story, the other clutching her doll tightly to her chest.

Finally, Mildred paused for breath. Julia leapt into the space. "We've eliminated this floor, haven't we? I feel good about that. How about you, Detective's Assistant?"

Mildred paused with her mouth open, arrested mid-story. She frowned, closed her mouth and glanced away for a moment, seeming to remember the reason they were together. After another moment, she looked back at Julia and nodded decisively. "He's not here," Mildred said. "I think we can be sure of that."

"Right. Where to next? Where else might a little boy hide?"

There was a slight flush to Mildred's cheeks that Julia assumed resulted from her animated storytelling. The girl thought about Julia's question for a moment and then gestured with her hand once more. "I'll show you another place we can look."

Julia nodded. "Lead the way."

Mildred giggled and pushed at Julia's hip with her small hand. "You lead this time."

Julia grinned. If the situation weren't so dire, she'd be enjoying herself.

CHAPTER FIVE

Merrick and Walt had begun a systematic search of the outbuildings surrounding the Bence's house. Mrs. Bence was convinced that Henry couldn't be outside.

"He's a delicate boy. He doesn't like bugs and dirt and that sort of thing." She wrinkled her nose while she explained.

As soon as they got outside, Walt asked, "What kind of boy dislikes bugs? I expect that was wishful thinking on Mrs. Bence's part."

Merrick nodded. "We'd best check out here anyway, despite what she says."

They divided up the yard into sections, Merrick gesturing with his arm. Walt checked a garden shed that housed rakes and shovels and other small pieces of equipment. He searched the garden itself, checking the snow cover for small boy tracks.

They checked under bushes, under low hanging evergreen trees. They checked the outhouse by the barn, though it was hard to see right down into the pit. Merrick made a mental note to go back inside the house and get a lamp. Gradually they moved their way across the yard, closely watching the snowy ground for footprints but finding nothing.

There was a small cabin set off to the side about 30 yards from the main house. Merrick suspected it was the original dwelling for whoever had built the Bences now large and imposing home. On their way out the door, Mr. Bence had explained that it housed two of the drovers who worked year-round on the property.

Eventually the two men made their way to the enormous rectangular barn. The side door, which could slide on a huge iron track at its top, was all the way open. Merrick and Walt split up, one going left, one going right down the centre aisle, checking all the stalls and under the mangers, and poking at the piles of hay therein.

Merrick entered a large box stall at the far end of the barn. It had a hay net in one corner and a feed bucket nearby. Beside this bucket there was a man sleeping on a pile of hay with a hat over his face. His arms hugged around his body and his feet were crossed at the ankles. Merrick tapped the bottom of one of the man's boots lightly with the toe of his own boot. The man jolted upright, knocking his hat rolling onto the stall floor. He looked around himself wildly, disoriented and sleepy-eyed.

Merrick leaned down and picked up the hat from where it lay and stepped across to hand it to the man. "Who are you?"

"Who's askin'?" The man's voice was rough with sleep.

"Constable Jack Merrick," Merrick said.

The man began scrambling to his feet. He was spindly, all arms, legs, elbows and knees. But he appeared to have very little control over his long limbs. As he tried leaping to his feet his boots slipped on the hay where he had been lying. He fell once and immediately began to right himself, only to slip again and bash his nose and forehead on the wall of the stall closest to him.

Merrick smothered a laugh. "Can I give you a hand there?"

"I'm fine. No problem," he muttered. He began struggling to get up again.

"Why don't you just stay down for a moment, and collect your-self? There's no rush."

"I'm perfectly fine, Constable." The man began to push himself into a sitting position.

When he had finally unfolded himself into a standing position, he cleared his throat. "I'm Amos Goddard."

Merrick nodded. "I take it you work here."

Goddard nodded.

His beard was at the itchy stage of three or four days growth. Its accompanying mustache was seriously in need of trimming. The teeth that he had, which seemed to be about every other one, were stained brown. His cheekbones stuck out high and tight on an ugly face with a crooked nose that had obviously been broken and probably more than once. Merrick could smell the man from where he stood, several feet away.

"Well, Mr. Goddard, we're looking for little Henry Bence, who..."

Before he could finish, Goddard began protesting. "Don't know nothin' about that. Haven't seen him. Don't know what he's been up to." He paused and narrowed his eyes at Merrick. "Nanny didn't say anything to you, did she?"

Merrick had no idea what the reference to 'Nanny' was about. He applied a trick that had worked for him in the past when seeking information and wishing to appear that he knew more than he did; he raised his eyebrows and gave the man a knowing look.

It worked.

"That bitch." Goddard spat a brown wad of tobacco juice toward the corner of the stall, however most of it dribbled down his chin and onto his jacket front. "She'd say anything to save her job, even if it meant getting an innocent man fired."

"Why don't you tell us your side of the story," Merrick said. He hoped that this would be enough to get the fellow chatting and he wasn't disappointed.

"It's never been my job to take care of that little brat," the drover said. "He's a cute kid, no question, but he's not my responsibility. That's what they pay the nanny for."

In the corner of the stall where he stood, Goddard looked like a rabbit run to ground by a wolf. He was jittery and anxious. He kept putting his hands inside his front pants pockets and then pulling them out again. When he wasn't doing that he was fiddling with his jacket sleeves and scratching at his scraggly beard. He had put his hat back on his head and from underneath it, shooting out everywhere at odd angles were wisps of long straight hair.

Merrick nodded as though he knew what the fellow was talking about and with his silence encouraged him to go on.

"She just dumped him on me that day. It wasn't my fault that I was busy. I'm supposed to be workin', not sittin' around watchin' a kid."

Merrick played along. "What day was this?"

"Oh, I don't know. Three or four days ago maybe?"

Merrick sensed that one day might run into another for this fellow.

"So earlier this week?"

The skinny little man thought about this for a moment and then shrugged. Goddard looked down and picked at the fraying edge of his coat. Merrick realized that his questions had shut the man down. He tried once more to encourage him. "So you were just doing your work..."

Goddard looked up. "That's right." He nodded, and Merrick could see him thinking back to the moment in time that he was so concerned about. He began again, speaking slowly, sullenly, but then warmed up to the sound of his own voice. "There was a lot going on that day. We was about to move the cattle from one pasture to another, and there was a hole in the roof I was supposed to be patching, and we had a hog was supposed to be butchered." Goddard sighed, his cross heavy. "And then who shows up at the barn door but bloody Nanny with the little tyke in tow. At first, I thought they were just here so the boy could play with the kittens what had just been born. But pretty soon she was bossing me around, the old cow, and telling me she's leavin' the boy with me while she did something else. I can't remember what her damn excuse was. I expect she just wanted the afternoon off." The man looked horrified and shocked at the injustice.

Merrick nodded.

Goddard continued. "He's a cheery enough little fellow. I don't mean to say that he's a pain. But the whole point of the situation is that I'm not his nanny. I'm out here doin' man's work. I tried to explain that to the boss when it all went to hell in a handbasket. I don't think the boss minded so much, but the missus was hysterical and looking to blame anybody her eyes fell on."

There were gaps in the story. What had gone to hell? Why was Mrs. Bence hysterical? Merrick tried the old silence trick again to keep Goddard's narrative moving and once more it worked.

"The boy was safe as houses, it turned out. He was just asleep there in one of the stalls we don't use much." He gestured with a spindly arm out into the aisle of the barn.

Merrick tried putting the pieces together of what he had heard so far. "So the boy went missing after Nanny left you with him, is that right?"

"Yeah, that's what I'm telling you. What are you? Thick in the head?" He tapped the side of his skull with two filthy fingers, clearly relishing the moment of having one-upped the police constable. "She shouldn't have left him with me in the first place. Like I said, I was workin'. I couldn't keep my eye on the boy every single second. I had him with me in the tack room for a while, but then I had to go to the outhouse and he seemed contented enough. I had given him an old curry brush to play with and he'd found an old horseshoe lyin' about, so he were fiddling with that. You know what little ones are like. He was pretending to brush himself and snorting like a horse." The drover gave a gentle laugh at the memory, and his face softened momentarily. But then he came to the point in the narrative that caused him the most bitterness. His face closed off again and he glared at Merrick as though he were responsible for the trouble. "Old man Bence nearly fired me. As though it were my fault. Bloody Nanny was shrieking, sayin' that I'd offered to take care of the little tyke. Which was bollocks, and she knew it. The missus was runnin' around here, cryin' her fool head off. It's a wonder they didn't come into town and alert you."

"But somebody found the boy, obviously."

"Yeah." The man sounded almost unhappy about it. And then Merrick heard why. "It was that nanny what found him. I had looked in the stall where the boy was, but I didn't see him. He had buried himself in a pile of hay, still pretending he was a horse, and he'd fallen asleep. So when I looked in there I couldn't see nothin' but hay. But Nanny found him." He paused for a moment thinking, "He's a little escape artist apparently. She did say to me after all the fuss died down that at least once a day she has to go looking for the wee bastard." He spat a wad of tobacco again and this time only about a third of it landed on his jacket front. "I wish she'd told me that beforehand. I only held onto this job by the skin of my teeth."

Behind him, Merrick heard Walt's boots on the floor. Out of the corner of his eye he saw the big man peer into the stall. He walked over to Merrick and held out his left hand, palm up. Merrick glanced down and saw lying there a small tin toy; a white horse suspended in a trotting motion, pulling a small two-wheeled cart with a man in uniform sitting in the seat. He looked at his friend.

"Where'd you find it?"

Walt made a motion with his head. "Tucked behind a basket of brushes in the tack room."

Merrick plucked the toy off Walt's hand and held it out to Goddard, who was watching them with narrowed eyes.

"Do you recognize this, Mr. Goddard?"

The man peered at it, considering. Merrick could almost see the thoughts running through his head as he decided what to say. He was holding his face in a mask of ignorance, but he was a terrible actor. "I think it might belong to the boy."

"You think?"

"Yes?" He made it a question, which destroyed his bid for confident nonchalance.

"Was the boy playing with this the other day when he went missing?"

"I don't know?" Another question.

Merrick sighed, exasperated. "We need to know, Mr. Goddard. Did the boy have this toy with him the other day? It's important."

Goddard began fidgeting again, taking his hat off and running his dirty fingers through his hair. His eyes flicked around from the toy to Merrick, to Walt, and back. Again, Merrick was reminded of the cornered rabbit. He considered what might be the best approach to get the truth out of Goddard. The man was concealing something; Merrick could see it on his face. But whether that was relevant to today's search, or some petty crime he had undoubtedly committed, Merrick wasn't sure. Goddard struck him as someone who felt guilty and persecuted even when he was innocent. And he obviously had a grudge against the nanny. Would he conceal the boy to get back at her for the trouble she got him in the other day?

"I think we need to bring your employer into this conversation, Mr. Goddard. Maybe if your job is at stake you'll be more willing to help us out and tell me the truth."

"But I...."

"Shhh." Walt hushed the two men.

"What?" Merrick turned to his friend impatiently, his mind focused on the task in front of him.

"Did you hear that?" Walt's eyes were staring past Merrick, his whole body on alert.

Merrick shook his head and was about to speak again when Walt held up a finger. And then Merrick heard it. A shout coming from the direction of the house.

CHAPTER SIX

When Julia and Mildred finished looking through the uppermost floor of the house, they proceeded down a back staircase to the floor just below them.

"Come and see my room," the little girl said. "I'll show you the doll that Grandmama sent for my birthday."

Julia's mind was preoccupied, trying to think of where else Mildred's little brother might be hiding, and wondering about exploring the house further. Was there a basement in this house? Where else might the family not have looked for the boy? But she was also feeling sorry for the little girl. It can't be any fun to spend one's birthday looking for one's little brother. Julia decided that a few minutes admiring the girl's new doll was the kind thing to do. *Perhaps*, she thought, *Merrick and Walt are having more luck than I am.*

Mildred led Julia down the hall, her boots tapping lightly on the dark stained floors. Julia shuffled along in her woolen socks, feeling rather silly. Though not as silly as she had felt in the Bence's fancy parlor.

Mildred's room was small but beautifully appointed. It had a narrow, child-sized bed with an iron headboard and footboard that were painted white. There was also a tall dresser with a small mirror on one side of the room, and in the opposite corner a small upholstered chair. Mildred made a beeline for the chair. She tossed down the cotton doll that she'd been carrying with her and picked up a China faced one with silken hair in ringlets that once again reminded Julia of Mildred's own hair. The doll's eyes were painted dark blue and she had pale pink lips and rosy cheeks. She had a beautiful yellow dress with delicate white lace at the sleeve cuffs and hem. Mildred proceeded to show Julia that the doll's china arms could move in their shoulder sockets, and that her boots were made from real leather. Julia was making admiring noises when from immediately behind them came a shrill voice that nearly brought Julia right out of her socks.

"Good heavens! There you are, Miss Mildred."

Julia turned as a woman swept into the room with a great deal of authority, and looked at Julia with a pinched and haughty expression. It was the children's nanny, someone Julia spotted briefly at the end of every day, standing in the street outside the schoolyard.

The woman was in her middle age, with an oversized bosom on a tiny frame. She had strands of grey liberally sprinkled throughout her dark hair, which was pulled back tightly and wound into a bun at the back of her neck. Her black dress was crisp and spotless and rustled slightly when she walked.

"Miss Mildred, where have you been? I've been looking all over the house for you."

Mildred's demeanor changed and Julia saw the sullen look that the girl had worn earlier in the day reappear on her face. She looked up at Nanny defiantly. "I was helping Miss Julia try to find Henry."

"Well," the woman glanced at Julia with disapproval in her eyes. She reached into a pocket and pulled out a handkerchief, which she used to roughly rub a spot on Mildred's cheek with what looked like an automatic gesture. The child winced but held still. This was obviously something she was used to enduring. "We'll leave that sort of thing to the grownups, won't we? It's time for your nap. Come on. Get up onto the bed."

Before Julia realized what was happening, Nanny had swept the doll out of Mildred's hands and placed it back on the chair. She bundled Mildred up into a sitting position on the bed and bent down and removed the girl's lace-up boots. Mildred gave few protestations despite the aggrieved expression on her face. To Julia, she did look as though she could use the rest. Her eyes had been drooping since they'd come into the room.

And sure enough, despite the quiet grumbling, the girl lay down so that Nanny could cover her with a small quilt. Almost before Nanny had stood up straight again to cast her baleful eyes at Julia, Mildred appeared to be asleep.

Julia opened her mouth about to say something, but Nanny pressed a stiff index finger to her lips and motioned to Julia to follow her out of the room.

They stepped out into the hallway and Nanny closed the door behind them softly.

"I'm assuming you and Mildred didn't find young Henry."

Julia felt like the sentence was a bit of an accusation. As though it was Julia's fault he was missing. She answered in her most polite voice. "I'm afraid not."

Nanny nodded. "I thought as much."

"Perhaps I could ask you about any ideas that you might have about where Henry could be?"

"I'm mending right now, so it's not a good time."

Julia thought this was an odd response. She had assumed the nanny would want to do anything she could to help find the young boy who was in her charge.

"Perhaps I could come and talk to you while you mend."

Nanny pursed her lips at this but couldn't seem to find any way to tell Julia that this would not be acceptable, so instead she just turned and walked down the hallway. After a moment's hesitation, Julia followed her to where she had disappeared into a room near the front staircase of the house.

The room was tiny and smelled of Borax and wet wood. It had one wooden kitchen chair, set by the window, which was where Nanny had landed. As Julia glanced around, she saw that this was a place that was Nanny's domain entirely. There was a tall sideboard against one wall that had been converted into linen storage. Neatly folded sheets and towels filled the shelves. Below this was a cabinet with two closed cupboard doors. Lying on the top were a few spools of thread, and a half-knitted mitten, the needles stuck through a ball of wool. There was a table in the centre of the room with dark stains along the top and a basket underneath filled with what Julia assumed were clean sheets waiting to be ironed. To one side of where Nanny sat, there was a drying rack in front of a small wood stove, a few socks drooped over its rungs.

From her seated position, Nanny picked up a piece of fabric from the basket beside her and proceeded with her work as though she hadn't been interrupted. She didn't glance up at Julia or encourage a conversation at all.

Julia plunged in anyway with what she hoped was an icebreaker. "How long have you worked for the Bences?"

Nanny ignored the question. "Why aren't you continuing your search for the boy? Wouldn't your time be better spent looking for him than talking to me?"

Valid question, Julia thought. "I just hoped I'd get a better understanding from you of what Henry's personality is like. Maybe I'll be able to help you to remember somewhere in the house that he particularly likes to hide." Julia stumbled to a stop, suddenly feeling self-conscious, and as though she were on trial.

Nanny glanced up now, though just for an instant, and then went back to her work. "It seems to me your time would be better spent looking for the boy."

Julia guessed that perhaps treading delicately with this woman was not the right strategy. She changed tacks. "What about you? Why aren't you looking for him?" *Take that, you old biddy.*

"Not that it's any of your business, but Mrs. Bence asked me to put Mildred down for her nap, and when I do that I like to stay within earshot in case she needs me. Besides, we've been through this before."

"What do you mean?"

Julia was surprised when the woman answered her. "Young Henry is something of a handful. I'm doing my best, but when I don't get help from the family, it's difficult."

"What sort of help?"

"I can't mold the child's character all on my own. When he's with his parents, they need to have a strong hand with him. He's a willful boy." Her tone told Julia this willfulness was a grave character flaw indeed. "They let him get away with everything. He can do no wrong in their eyes. He's the prince of the kingdom, you see."

Julia hazarded a guess. "The first boy in the family."

"The only boy." Nanny tugged sharply at her thread. "Mrs. Bence has a terrible time when she's," her voice dropped to a whisper, "in the family way."

Julia murmured an understanding noise and was thankful when it seemed to encourage more sharing.

Nanny continued, "She lost several babies before Mildred was born. Two of them were full term, and they were born dead." She shook her head, remembering. "And she confided in me when she finally did bring a child to term, that it was such a disappointment to Mr. Bence when Mildred was a girl. Mrs. Bence was in tears after the birth realizing she'd have to try again to have a boy." Nanny tutted and kept stitching. "So, once Mildred was a year old, she tried again. It was worse this time. She lost three babes, though fortunately, none went full term."

Julia shifted on her feet, feeling both sad for Mrs. Bence and uncomfortable about the topic.

Nanny continued, "Finally, finally, she was gifted with Henry. Thanks be to God. Oh, the rejoicing on that day. There was practically a 21-gun salute." The hint of a smile crossed Nanny's face at the memory, but then her expression clouded over again. "So they let that boy run wild, and they treat him with kid gloves. It's not right, I'm telling you. They'll pay for it sooner rather than later. Well..." she looked up at Julia, "it looks like they're paying for it now, doesn't it?"

"Do you think Henry has run off on his own?"

"I can't say, young lady. I can't say." She shook her head while she tied a knot in her thread and reached for the scissors in the basket. "All I know is, I'm sick to death of having my authority undermined. Henry knows he doesn't have to listen to me. He goes running to his papa anytime I try to discipline him, and once he's done that he can have whatever he wants." She dropped the scissors back in the basket and looked up at Julia. "I might as well not be bothered."

Julia watched the nanny while she put the sock on a low table in front of her and began fishing around in the basket once more, looking for its mate perhaps.

The lack of concern Nanny was showing was setting off alarm bells for Julia. Her justification that she needed to stay within earshot of Mildred seemed weak. Mildred was a child, but not a toddler. It was unlikely that at nine years old she needed around the clock supervision. Could Nanny be hiding the boy from the family to make a point about his willfulness and his special place in the household? That would seem a rather dramatic course of action and one that was sure to get the woman fired if she was found out. On the other hand, if she ended up 'finding' the boy, it might gain her the respect she felt she was lacking.

Julia pondered these thoughts, one chasing another ineffectively around inside her head, like chickens in a yard. Nanny found the sock she was looking for and set it in her lap. She looked up at Julia.

"Anything else, young woman?"

Julia felt that the subtext of this question was that she was being dismissed, but she asked another question anyway. "Has Henry ever gone missing before?"

"Before today?"

Julia thought this an odd follow-up. It felt like Nanny was stalling for time. "Yes," she answered patiently, "before today."

"Well." Nanny's eyes dropped to the sewing in her lap and she shifted slightly in her chair. This was the first time Julia had noticed Nanny not being in complete command of herself, and also of Julia. "There was a bit of a barney last week."

She didn't continue, so Julia prodded. "What happened?"

The nanny sighed. "It had nothing to do with me, you understand." Her tone was defensive and angry. "That fool of a filthy man in the barn caused all the trouble."

"What trouble?"

"Oh, he insisted he wanted to play with the boy when we were out for a bit of a walk. Stupidly, I agreed and turned my back for five minutes. Well!" She looked up at Julia, her brows pulled together and her mouth pursed, a shape Julia was learning that her lips found very often. "That idiot lost the boy almost immediately. The Bences were frantic, of course." She shuddered at the memory. "Luckily, I found him."

Julia didn't miss the emphasis on the first pronoun in that sentence. She wondered if this confirmed earlier suspicions about Nanny creating a problem so that she could solve it and seem the hero. She was just about to ask for more details when there was a loud cry, almost a scream, from downstairs, and then the sound of raised voices and someone running along the wooden floors below them.

Nanny dropped her work into the basket. "Maybe the boy's been found."

It hadn't sounded like a happy cry to Julia. She turned and ran out of the room as fast as her sock feet would carry her.

CHAPTER SEVEN

As Julia came down the staircase at the front of the house, her socks sometimes sliding on the polished wooden runners in her haste, Merrick and Walt burst through the front door, panting.

Merrick met Julia's eyes. "What's going on?"

Before Julia could answer that she had no idea, Mrs. Bence appeared in the doorway to the parlor looking terrified, tears streaming down her cheeks. She was holding a small toy in her hands.

She began to speak, addressing Merrick. "This is Henry's elephant. I just found it in the fireplace."

Merrick and Walt were both unlacing their boots. As soon as he was in his sock feet, Merrick walked toward Mrs. Bence. "Show me," he said.

Julia, Nanny, and Walt followed the two like a small parade down the hallway and into the parlor where they had met just an hour earlier. Julia could see that Mrs. Bence was shaking as she told Merrick the story of what she'd found.

"It was just there," she pointed, "lying on the grate. I'm sure it wasn't there before. I would've noticed it." She was clutching the toy tightly to her chest.

Merrick held out a hand. Mrs. Bence hesitated for a moment and then gave him the toy. To Julia, it looked to be made of light brown velvet. It had glass eyes and an upturned trunk and was a little smaller than one of Julia's regular boots.

From a doorway at the far side of the room, Mr. Bence came rushing in, taking in the scene with wild-eyed looks around the room. "What's happened? Have you found Henry?"

Julia wondered where he'd been.

Mrs. Bence started to cry again. Her husband crossed the room and put his arms around her, still looking to Merrick for answers to his questions.

"Oh my, oh my." Millie Jones sat in a wingback armchair in a corner of the room, observing everything that was going on. Julia noticed she could hardly conceal the delight on her face at all the drama. She was fanning herself with a copy of The Lady magazine while dabbing her forehead with a handkerchief held in her other hand. "This is a turn of events, wouldn't you say, Constable?"

Merrick ignored her. He stepped over to where the large fireplace occupied the longest wall in the room. It was quite a showpiece, made with large river rocks. A low iron grate stood on its floor, and there were fresh logs and kindling laid out, ready for a fire to be started. The floor of the fireplace was devoid of ash. Julia, not for the first time, remembered how nice it was to have someone to do those dirty chores for her. She hated the job of cleaning out her wood-stove and had recently ruined more than one skirt doing so.

Merrick knelt down in front of the fireplace and then looked back at Mrs. Bence. "Can you tell me exactly where the toy was, please." He looked directly at her and spoke in his calm, problem-solving tone.

Mrs. Bence's crying had slowed, but she was hiccupping softly with her face buried in her husband's shoulder. She raised her head and pointed in a vague way toward the logs on the grate.

"Here?"

Mrs. Bence nodded and Merrick turned back and lay the elephant down on top of the narrow pieces of kindling. "Like this?"

Mrs. Bence shook her head. "A little more that way." She waved her hand toward Merrick's right.

The large man moved the elephant over. "Here?"

"More." Mrs. Bence waved her hand again.

Merrick moved the elephant as far over on the right-hand side of the pile of logs as it would go. He looked back at Mrs. Bence once more.

Helping Merrick with this part of the investigation seemed to be calming the mother. She took a deep breath and dabbed at her face with her husband's handkerchief. "It was sort of hanging off the side of the logs there."

Merrick positioned the elephant as she had instructed and the woman nodded.

The room was silent while Merrick leaned in and peered around the logs and the grate and at the crumpled paper that was underneath the kindling wood. Julia felt like she was holding her breath, and forced herself to take a deep inhale. The grandmother clock that was standing against the wall behind Millie Jones's chair tick-tocked loudly. Julia hadn't even noticed it in the room previously, but now with this high tension and nerves strained to the point of breaking, it sounded as loud as though someone was banging a drum in the room.

Merrick leaned farther into the cavern that formed the chimney that led up to the roof of the house. He twisted his head, peering into the darkness, his eyes squinting. After a moment he pulled his head out again and turned to Walt. "Get me a lamp or a lantern, would you?"

Mr. Bence started to move but Walt said to him, "Just tell me where I can find one." Mr. Bence pointed to a sideboard at the end of the room between two tall windows. In three long strides Walt stepped over to the sideboard and found the matches lying on top.

He lit the lamp, replaced the glass chimney, and carried it over to Merrick.

Merrick traded Walt the elephant for the lamp and then, carefully, without bashing the glass into the lip of the fireplace, leaned in again, his left hand braced on the floor. The light from the lamp disappeared as he raised it up inside the chimney. His head disappeared as well.

Julia reminded herself to breathe again.

After a moment, Merrick carefully lowered the lamp and pulled his head out of the chimney.

"There's something up there," he said. "Hold this, will you?" He handed the lamp back to Walt.

He shuffled forward on his knees and leaned into the fireplace once more, and then once again his head disappeared up into the chimney. This time he reached his arms up as well, though he had trouble almost immediately. Julia could see that he was pulling his wide shoulders into his body as much as he could, but it was still a tight fit.

In the ensuing quiet, while the room waited, Millie Jones whispered to her husband, "I must say, if this isn't the most exciting thing to happen on a Saturday afternoon, I don't know what is."

Julia wasn't sure if Millie knew how inappropriate some of the things she said were and she just didn't care, or if she was missing the sensitivity required to recognize her error. Or maybe she enjoyed the drama that often resulted from her words. *Perhaps it's a bit of all three*, Julia thought.

From inside the chimney came Merrick's muffled voice. Julia thought he said, "I see what's happened."

There were some grunting noises from Merrick and then Julia thought she heard the sound of a piece of fabric being torn. She glanced around the room but couldn't see where the noise could've come from.

"Shit." This from Merrick inside the chimney. There was a long pause while the whole room waited. Finally, Merrick's voice came again. "Walt?"

Walt, still holding the elephant and the lamp, answered, "Aye?"

Merrick's left arm began to wriggle. Julia could see him working his shoulder. He shuffled on his knees once again to his right, seeming to make space for the arm. After a few seconds his elbow appeared, followed by his forearm and then his hand.

"Pull on my jacket, will you?"

Walt stared at Merrick's back and looked puzzled. "What?"

"Pull on the cuff of my sleeve. I need to take my jacket off."

Walt glanced at Julia and she shrugged in response, not understanding either. He turned and walked the lamp and toy over to the sideboard and set them down. He went back to the fireplace and bent down, resting his hands on his thighs. "What in the hell, Merrick?" he said in a near whisper. "What are you playing at?"

There was another long pause, and then in his muffled chimney voice Merrick said, "I'm stuck."

MERRICK HAD DEDUCED that the elephant had been hanging from a nail that was about three feet up in the chimney wall. Once Walt got the constable out of the left arm of his jacket, Merrick was able to maneuver himself to pull his right arm out of the sleeve that was caught on the nail. He slowly backed out of the chimney, leaving the jacket hanging where it was.

His white shirt was spotted with soot, as was his face. At the sight of this, a whispery thought ran through Julia's head, but she wasn't able to catch it. When he turned around and stood up, Merrick had a thin ribbon in one of his hands, it's original color now blackened with soot. He held it out to Mr. and Mrs. Bence.

"It looks like someone hung the toy from that nail using this ribbon. Do you recognize it?"

The Bences looked at one another and then back at Merrick and both shook their heads.

"Who would do that?" Mrs. Bence said. "Everyone knows that Henry hates to be separated from Elly."

Merrick and the Bences went back and forth, trying to see if they could figure out the origin of the ribbon. Mrs. Bence insisted that Elly normally didn't wear any decoration.

"When Henry got him last year for Christmas, Elly came with a red bow around his neck." A ghost of a smile came to Mrs. Bence's lips at the memory. "Henry took it off immediately. He said that Elly was a boy and that boys didn't wear ribbons."

The parents looked at each other. Mrs. Bence began crying in earnest. "What does this mean, Edwin? Where has he gone?"

For a moment all the voices in the room receded from Julia's ears. It was like gears were clicking in her head, blocking out the sound of the conversation. Millie Jones was chiming in, saying something rude, but Julia barely heard her.

There was a memory tickling at her, something she couldn't quite catch. She stared off, her gaze falling down to the carpet in the corner of the room, although she didn't see anything at all.

She looked up at Merrick's face, smudged with soot. And then it came to her.

"It's the ribbon!" she said.

Merrick looked over at her. "Yes, Julia, it's a ribbon. Sort of silky." He rubbed the object between his thumb and forefinger.

"No," Julia looked around the room at all the eyes staring at her. "I mean, I know where Henry is."

CHAPTER EIGHT

Once again, just as when they had gone into the parlor, the party formed a little parade and followed Julia out of the room. Stepping lightly in her sock feet, Julia led the group toward the front door and then turned and went up the wide wooden staircase toward the second floor.

"Miss Thom," Mrs. Bence pleaded, "please tell me where Henry is."

Over her shoulder, Julia smiled at the mother who had caught up to her. Julia reached back and took the woman's hand and gripped it in a comforting way. "I'll do you one better," she said. "I'll show you where he is."

"Is he safe?"

Julia nodded. "Oh yes. I think you'll find he's quite safe."

When they got to the top of the stairs, Julia turned as the group gathered around her. "Nanny, I wonder if you would wake Mildred? I'm sure the detective's assistant will want to be in on this."

The nanny glanced at Mrs. Bence, still holding Julia's hand. She nodded.

When Nanny and Mildred had joined the group, Julia led them

to the staircase that went up to the third floor. At the back of the line, Julia heard Millie protesting to her husband. "I wonder if we'll ever get the lunch we were promised?"

When they reached the top of the staircase, Julia turned to her left. She led them all down the hallway toward the dormer window that looked out to the west of the property. It was late afternoon and sunlight was streaming in through the windows, showing off glittering bits of fluff and dust floating through the air, an effect that always reminded Julia of snowfall. She walked down to the very end of the hallway and stood in front of the wood-paneled wall that was butted right up against the wall perpendicular to it that held the window.

Julia squeezed Mrs. Bence's hand and then looked at her husband. "Do you know about the secret room that's hidden here, Mr. Bence?"

The man looked at her with a lack of understanding in his eyes. He shook his head and looked at his wife. Julia turned toward Mrs. Bence and she shook her head as well.

The hallway was silent, the only sound was Mayor Jones' wheezy breathing from the trip up the stairs.

"Secret room?" Nanny scoffed from her position behind Mayor Jones. "Don't be ridiculous." Julia glanced at her and saw a mixture of contempt and fear on the woman's face, a combination that surprised Julia.

Beside Nanny, Mildred was leaning sullenly against the wall, looking bored, rubbing at one of her eyes.

"Mildred, why don't you show us?"

Mrs. Bence gasped. Julia squeezed her hand reassuringly again.

The birthday girl dropped her hand away from her face and stood up a little straighter. Her eyes were wary. She shook her head once at her teacher.

"Are you sure?"

The child stood, frozen. Then she reached out and found her father's hand and pushed herself in beside him, hiding her face behind his elbow.

Julia let go of Mrs. Bence's hand and turned so she could feel around on the wall beside her. In a moment, she found a little metal latch that was lying flush with the wood. The way the wood-grain lay, combined with how the latch was flat and sunk into the wall, made it nearly impossible to see. She pushed on the top of the latch so that the bottom of it popped out. She grabbed this and pulled. A small door, about half the size of a regular doorway, swung out from the wall on invisible hinges and blocked out part of the window to Julia's right shoulder. Mrs. Bence let out another little gasp.

At the back of the group, Millie Jones said, "Move out of the way Billy, I can't see. What is it?"

Julia held out her hand to Mrs. Bence once more and led her into the opening where the doorway had been. Single file, the two women went up a narrow little set of stairs that was almost like a ladder. When they got to the top, they found Henry lying on a small cot under a window, fast asleep.

Mrs. Bence gave a little cry. She took two short strides and dropped to her knees beside the cot. She began sobbing on top of her son. The boy woke up, bleary-eyed with sleep.

"Mama," he said. "Where have you been?"

CHAPTER NINE

It was almost dark so Mr. Bence loaned Merrick, Walt, and Julia a lantern to help guide them back to Horse. They were fortunate as well that the moon was bright, although Julia suspected that Earl could likely find his way back to the livery in pitch black even if he were wearing a blindfold. Behind her, Julia could smell the very pleasant piney smell of the tree that they were carrying with them back to town. With the sun gone it was colder than it had been earlier that afternoon. Julia's feet were warm in her over-sized boots, but she shivered a little and tucked herself down deeper inside the high collar of her coat. She pulled the blanket that was over her knees up a little higher in her lap.

There had been much rejoicing and many tears from the Bences when Henry was found. But not so much from Mildred.

Mr. Bence hadn't been able to hold himself back when he heard the reuniting occurring in the small attic room. He pushed his way up the staircase, though he couldn't fit in the room and had to stand a few rungs down, glancing around at the small, dimly lit space. When he absorbed what was happening, his face softened with relief. He looked up at Julia. "How did you know?"

"Let me come down and I'll tell you."

Mr. Bence had backed down the narrow staircase and Julia followed him, carefully picking her way down the narrow treads. They left Mrs. Bence cuddling her sleepy and confused son.

Julia had emerged into the hallway. Everyone from the mayor and his wife to Nanny to Merrick and Walt watched her and waited. Mildred peeked out at Julia from behind her father's elbow and then disappeared again.

"All right now," Mr. Bence said. "Tell us how you knew where Henry was."

"It was the ribbon on the elephant that Merrick pulled out of the chimney," Julia said. "I recognized it as the kind that Mildred had in her hair earlier in the day."

"But how did you know Henry was here specifically? I had no idea this room even existed."

Julia had explained. "A couple of things led me here. When Mildred and I searched the rooms on this floor, she was extremely helpful and cooperative. Until we got to this end of the hallway, that is. We ended our search here," she gestured to the open door, "and she began chattering more than she had been. In hindsight, I realized it was like she was trying to distract me. But from what? Then I remembered that while she had been leading me through our search up to that point, when we finished she insisted I leave this part of the hallway first."

Julia gestured to the door that opened up from the wall. "Mildred was standing with her back against that wall, which didn't seem odd at the time. But earlier today I had been thinking of my own family and our Christmases. When Merrick produced the ribbon, I recognized it as one that matched those in Mildred's hair. And then his soot covered face reminded me of a moment I hadn't really registered earlier, when Nanny had wiped something off Mildred's face before her nap." Julia looked over at Nanny. "Was that a spot of soot?"

Nanny nodded.

Julia shook her head to herself. "I'm amazed I didn't notice it myself. I suppose I was too focused on our room-to-room search."

She took a deep breath. "So I began to suspect that Mildred was involved. But I wasn't sure where she could have hidden her little brother. This house had been searched from top to bottom, more than once today."

"We looked everywhere," Mr. Bence confirmed. "I had absolutely no idea that little room existed."

"It was only providence that led me to remember the tiny, hidden room we had at the top of our house, where my mother kept all her Christmas decorations," Julia explained. "Without that memory, I doubt I would have thought of looking for that latch."

"Well, my dear," said Mr. Bence, "I'm at a loss for words. I am so grateful to you."

Julia, slightly uncomfortable with the attention, murmured that it was her pleasure to be able to help.

From the back of the little cluster of people in the hallway, Nanny said, "Why did you do it though, Mildred? Why hide Henry from us?"

The little girl was silent, and Julia now felt sorry for her. She looked over at the imperious woman in the black dress. "I think you know that better than anyone, Nanny. You said yourself that Henry tends to receive a lot of attention and focus from his family." Julia was treading softly, not wanting to offend Mr. Bence. "I think Mildred wanted this day to be about her."

Merrick looked puzzled. "But the day became about searching for the boy. Mildred's party was ruined."

Julia nodded. "If I had to guess I'd say that in her nine year old way she simply saw a problem - her annoying little brother taking away attention from her - so she got him out of the way. Not realizing, and not thinking ahead, that everyone would be looking for him. Maybe she hoped no one would notice."

Mr. Bence had been listening intently to Julia. Now he scowled. "That can't be true." He looked down at his daughter. "Mildred loves her brother."

"Of course she does, Mr. Bence. Love and jealousy can co-exist."

But the father seemed unable to grasp what Julia was saying. He had shaken his head and then ushered everyone back downstairs. "Time for a celebratory drink, I should say. Join us please, won't you, Constable. You too, Sheehan. I've got some fine port that just arrived from Spain."

The three men had walked away from Julia, chatting amongst themselves. Mildred clung to her father's hand and didn't look back at Julia. The Jones' followed, Millie gnawing on her husband's ear, as usual. Julia wondered how Billy did it, listening to the odious woman day and night. Perhaps it explained his overly developed fondness for food and drink. Julia didn't blame him. She'd drink excessively too if she spent every day with Millie.

Nanny surprised Julia and stayed with her while the others disappeared downstairs. When the crowd was gone, she leaned in toward Julia and said quietly, "I think you've assessed the situation exactly right."

"Why thank you, Nanny."

"Father simply doesn't want to hear that one of his children could be so calculating."

"It's not easy, is it? To see the flaws in the ones we love and continue loving them anyway."

JULIA REFLECTED on this as the sleigh slid through the darkening day, the muffled clopping of Earl's big feathered feet on the snow hypnotizing Julia slightly.

"I have one more question," Merrick said, breaking her ruminative thoughts.

"Yes?"

"What about that toy Walt found in the barn?"

"What toy?"

Beside her Walt grunted and began rummaging around in one of his coat pockets. He pulled out a small tin toy and lay it flat on his palm to show Julia. The sleigh hit a bump and the toy bounced, threatening to fall off Walt's hand. "Perhaps it was from the day last week when the boy went missing," the blacksmith said. He tucked it back in his pocket.

"Nanny mentioned something about that," Julia said. "But I didn't get the whole story. Something about a worker in the barn wanting to play with Henry."

"Yes, well," Merrick sighed, "we got the opposite side of that story. If I didn't know any better, I'd wonder if Nanny and Mr. Goddard were making excuses to see one another."

"Who?" Julia asked.

"Doesn't matter." Merrick took his eyes off the trail and smiled at her.

In the distance, Julia could see the faint twinkling of a couple of lanterns in the town. On either side of her, the two men were quiet now, perhaps lost in their own thoughts. Julia wondered if they were reflecting on Mildred and the motivation for her small crime.

Merrick was the first to break the silence. "Christ, I could eat the hind leg off a moose,"

"Aye," Walt chimed in. "Whatever Finnegan has on the menu today, I'll have two."

Julia smiled to herself. Reflection on others' characters, it seemed, was her preoccupation, not that of her two large friends.

CHAPTER TEN

Merrick pulled the sleigh up outside the schoolhouse, and Julia walked up the stairs, mindful of the extended toes of her boots. She opened the outside door and walked through the small foyer with its rows of coat hooks on the side walls, into the large room that served as schoolroom, dancehall and church.

She heard her two friends grunting and gently negotiating about the best way to bring the tree up the stairs. Walt was convinced that they should bring it up trunk end first. Merrick didn't seem to agree with this plan.

Julia waited a little impatiently and eventually the matter was resolved. They came up the stairs just as Walt suggested - a rare victory - and wrestled the tree in through the two doors and down the length of the schoolhouse room.

Before they had gone out into the woods, Walt had brought over a cast iron tree stand that he had forged. Its wide base formed a crisscrossed Celtic knot pattern. While they were in the forest, Walt had sawed off some bottom branches from their conquest so that the tree had a nice clean trunk that would fit into the cup that rose out of the middle of the stand. While the men held the tree in place, Julia crouched down and tightened the screws into the tree's trunk to hold it upright.

Julia stood and the three of them each stepped back to admire their handiwork. The top branch of the tree very nearly touched the ceiling.

"I told you it would fit." If Merrick had been a child he would have stuck his tongue out at his friends.

"Aye, but Julia's going to need a great jeezly ladder to get decorations right up to the top." Walt winked at Julia as he said this.

The tree did look beautiful. It had been a good choice, despite its homicidal aspirations. The branches were full, and the tree was a perfect triangular shape, filling out the corner where it stood. Julia knew that on Monday morning the children would be beside themselves with excitement at seeing this treasure, and at being allowed to decorate it.

The thought of decorating tickled her memory. She groaned. Walt and Merrick looked at her.

"What is it?"

"My pinecones." Julia sighed and closed her eyes. "I left them at the Bence's."

WITH THE TREE SET UP, and despite the loss of the pinecones, Julia was feeling at peace with herself. She was pleased that they'd been able to figure out where Henry was before the Bences had been caused too much stress. As she walked home down the dark, silent streets that led to her little one bedroom house, she reflected that she was glad she was only Mildred's schoolteacher and not her mother. The girl was clearly going to be quite a handful.

Julia was an only child and didn't entirely understand the jealousy Mildred must have felt that caused her to hide her brother away. But she did understand complicated family relationships that sometimes make us do extreme things.

Walt and Merrick had taken the sleigh back to the livery and would be bedding Earl down for the night before they went to Finnegan's hotel for supper. They had offered to drive her home, but Julia had declined, wanting to stretch her legs. She was looking forward to a quiet night. She would light a fire, heat up some soup and read a new book that she'd borrowed from Mrs. Thoreson.

She felt rather than saw the walkway to her house appear, and followed it up to the front door. She was about to step inside when her toe hit something set down in front of the door. She bent down and peered at it in the dark. It was a small parcel wrapped in brown paper and tied with string. She picked it up and found a piece of paper tucked under the string.

Once she was inside, Julia set the parcel down on the kitchen table and lit the lantern. Still wearing her long coat, scarf, and hat, she pulled off her gloves and opened the note. It was in tidy feminine handwriting.

"This came for you on the stagecoach today.

Betty"

Julia took a knife from the wooden tray where they lay and cut the string, which fell away from the package. She recognized, to her surprise, her mother's handwriting on the parcel.

She pulled at the brown paper until it fell away, and in her hands was a dark blue lidded box. She pulled open the lid and laying on top of a mound of cotton wool was a note card that Julia recognized as one of her mother's. The note read,

"Your father misses you.

We hope that you have a Merry Christmas.

Kind regards,

Mother."

Julia smiled at her mother's formality and was comforted by it. She would have been alarmed if the note had been emotional or sentimental. She set it down and began digging through the cotton wool in the box. Eventually her fingers found something slightly sharp and hard. She grappled around and found purchase on what felt like a piece of ribbon. She pulled it up into the air and the rest of the cotton wool fell away.

It was a Christmas tree decoration; a ball decorated with frilled ribbons and pearl-headed pins. A small bell hung from the bottom by a red string and tinkled when the ball moved. It was not a decoration that Julia recognized from her childhood. Her mother must have made it for this occasion.

It seemed Mrs. Thom had defied her daughter's expectations and offered the first olive branch.

Julia's eyes welled up and tears spilled over onto her cheeks. "Oh, Mother," she sighed, speaking to the empty kitchen. "Thank you."

the end

~

Would you like to read another short mystery in this series for free?

For a limited time you can go to AlexandraAmor.com/Ukee and grab your copy of *Charlie Horse* today!

ABOUT THE AUTHOR

Alexandra Amor is the award-winning author of a memoir about ten years she spent in a cult in the 1990s, as well as the Juliet Island Romantic Mystery series, Town Called Horse historical mystery series, and four animal adventure novels for middle-grade readers.

Alexandra lives in a small fishing village on the west coast of Vancouver Island, where she writes every day.

Learn more about her books, including the next Town Called Horse Mystery, at AlexandraAmor.com.

Learn more
www.AlexandraAmor.com
info@alexandraamor.com

ACKNOWLEDGMENTS

Copyedit by Jennifer McIntyre

Cover design by Streetlight Graphics

Thanks as always to Bob Sirrine for his amazing proofreading skills.